The Affair of the Porcelain Dog

The Affair of the Porcelain Dog

by

Jess Faraday

A Division of Bold Strokes Books

THE AFFAIR OF THE PORCELAIN DOG

ISBN 13: 978-1-60282-230-6

THIS TRADE PAPERBACK ORIGINAL IS PUBLISHED BY
BOLD STROKES BOOKS, INC.
P.O. BOX 249
VALLEY FALLS, NY 12185

CREDITS
EDITOR: GREG HERREN
PRODUCTION DESIGN: STACIA SEAMAN
COVER DESIGN BY SHERI (GRAPHICARTIST2020@HOTMAIL.COM)

Printed in the U.S.A.

Acknowledgments

Many thanks to:

Roy, who took my scribbling seriously, even when I had my doubts,

Helen, whose work-sharing scheme made authors of us both,

My writing group: Crystal, Heidi, Helen, Jen, Kam Oi Lee, N.J., and Wendy, for suffering through four drafts and always managing to come up with new and helpful observations,

Erastes, Hayden Thorne, Phyl Radford, and Babette Sparr for professional advice—even when I didn't always follow it,

And my editor, Greg Herren, who helped make this manuscript the best it could possibly be.

JF 2011

Chapter One

Wednesday, July 3, 1889

Wednesday's letter arrived in the evening post—a brief but pointed threat scrawled across ordinary white stationery in a startling lavender ink. But Goddard hadn't filed this one neatly behind the gilded cigarette box on the mantel with its predecessors. Instead, he had cast it down like a gauntlet onto the table between our twin armchairs. Hours later it remained like an uninvited guest.

"'I know what you are.'" Goddard picked it up and read aloud. "'Soon, the police will know as well. Unless.'"

"Unless what?" I asked.

Not that it mattered. Cain Goddard, a.k.a. the Duke of Dorset Street, did not negotiate with blackmailers. At that moment, his entire network of spies, cracksmen, bludgers, urchins and whores was scouring London in search of the person who dared threaten a criminal of his stature. When they found him, his skin wouldn't be worth a farthing. But what if they didn't find him? I imagined being led away in shackles, never again to put my feet up on the mahogany desk before the window, run my fingers over the leather-bound volumes lining the walls, or drape myself across the olive-colored velvet divan where Goddard had taken my hand and asked me to stay. At that time, I swore I would never return to Whitechapel. But even Whitechapel would be preferable to prison—and prison it would surely be, should the police learn the nature of Goddard's and my domestic arrangement.

The grandfather clock in the vestibule struck eleven. Goddard fingered his mustache thoughtfully, then shrugged.

"To convict us of criminal sodomy, dear boy," he said, patting my cheek on his way to the drink cart, "would require evidence that simply does not exist. Whisky?"

I nodded.

I relaxed as the liquor burned its way toward my stomach. We'd been discreet. Only Goddard's manservant had any inkling I was anything but a confidential secretary. Though the man had never liked me, Goddard paid too well for him to go telling tales.

"To convict me, on the other hand," he continued.

"What?"

How he could laugh when the cold fingers of panic were reaching for my throat was anyone's guess. Thus far, no one outside of Goddard's tight *coterie* connected Dr. Cain Goddard, the self-effacing night lecturer at King's College, with the hated, feared Duke of Dorset Street. But once the police had him for buggery, it would all come out. Even if I did manage to slip away into the night, I'd be back on the streets—two years older, broke, and far too spoilt to go back to selling my arse.

"Ah, the mistakes of youth," Goddard said. "I'd hoped it wouldn't come to this, but now that it has, how fortunate I am to have a nimble-fingered young protégé to set things right."

He glanced at me over the cut crystal glasses.

"You can't mean me," I said.

"Come, now. I need you, Ira. Not to warm my bed this time or run messages on the wrong side of town. I need you to retrieve something for me, something I'd feared lost, but which has now been found. My freedom, and, I daresay yours, depends on it. Can I depend on you?"

I looked around our beloved morning room. The armchairs in front of the fireplace, the rack of expensive, unused rifles over the doorway, the dearth of gewgaws and knick-knacks with which most people felt the need to litter their living spaces—after two years ensconced in this unspeakable luxury, how could I go back to doorways and doss-houses?

"I—I suppose," I stammered.

"Excellent. My carriage is waiting outside. The driver will take you to a pawnshop on Dorset Street, where you will find a black porcelain hound of unusual repugnancy. Bring it back, and our blackmailer won't have a wooden leg to stand on."

"That's all?"

I laughed. A simple burglary in my home territory. With my talent for locks, it would be easy. Goddard smiled. It was a rare expression, but it transformed his purposefully bland face into something beautiful.

"Do this, and you'll have roast beef and Islay malt for breakfast, lunch, and dinner for the rest of your days, and all the books of Greek art your delicate arms can carry."

The tightening in my chest eased. It's sad how easily I can be convinced. But being a mere two years off the streets, the simple promise of even these small luxuries was enough to fortify me for the task.

"But who's sending the letters?" I called as he stepped out into the vestibule to fetch my coat. "What does he want?"

What he came back with was not my coat, but he draped it around my shoulders anyway.

"Never mind that, dear boy," he said, buttoning the ratty tweed across my chest. "Just get the dog."

"In this?"

In addition to its shabby condition, the so-called coat was much too large and stank of another man's tobacco. Moreover, it was July and anything heavier than linen was going to be hotter than hell. Goddard liked to dress me up sometimes, but never in secondhand rubbish ten years out of fashion.

And never in tweed.

Ignoring me, Goddard tucked his Trinity scarf beneath the collar and the lavender letter into my trouser pocket with a satisfied nod.

"The pockets are deep and have more give than a whore's bedsprings. Besides," he said with a smirk, "it'll make you look like Andrew St. Andrews."

"St. Andrews!" I sputtered.

That meddling popinjay of a detective had never rolled up his sleeves to pick a lock, or hiked up his coat-hems to keep from tripping across a doorstep. Being the third son of an earl, he'd never had the need to burgle. And if he were to do it for kicks, he'd no doubt commission a special garment for the adventure.

The question at the front of my mind, though, was why Goddard would compare me at all to someone he so loathed. The question was answered by Goddard's teasing chuckle.

"St. Andrews, indeed," I grumbled.

Goddard patted my arse, slipping my silver flask into the pocket of the coat. There was a faint tinkle as the flask hit bottom. He'd even remembered my picklocks.

"Remember," he said. "A porcelain dog, half as long as your forearm, black as sin and twice as ugly. Now go."

With a sniff, I swept the horrible thing around me. Then, feeling a bit ashamed—it was an easy job, after all, and most of the time, Goddard didn't ask much of me—I pecked him on the cheek. When the carriage pulled away from the big house on York Street with me inside, Goddard was still standing in the doorway, running his fingers thoughtfully over his jaw, a little smile pulling at the edges of his lips.

What self-respecting housebreaker sets off wearing a Trinity scarf, you might ask? Blame Goddard's sentimental streak. He had taught at Cambridge once, and though he refused to talk about the experience itself or the circumstances of his dismissal, the scarf meant a great deal to him. You might also wonder what sort of imbecile takes a shiny private hansom to the building he intends to burgle. A necessity, I'm afraid, unless he intends to walk. The pawnshop stood nearly five miles away in Miller's Court, and no cabbie in his right mind ventured down that wicked quarter mile after dark. The streets were deserted, and the weather was clear. Not half an hour later, we had left the red brick houses and well-tended gardens of York Street behind, and the rubbish-strewn East End closed around us in a cocoon of filth and desperation.

I instructed the driver to let me out in front of the Blue Coat Boy pub, two blocks removed from my destination. An excited throng had gathered around the entrance—another fight, no doubt—and I was able to pass by unnoticed. Closer to the shop, jolly old Do-As-You-Please Street, possibly the most lawless quarter mile in London, was quiet. I strode up to the front door as if I owned the place—the only way to break into a building in plain sight—slipping my picklocks into my hand. Seconds later, I nudged the door shut behind me. Silence descended, and I relaxed, knowing I'd be able to go about my work in peace.

The word "dollyshop" might conjure images of china-faced pretties with real hair for a little girl to comb, and blue eyes that open and close. This shop belonged to a grubby matron who doled out ha'penny loans against objects that were hardly worth that. Crates of rust-scabbed metal were stacked as tall as a man along the back wall. The other walls were lined with ill-fitted shelves, bowing under haphazard loads of mildew-encrusted boots, stiff and stained rags, salt-encrusted horse collars, and what appeared to be bones. In the center of the room, piles of rubbish sat where they'd been dropped, layers of dust testifying to how long they'd been there. An attempt had been made to organize some of it into bins, but the bins were already overflowing with towers of detritus threatening to topple at the slightest breath. The dog could have been anywhere in that mess.

Tugging at my waistcoat, I picked up a fireplace poker with a missing handle and began prodding the chaos, listening for the telltale *clink!* of metal against porcelain. Forty sweaty minutes later, I was bored as hell and my eyes burned from the dust. I was tempted to declare the mission a failure and take the carriage back to York Street for whisky and a sympathetic fuck. But if we didn't put paid to the blackmailer, it would be the end of both whisky and fucking for a good long time. Sighing, I fixed my eyes on a stack of bedding gradually being devoured by mildew and raised the poker.

It was then I heard the footsteps.

I mightn't have noticed them at all, had they not been the only footsteps that I'd heard since I'd arrived. Quick and sure, with the weight of a man and the confidence of someone who could afford a stout pair of boots, the footsteps stopped directly before the door.

Fuck me, had I remembered to lock it?

I flew back to the front of the room, dodging perilous mountains of rubbish, and flattened myself against the doorjamb. The footsteps didn't have the righteous clip-clop of a Whitechapel bobby. But what were the chances someone else would decide to burgle, on the same night as I, this down-at-heel junk shop? I swiped a damp clump of curls from my forehead, chafing against the overcoat. A prickling sensation crawled over my nether regions—the itch that had come to plague me over the past few weeks was making its presence known. Just in case I'd forgotten. Resisting the urge to claw at myself with my free hand, I felt instead for the sharpened length of pipe I used to carry on my belt during my Whitechapel years.

It was, of course, in my trunk back at York Street, sod it all!

From somewhere near my right hip came the grind of metal against metal. Slowly, the door creaked open, spilling a stream of gaslight across the dusty floor. My muscles tensed with the urge to flee. I'd not courted physical confrontation since Goddard had taken me into his home two years before. I hadn't missed it. A single, shiny boot breached the doorway before stopping, suspended as though testing the air.

I swung the poker with all my might.

"What in blazes?" the other man exclaimed as the poker swept his cap back onto Dorset Street and smashed into the doorjamb with a force that left my left side ringing.

While I was still picking splinters from my teeth, the man sprang up next to a box of unraveling straw bonnets, straightening his jacket and smoothing his neat mustache with indignant little grunts. He squinted in my general direction, his expression registering confusion and then irritation.

"Adler?" he sputtered. "What the deuce are you doing here?"

"Lazarus?"

Only Timothy Lazarus would respond to such an attack with euphemism—and with a perfectly executed defensive roll. Disgusted, I kicked the door shut and slammed the bolt home.

Lazarus, too, had dressed for Whitechapel. A once-white workman's shirt hung from his muscular shoulders and bagged around his toned middle. Charity-box trousers rode low on his slim hips. Only the fastidious cleanliness of both clothing and man betrayed Lazarus's middle-class origins. One might have dismissed his attention to hygiene as a consequence of his work as a physician in the most pestilent, lice-ridden corner of London. However, having known the man in the most intimate way possible, I can assure you his enthusiasm for soap went straight to the core.

"Ira Adler," he said. "I suppose it was to be expected."

"You can't mean that you knew I'd be here," I scoffed.

He spat into his palm, smoothed back a section of dark hair that had been disturbed by my assault, then met my eyes.

"St. Andrews asked me to retrieve something for him. Considering Goddard's uncanny record of predicting what St. Andrews might consider important, and snatching it from under his nose, it stands to reason I'd meet one of Goddard's errand boys tonight. I suppose I should consider myself lucky it wasn't someone with better aim. Now, shall we find the dog together, or are you going to subject me to another tiresome display of violence?"

How the devil?

No matter. The statue was Goddard's, and I'd be buggered if I'd let it end up with Lazarus.

"Dog?" I asked innocently.

Lazarus sighed again. "A black porcelain statue, terrifically ugly, and somehow to do with the letter you're rubbing like a talisman between your thumb and forefinger. At least I hope that's what you're doing."

I yanked my hand out of my trouser pocket, sending a shower of coins across the floor. The itch had doubled its strength; my entire genital region was crawling. As I straightened my waistband in an attempt to regain a bit of dignity, the blackmail letter fluttered gently to my feet. Lazarus snatched it out of the dust before I could protest.

"'I know what you are,'" he read, flicking a bit of fluff from the corner. "Hmm. It seems the blackmailer expended his store of clever synonyms for 'sodomite' in his previous letters."

"How do you know what the other letters said?" I demanded.

Lazarus held out the paper as if it were a soiled handkerchief. In the gaslight glowing through the dust-smeared window, the lavender ink looked like blood.

"Because, Adler, we've been getting them, too."

"You've—"

"Now, where do you think it could be, hmm?" he asked, as if we were somehow working together. Then he took my poker.

"It's not in here," I said, as he made a tentative jab at a stack of books that looked as if they'd been burnt. "I looked."

"Shh."

He carefully stepped over the books. After surveying the rubbish for a moment, he knelt down over a tray of bent nails. He spent so much time picking over them at one point I thought he'd found the bloody thing.

"So…it wasn't St. Andrews sending the letters?" I asked, relieved, when he moved on to a bucket of wooden bucket handles.

"Adler, be quiet."

It wasn't impossible. For whatever reason, St. Andrews had cast Goddard as the villain in the solipsistic drama that was his life. For reasons of his own, Goddard reveled in that fact. That my own nemesis had ended up sharing rooms with Goddard's could only have been some sort of divine joke.

"St. Andrews would cut off his left testicle before turning anything over to the police," Lazarus said. He sighed, tucking the poker under his arm. "Though admittedly, either option would result in a lot less trouble for everyone than his misguided pursuit of crime where half the time there is none. Actually, my first thought had been to blame you for the letters. But then I remembered that you're illiterate."

"Am not," I said.

"Oh, really?"

"But it wasn't me."

"No."

I followed him around the perimeter of the room, watching as he continued to jab and lift and tease. He eventually worked his way to the far side, where a narrow door was half-hidden amid boxes of metal scraps..

"Even if I hadn't already deduced your innocence, Adler, your presence here proves it. Aha," he said, producing his own set of picklocks, "now I think we might be getting somewhere."

The door opened onto a small room lined on two sides with floor-to-ceiling shelves. A small curtained window looking out onto Miller's

Court was on the bare opposite wall. Behind the curtain, the single gas lamp Her Majesty had provided to illuminate the vast courtyard glowed anemically. Lazarus laid a hand on my elbow as I stepped past him to let in a bit of light.

"Not so fast," he said, withdrawing a long metal pipe from his waistband.

I stepped back in surprise.

"It's not what you think," he said. He flicked a little switch on the pipe. One end lit up and filled the room with a bright glow. "Just a little something I've been working on. There's a dry cell battery inside, and an incandescent bulb. Blast!" he cried as the light winked out.

He shook it tentatively before giving it a solid smack with his palm. The light blinked on, but died just as quickly.

"I think you should keep working," I said as he pushed past me. Obviously embarrassed, he pulled the curtain back an inch.

Gaslight brought the walls alive with the eerie light of a thousand porcelain eyes. The place was crawling with statues, each more loathsome than the last. A matched pair of warhorses with lions' heads pranced near my shoulder. A spiky-backed sea monster reclined nearby, and next to it, a serene-faced woman stood with her foot on a dragon's neck.

"I say," Lazarus said, "it appears we've stepped into the devil's own curio cabinet."

"Imagine anyone actually paying money for something like this," I said, waggling a gilded harpy in his face. He ignored me.

"Blast and blunder," he said. "How is one meant to distinguish any one of these monstrosities from the others?"

I stashed the harpy between a dragon and a fierce-looking bull. As Lazarus examined the statues on his side of the room, I continued scanning the shelves on mine in a halfhearted manner. Each of the horrible things had been endowed with a curl of lip or roll of eye making it look simultaneously of this earth and not. If Goddard was thinking to display his precious porcelain dog anywhere in our house, he had another thought coming.

"Ira," Lazarus said with suspicious joviality, "isn't there a hot toddy and a pair of beaded slippers waiting for you back at York Street?"

"How did you know about my beaded slippers?" I demanded.

"Just a guess."

Lazarus was examining the middle shelves with more than casual interest. He cleared his throat, eyes darting around nervously—a sure sign he'd found something.

"What I mean to say," Lazarus said, leaning closer to the shelves, "is surely you've better things to do on a Wednesday night. We both want the dog for the same reason—to render our blackmailer toothless. If you think about it, it doesn't matter who actually finds it. Now," he said, looking over his shoulder with a patronizing smile, "why don't you go home and leave this to the professionals?"

"What, like you? Just how many locks have you picked in your life, Doctor?"

I pushed my way over to where he was standing. He had found something, but wasn't going to leave with it.

His shoulders tensed as I came up behind him. "Because surely if St. Andrews considered you a professional like himself," I continued, placing my hands on his waist as I examined the shelves over his shoulder, "he'd have told you why you were looking for a porcelain cur, instead of just sending you out. Like an errand boy."

I whispered this last part into his delicate ear, smiling as it went red. Slippers and buttered rum, indeed! And then I saw it: a black, grimacing dog with bulging eyes, razor teeth and the mane of a lion; it could be nothing else. It was sitting on its haunches on a block carved with the illegible scrawl of some or other savages. But even seated, it was exactly half as tall as Lazarus's forearm was long. I reached for it.

And my midsection exploded in pain.

"Thank you, Adler," Lazarus smirked, rubbing his elbow as I went down. "I was wondering which of these repugnant things it actually was." He plucked the statue from the shelf.

"The elbow strike is a lady's move," I gurgled.

"But it worked," he said.

I'd been training with Goddard's Oriental Fighting Society a little over a year. Lazarus clearly had been working on something similar, only his performance left no doubt he was the one the instructor called on to demonstrate techniques, rather than the reprobate whose appalling lack of talent made the demonstration necessary. Stepping over me, Lazarus paused as if contemplating stomping my face for good measure. He'd have been well within his rights, I suppose. We'd not parted on the best of terms.

Dr. Lazarus and I had met at the Stepney Street Clinic. We'd started chatting while he stitched me up after a meeting with a sadistic, albeit well-paying client. As far as clients went, Lazarus himself turned out to be far from sadistic. Sometimes he'd even buy me a meal before disappearing guiltily into the night. How was I to have known that our paid assignations had, to him, signified something more?

Though one might argue he'd brought it on himself by maintaining unrealistic expectations, one wouldn't be far from wrong in saying I'd been a bit of a shit.

I grabbed his leg and pulled until he tumbled over me like a load of bricks, pulling me on top of him.

"Give me that dog, Tim."

With astonishingly little effort, he flipped me onto my back and pinned my wrists to the floor with his knees, while clutching the dog to his chest. I got my leg under me and pushed off from the floor, sending Lazarus into the wall with a foundation-shaking thud. A statue crashed to the floor behind me, and the air was suffused with sweet powder.

"Opium," I wheezed.

My eyes watered. My throat burned. From where he was, Lazarus had probably just got a whiff. I'd had a right snootful, but I wasn't so much feeling the drug as the weight of the memories attached to it—memories that I'd gone to a great deal of trouble to suppress. But more importantly, Goddard had said the statue contained the evidence that the blackmailer needed to put him away. These contained opium, which was not only legal, but was the cash cow of Goddard's enterprises. He certainly didn't need me to steal it for him. That meant there was something else inside the cursed cur.

Against the back wall, Lazarus was groaning and stirring. I lunged, grabbing the statue with both hands this time. He rolled on top of me again—but he was weakening, and I had the bloody thing, by God.

"Give it, Tim," I growled.

"I'll give you my other elbow if you don't let go."

I did let go—with one hand, to smash thc base of my palm into his nose. I flipped over on top of him with a roar. Blood streaming down his face, he rewarded me with a cupped hand to my ear.

"You slap like a lady, too," I muttered, trying to pop my jaw back into its hinge.

"How does Goddard slap you?"

"Give me the damned dog."

He bucked me loose, sending me rolling into the wall this time. Statues rained down from the shelves, smashing on the ground all around me. I scrambled to my feet as clouds of opium powder rose from the floor. But the son of a bitch still had the dog.

"I don't think so, Adler," he said as I lurched back toward him.

He grasped my hand with a surprisingly effective wristlock and brought me down on my back. Gore dripped from his half-mad face as he grinned down at me. Eleven years separated the good doctor and myself, but in contrast to my luxury-atrophied state, Lazarus was in the pink of health. He might actually have gained the better of me that night had a sharp voice and frantic pounding at the front door not interrupted our struggle.

"Police! Open the door!"

"Oh, Constable, thank God!" I shouted, a little too enthusiastically.

I reached up and tweaked Lazarus's nose. He let go of my wrist with a cry, both hands instinctively flying to his injured snout. I rolled him off, and the dog fell neatly into my hand. I shoved it deep into the generous coat pocket and sprang to my feet. In a moment of inspiration, I pulled out my silver flask and gave Lazarus a face full of Goddard's best whisky. It was a sacrifice, but when the constable finally did pound down that door, I doubted the guardian angel of Stepney Clinic would care to explain how he'd come to be reeking of opium and booze and beaten to a pulp by a known male prostitute.

With a last backward glance, I thrust the window up and clambered out.

Chapter Two

Miller's Court was a depressing stretch of crumbling pavement walled in by tenements. A single gas lamp illuminated the weeds sprouting from the cracks, turning pools of broken glass into diamonds beneath my feet. I'd spent my share of evenings there—furtive fumbles in shadowy stairwells, an hour of stolen sleep here and there in an alley—but this was no time for reminiscing. Inside, Lazarus was pulling himself to his feet. People were gathering back near the water pump where I'd performed my ablutions more times than I cared to remember. Suppressing a shudder as I passed by the room where they found poor Mary Kelly last November, I made to lose myself in the crowd.

On the far side of the yard, surrounded by a jeering throng, two men were tormenting a bear on a leash by whipping its hind feet with strips of leather to make it dance. It was a matted, malodorous brute with runny eyes and a dazed expression. It lurched as it stumbled in time to an accordion's dissonant wheeze. Bear and men wore matching waistcoats and hats, though the men's teeth had not been filed to stubs, nor had their fingernails been pulled out with maiming force. As many times as I'd listened to Goddard's argument that nature was ours to do with as we wished, I couldn't help but think that if there were any justice, the creature would one day have its revenge.

I pushed my way through the knot of unshaven, gin-smelling men, rough-faced women, and given the time of night, an astounding number of children. I tossed a few coins into the hat for the poor beast's upkeep.

No sooner had my hand gone back into my pocket than a voice at my shoulder said,

"'Ello, there."

Before I could respond, a young woman threaded her arm through my elbow.

"You look familiar," she purred as she steered me out of the crowd and into the shadows.

"Anyone would look familiar who had enough money, I'd wager," I said.

She was about my age, mid twenties, and at first glance looked like any of the women one might encounter in Miller's Court this time of night—greasy hair loosely piled on top of her head, a week's wardrobe layered about her person, tattered hems dragging the ground.

"Lookin' for someone?" she asked.

"Not in the sense you mean."

"Don' 'ave to mean nuffin'," she simpered.

I shot her an irritated look as I disentangled our arms. Her face stopped me in my tracks.

She was Chinese, though she was trying to hide the fact with hair, clothing, and Cockney that was a bit too perfect. There were quite a few Chinese in London, but they tended to stay down in Poplar and Limehouse. One seldom encountered the women outside of these enclaves. One never encountered them unaccompanied and dressed like a common doxy.

"A little far from home, aren't you?" I asked as she reached again for my arm.

Her grip was strong. Even beneath the layers of clothing, I could see that she was unusually muscular. I glanced toward her throat for the telltale bulge, or a scarf hiding it, but found no evidence that she was anything but a natural woman.

Again I tried to wiggle out of her grip, but she held fast, pressing herself lewdly into my chest as if she intended to climb into my trousers with me.

I gave her a push.

Normally, I'm loath to strike a woman, but she was not what

she appeared to be. She didn't belong there, and it was making me nervous. Now free, I walked quickly toward Commercial Road while she followed, keeping up her prattle.

"I could be anyfing you want me to be," she wheedled. She caught my arm and renewed her assault. "Come on, now. Wot's the gen'l'man's fancy this evenin'?"

"I prefer bull to cow," I said, as she made another attempt on my waistband. I twisted away and caught her wrist in a lock—the second time Goddard's training had come in handy that night. I pushed her off, harshly this time. Anger flashed across her face. Then a smug grin.

"You wait right 'ere, then. Maggie knows just wot you needs."

With a wag of her finger, the woman melted back into the shadows. I suppose she expected me to simply stand there and wait for whatever mischief she had planned for me. Not fucking likely. Commercial Road lay before me—a deserted path of cobblestones between walls of darkened shops. Unfortunately, Goddard's hansom was nowhere to be seen.

I ran.

I had once known the shadows and passages of Whitechapel like the back of my hand. I flew past boarded-up stores, massive tenement blocks, and locked warehouses. I sprinted through twisting alleys and even vaulted over a wall, blackening my hands and coat. My heart pounded with excitement—and no small relief that my street skills hadn't completely deserted me. Fewer than five miles stood between Miller's Court and York Street. It felt like coming up from the bottom of the sea as the dark, dangerous streets gave way to even pavement and well-maintained gaslights. I slowed to a walk. I might have kept running right past Regent's Park, but experience had taught me that doing so would have resulted in the immediate descent of all of the constables who should have been arresting murderers in Whitechapel.

As I rounded the corner of York and Baker Street, I almost cried out with relief. Our neighbors slumbered on behind red bricks and lace curtains, but Goddard had left his house lights blazing. I tried to calm my breathing as I ascended the scrubbed stairs, leaning briefly against one of the whitewashed columns that stood on either side of the porch.

A warm rainbow of light shone through the stained glass panel Goddard had commissioned for the front door. I'd have collapsed against it had Goddard's man, Collins, not opened it just then.

"Mr. Adler," he said, as I slipped in under his arm.

Collins was an ox of a man, twenty-five years my senior, but fifty pounds heavier. I'd heard tell he'd been an amateur boxer in his youth. He'd never liked me, but he knew his place. At that moment his place was standing there on the black and white checked tiles, patiently waiting to take my coat over his tree trunk of an arm. Bent double in the vestibule, I panted like a dog and grinned. Two years of clean sheets and Egyptian tobacco, but I could still crack a lock with the best of them before sprinting five miles home.

"Your coat—" he began.

"Burn it."

I sloughed off the horrible tweed. Collins made no comment, probably because, all things considered, burning the coat was the most prudent course of action. He folded it over his arm and turned toward the servants' stairs.

"But before you do that," I said. "I should probably give Dr. Goddard his prize."

I stopped for a moment to appreciate the comforts of our home—the gentle hissing of the gas lamps behind their frosted glass sconces, the whiff of the excellent pork supper for which we'd unfortunately had no appetite, the vase of heavy-headed flowers on the vestibule table. Next to the vase was a silver tray upon which Collins bore in the post, three times daily—including, for the past four days, the lavender letters. Because of me, it was all safe—that is, once I turned the statue over to Goddard.

But where was Goddard?

Straight ahead of me the morning room door was shut tight, the lamps extinguished for the night. Neither footsteps nor creaking bedsprings sounded overhead. I glanced down the corridor to the left to the door of Goddard's study. A dim light shone beneath the door. Clearly, he'd lit his desk lamp instead of the wall lamps, whose generous light he usually favored. Did he not wish me to know he was there?

"The master is engaged, Mr. Adler," Collins said.

I frowned. I could hear the muted voices of two men behind the study door. Unusual visitors at unusual hours were part and parcel of sharing a household with the Duke of Dorset Street. But Goddard would sooner have entertained Her Majesty in his smallclothes than allowed the usual lowlife into his *sanctum sanctorum.*

"Who's there with him?" I asked.

"I've taken the liberty of laying out a new set of pajamas," the manservant said. "The master commissioned them for you last week." He grasped my elbow, managing to pull me back a few steps before I dug in my heels. "Green silk with an embroidered dragon. I think you'll find this particular shade quite becomes your complexion—"

"Collins, who's in there?" I demanded, shaking free of him.

At that moment, the door cracked open.

I only had a glimpse of the visitor—a middle-aged man with the build of a scarecrow, a deerstalker cap and a newer version of the voluminous tweed hanging over Collins's arm—before Goddard's pale hand appeared on the man's shoulder and pulled him back.

"What the—St. Andrews?" I demanded, wheeling around. "Was that Andrew St. Andrews?"

Lazarus's particular friend was obsessed with Sherlock Holmes. He'd spent the last few years trying to get the press to refer to him as the Holmes of St. John's Wood, and now he was even dressing like him. No doubt he'd come here to accuse Goddard of sending the lavender letters. At least his arrogance had kept him from bringing along a couple of pet constables. Though that might not have been quite as bad in the end. Now that Goddard had set him straight, St. Andrews had an actual case to sink his teeth into: two sworn enemies receiving identical blackmail letters. But why didn't Goddard want me to know he was there?

"Shall I bring up the night tray after your bath, sir?" Collins asked, as if it hadn't happened.

"The devil take the night tray!"

Goddard had his secrets. It would have been laughable to expect a criminal of his caliber to share everything, even with his closest companion. And yet who was it that had taken an elbow to the gut over that sodding statue? I wouldn't embarrass him in front of St. Andrews, but Goddard would tell me everything before the night was out. Ira Adler is nobody's errand boy anymore!

"I will have that bath after all," I said primly. "With eucalyptus. And leave the jar."

Eucalyptus leaves were expensive. While Goddard had his little tête-à-tête with the Holmes of St. John's Wood, I'd use the rest of them.

"Certainly, Mr. Adler."

"And if Dr. Goddard finishes with his guest before dawn, inform him I've retrieved the object he sent me for. It's in the pocket."

I nodded toward the coat. Collins searched both pockets and turned to me with a frown.

I snatched back the coat to see for myself, but fuck me! The only things in there were my picklocks and flask.

"I don't understand," I said. "It has to be here somewhere."

But it wasn't. Not in the coat, not in my trousers, nowhere.

"Perhaps it fell out," Collins suggested.

"A great ugly thing like that? Don't you think I'd have noticed?"

I went over the evening's events in my mind. First Lazarus, then the bear, and then that woman, so out of place and yet attaching herself to me with such purpose.

"Blast and buggery!" I cried.

She hadn't been after my custom at all—nor my silver flask or money.

The doxy-that-wasn't had been after the statue all along. And I'd fallen for the oldest pickpocket's trick in the world!

CHAPTER THREE

A good, long soak in our mahogany-encased tub would have gone far toward soothing my injured dignity had I not been terrified of what Goddard would say. Not only was the porcelain dog no longer where he thought it was, but there was no way of knowing where it had gone. Putting aside the embarrassing fact it had been lifted off me by a girl—and who the devil knew what she wanted with it—Goddard was in shit's creek to his neck, and having lost the abominable thing, I was in it to my eyeballs.

And there was Goddard's sworn enemy St. Andrews, here in our very home. From what Goddard had said in the past, St. Andrews would have happily pushed him under a carriage. The feeling was mutual. So what was he doing in Goddard's study? And why did Goddard want to conceal this fact from me?

Apart from their mutual antipathy, the only thing Goddard and St. Andrews had in common was their preference for their own sex. Labouchere's law had made it possible to jail either one of them on just a rumor of indecent behavior. St. Andrews was so obvious it was only a matter of time before some enterprising blackmailer tried his hand. But Goddard was pathologically careful. I could count the number of people who knew about us on one hand—and they were all well bought.

Who would go after them both? Together? And why?

A timid knock on the bathroom door brought me back to tepid water with sodden eucalyptus leaves floating on the top, cooling embers in the fireplace, and the magazine of dreadful stories which Eileen, our girl-of-all-work, had left the night before for my enjoyment. I'd set the latter aside in favor of my melancholic ruminations, and it now hung limply over the side of the tub, one corner dragging the surface of the water.

"Mr. Ira, sir?" called this same Eileen from the hallway. "I've brought your water."

The water heater in the corner of Goddard's bathroom was no smaller than any other in London. Considering the novelty of indoor plumbing, I should have been grateful for even its miserly capacity. But when one has spent his childhood washing knees to chin in a copper basin behind twenty-seven other workhouse urchins, somehow filling the tub just once never seems quite adequate.

"Mr. Ira?"

I glanced guiltily toward the door, behind which I could hear her struggling with the hot water–filled jug. The sound of Collins running my bath had no doubt awakened her and she'd sprung out of her narrow bed to get the vat on the stove. But I didn't want more hot water. The eucalyptus had irritated the skin between my legs mightily.

And Goddard was still entertaining his nemesis. I just wanted to go to bed.

"Thank you," I called. "Just leave it outside the door."

"Yes, sir," she said with relief. Eileen was sixteen and devout. No doubt she'd have put out her own eyes before accidentally catching a glimpse of a man in his natural state.

I waited until I heard her scurrying down the stairs, and hauled myself out of the deep tub. My head was still a bit spinny from the opium, and I'd pulled something during the struggle with Lazarus. By God, I was going to feel it all in the morning. I gingerly touched my abdomen, where the doctor's elbow had done its worst. *Do no harm*, indeed! Sighing, I dripped across the dragon-patterned rug to the chair by the fireplace, helping myself to a warm towel. After applying a second towel to my sopping curls, I wrapped myself in the green silk pajamas Collins had hung above the chair. I found my slippers and clacked off to bed.

Goddard's bed was just a bit too small for two. It felt enormous, cold, and empty without him in it. I slipped between the silk sheets and let my bones settle into the gentle depressions that had gradually appeared on my side of the mattress over the past two years. Outside, the street was silent. If I focused, I could hear the voices of Goddard and his guest downstairs but couldn't make out their words. If St. Andrews still thought we were behind the letters, he'd have stormed out by now and returned with as much of Scotland Yard as his family's money could purchase. Yet both men's tones sounded civil. No doubt Goddard had told him the matter was resolved and the dog in our possession.

Fuck me.

Stress and exertion eventually took their toll and I fell into a black, dreamless sleep.

I was awakened some time later by furtive tugs at the covers as Goddard attempted to crawl into bed without waking me. He had opened the curtains and the window. The glare from the street lamps below cast our room in an orange haze.

"Is he gone?" I asked.

"Who?"

"St. Andrews."

I propped myself up onto an elbow, rubbing my eyes. Goddard slid beneath the covers, punching his pillow into submission, and rolled onto one side to face me.

"I ran into his little friend Lazarus at the dollyshop," I continued. "He said they're getting the lavender letters, too."

"Indeed," he said.

He was forty-two to my twenty-five, but the soft light smoothed the lines around his eyes, giving his face a porcelain vulnerability that made him seem much younger.

"Why? Who's doing this? What does he want?"

Goddard drew a long breath.

"Do you trust me, Ira?"

"Of course," I said. "I—"

"Then don't ask these questions, I beg you." He let out a long breath and began amusing himself with my curls. "Besides," he said, "none of it matters now that you have the dog."

"Um."

The gloom seemed to close around us. I hadn't thought it possible this could be even more difficult than I'd imagined. My imagination was second to none when it came to predicting the worst.

"You did find it," Goddard said.

"Yes, I…found it."

"And you brought it back?"

I sucked in my breath. He sat up.

"Ira, where in God's name is the dog?"

His voice rose in a way that would have sent his stoutest thug diving under the sofa. My gut clenched, but I held my ground. Goddard shouted occasionally, but had never laid a hand on me.

Yet.

I watched, heart pounding, as he forced himself to inhale deeply and count. He exhaled with excruciating deliberation. He looked down at me with nothing more than simple expectation.

"It's no longer in my possession," I admitted.

"That much is clear, but—"

"I'll get it back, I swear. I just need a few hours' sleep."

And for the sickly sweet smell of the lotus to clear out of my nostrils.

"Hmm," he said doubtfully. Then his gaze fell to my midsection. He teased open the front edges of my pajamas to reveal a large bruise blooming beneath my sternum. "What the devil is that?"

"Sodding Lazarus." I pulled my pajama top closed. "He's quite good with his fists, you know."

"So Lazarus took the dog from you."

He sounded relieved.

"Not exactly," I said.

"Then who did?"

It would have saved everyone a lot of trouble, had I told him everything at that point. I could still see the woman in my mind's eye—her coarse, dark hair and almond-shaped eyes. I could hear her too-perfect Cockney, feel her strong, mannish hands rifling through my pockets. If she was staying in Whitechapel, Goddard's men could have had her on our doorstep by luncheon.

But the shame of my failure would have killed me. Goddard had given me so much—a home, an education, companionship, and material generosity that knew no limits. And in return, he'd asked one simple errand. Even if we did both somehow escape prison now, I'd never be able to live with myself if I didn't at least try to complete it.

Moreover, the woman had nicked the statue off me as easily as if I'd been some Piccadilly fop with no more street sense than an infant. She could not be allowed to get away with it.

I could make this right. By God, I would.

"It's a long story, but I'll get it back by day's end," I swore again.

"All right, all right. Rest now. You've had quite a night."

He patted his thigh, and I gratefully laid my head down upon it. Now that his anger had run its course, he was thinking. He hummed softly as he teased the tangles from my hair, pausing to run his manicured fingernails over my cheek now and then. His skin smelled of bergamot, jasmine, and musk. If I weren't so knackered, it would have made me harder than the Rock of Gibraltar.

"It's almost dawn," he finally said. "A few hours won't make a difference, and you're useless without your beauty rest." A smile crept into his voice. "But you must find it, Ira. Our blackmailer mustn't get his hands on it. And that goes double for that prick, St. Andrews."

"Why?" I asked.

I tried to sit up, but he gently held my head against his thigh. The rhythmmic stroking began again, and he said, "The mistakes of youth, dear boy. That's all I can tell you right now. Please trust me."

His hands wandered down, over my shoulder, over my chest, drawing back the edges of the silk pajama top. Gently, his fingers began investigating my bruise. He pulled back quickly when I gasped.

"I don't like this," he said. "I'll summon my physician in the morning."

"'S just a bruise," I said sleepily.

"No arguments. Will you have a drop of laudanum for the pain?"

"I think I've had enough already," I mumbled.

I'd have refused even if I hadn't choked down my weight in *pulvis opii* that evening. Laudanum was safe enough, but I'd seen enough of the damage opium could do during my Whitechapel years. I wanted nothing to do with it in any form.

What the devil would have inspired someone to pack those statues with opium powder, anyway, I wondered. The obvious reason would be to smuggle it somewhere. But why—when even a child could walk into a chemist's shop and purchase the stuff in any of a hundred different forms?

"Cain," I said. "Who does that storeroom belong to?"

"The owner of the pawn shop, I'd imagine," he said.

"And the statues?"

"Why?"

"Because some of them were filled with opium powder."

For several moments, he was absolutely silent. "That is curious," he eventually said.

His tone gave nothing away, except for the fact he'd nothing more to say to me on the matter. There was a bit of jostling as he arranged our pillows between his back and the iron headboard. He turned the bedside lamp on very low, and I heard him shake out the pages of his trusty *Literary Quarterly*.

As I drifted off in the warmth of his lap, my thoughts turned to the Chinese woman who had accosted me in Miller's Court. The Chinese dealt in opium, as did Goddard. Could the blackmailer be one of his rivals? Goddard guarded his personal life so meticulously I couldn't imagine it. And what had he said about "mistakes of youth"?

I rubbed my eyes, trying to clear away the fog of fatigue and lotus. Goddard stroked my hair.

"Whatever you're thinking will keep until morning," he said. "Sleep now."

CHAPTER FOUR

Morning arrived all too soon. From Goddard's expression, I could tell that he was thinking the same thing. The Duke of Dorset Street typically greeted daybreak with more enthusiasm than a crime lord reasonably should. In the gray light streaming through our bedroom window, I could see the wee hours had treated Goddard even more miserably than they had treated me. His face was pale and his dressing gown hung heavily from his compact, muscular frame. He was clutching the curtain so tightly that even from across the room I could see that his knuckles had gone white. This quiet vigilance was as close to panic as the Duke of Dorset Street ever got.

It didn't suit him in the least.

Outside the sanctuary of our chamber, the manservant's footsteps creaked up the stairs, stopping outside our door.

"Coffee, Collins," Goddard called through the door. "And summon my physician as soon as is decent."

"Yes, sir."

Down on York Street, the day's first carriage rattled by. Goddard pulled back from the window as if the carriage were a police wagon coming to take him away for the crime of lying with a willing man in the privacy of his own chamber. I wanted to put a hand on his shoulder and tell him that it would all work out in the end—even if I couldn't see how it would.

"So Lazarus doesn't have the dog," he said once the carriage had passed.

"No," I replied.

"Bloody hell."

Goddard let the curtain drop with a worrisome resignation, considering he believed every man to be the captain of his own fate. He turned from the window. His gaze wandered from the bed where I was sitting to the spindly bedside table to the wardrobe on the opposite wall. As far as furniture went, Goddard favored clean lines and unvarnished wood, with a few discreet Oriental flourishes. He had commissioned all of his furniture to reflect these tastes, giving the house an elegant, masculine feel I adored.

Footsteps shuffled by along the sidewalk on the street. Someone mounted our front steps and rang the bell. I heard the front door open and muted voices. Collins thanked the visitor—one of Goddard's messengers, I'd have wagered from the brevity of the exchange—and shut the door.

"I'll get the dog back," I said.

"You're damned right you will." Goddard turned. Some of the color was coming back to his face, and the familiar arrogance returning to his voice. "But first, Dr. Hendricks will have a look at that bruise."

I opened my mouth to protest, but the door opened. The room filled with the rich aroma of coffee that Goddard chose himself, and which Collins roasted and ground to specification.

"Just put it on the bedside table," Goddard said.

Goddard walked over to the wardrobe and opened it, sighing as if he'd expected something other than the row of identical white silk shirts facing him. Laying out the day's clothing was Collins's job, and before remembering the tray in his hands the manservant started toward the wardrobe.

"On the table, please, Collins," I said.

The manservant regarded me with a disdainful flick of his eyes, but eventually crossed to the bedside table. He reverently placed the *Literary Quarterly* into the table drawer before setting down a small pot and a single china cup, sparing me not so much as a sneer. Goddard and I had shared a bed for two years. The manservant had to have seen me in that very spot a hundred times, in a hundred different states of undress. Yet each time he addressed Goddard as if they were the only ones in the room. Like his adamant refusal to call me "Mr. Ira," which would have indicated he considered me a member of the household rather than a fellow employee, pretending that I wasn't actually in Goddard's bed was a subtle but unmistakable snub.

"Sir," Collins began.

"I thought I said…"

Goddard's voice trailed off when he saw the envelope that Collins was tapping against his fleshy palm: white stationery with dark ink. My heart stopped.

"Good God, not another one," Goddard said.

"No, sir," Collins replied, his tone reflecting pleasant surprise. "Actually, it arrived just now from the chancellor's office."

Goddard sucked in a sharp breath.

"Then that's it," he said. "They've decided."

"I daresay it appears that way…Professor."

Though Goddard's criminal enterprises had brought him wealth beyond measure, he'd always felt that his proper place was in the ivory tower of academia. It sounds strange, I know. And yet he'd undertaken my own education with such thoroughness and patience that he'd convinced me as well. It was a shame the rest of the world didn't see it that way. Since his dismissal from Cambridge he'd spent as much time trying to insinuate himself back into the academic fold as he had buying judges and brothels. Yet no matter how many brilliant monographs he produced, it seemed clear that he was never going to go further than occasional evening lectureship at King's.

Until now.

"Phillips is retiring after this term," Goddard said as I pushed my way between them. "They have to give his post to me. The rest of them have five years' experience between them, and a handful of articles, if that. I can't look, Ira. Read it to me."

He thrust the paper into my hand. My heart raced as I took in the symbol of the college—the shield with its blue bar, red cross, and the tome at the top, covers splayed out like wings.

"'Esteemed Dr. Goddard,'" I began. I smiled at him. "That sounds promising."

He began pacing, his crimson dressing gown billowing behind him. I tried to read ahead, to soften any blows before they came.

"Well?" Goddard demanded.

"He wants you to meet with him at ten o'clock this morning in his office."

He stopped."That's all?"

I held up the letter. His dark eyes darted over the lines once, twice.

"Of course. He would want to tell me the news in person. Yes, quite."

Goddard raked his fingers through his rumpled hair. Between his avid pursuit of the fighting arts and his meticulous diet, he had not only managed to retain the physique of a much younger man, but also to keep the gray hair confined to a distinguished dusting at each temple. The combination of power and dignity never failed to stir me. I wondered what sort of salary a professor commanded.

"Leave us." Goddard dismissed the manservant with a wave. "Have some coffee, Ira."

"I'd prefer buttered rum," I said.

"*Buttered rum*?" He laughed as if I'd been joking, while filling the little china cup. "Why, the day is just beginning, dear boy. The time for sleep is over. Drink and be refreshed. So Lazarus took the dog, but he doesn't have it anymore?"

"That's about the size of it," I said.

"Hmm."

The prospect didn't seem to vex him as it had in the dead of night. Now he stroked his mustache as if entertaining a philosophical question. I watched him cross back to the wardrobe, where he withdrew one of the identical silk shirts and held it up before discarding it onto the floor. When a second shirt joined the first, I realized that he'd simply traded one vexation for another. When he picked up a third, I set the coffee down.

"Cain, that's no way to treat silk."

Goddard was a man of contrasts. One of the most powerful men in London, he was consumed with concern about what to wear to a meeting with a stiff-collared chancellor whom he could buy and sell a thousand times over.

And though it was no little relief for my failure to be forgotten for the moment, I did hate to see him suffer.

"First," I said, taking the third shirt from his hands and replacing it in the wardrobe, "we choose the suit. Large details before small."

I might have spent the first twenty-three years of my life wearing other men's rags, but Goddard knew no valet could put together an ensemble better than I. He relaxed visibly while I chose a jacket and trousers in charcoal. The matching waistcoat also got the nod, though the crimson flecks did give him a moment's hesitation.

He balked when it came to the bright crimson cravat, however.

"No," he said. "Absolutely not."

"Trust me."

I opened a small drawer atop one of the wardrobe shelves, drawing out a silver stickpin with a ruby tip. I held it against the cravat. I considered putting the pin back in the drawer, but imagining how smashing it would look against the black silk I'd later tie around my own neck, I pocketed it instead.

"The suit is somber enough for the occasion, but not so formal as to let the chancellor think that he has the upper hand. The pattern of the waistcoat may seem a bit *outré* to your conservative tastes, but it makes you look like a man of the world."

"But the *tie*."

I smoothed the satin lapels of his robe.

"I bought it for your last birthday," I said.

"Oh. Well, then." He paused to smooth an errant curl from my forehead. "Dear boy, with you in my corner, how can I fail?"

"Now we're ready for a shirt," I said. "Might I suggest the white one?"

I leaned against the iron footboard and watched him put on the outfit I'd assembled. Sometimes our interactions took on a semblance of domestic routine that would have made it easy to forget my place. Goddard and I might be lovers, but I had begun as his whore. At some level, he still thought of me that way.

And whatever affection I might feel, the worst mistake a whore can make is to fall in love with a client.

"So," Goddard said, tucking his shirt into his trousers, "how do you intend to get the dog back?"

"I thought I'd start by asking at the clinic."

He had slid one arm into the waistcoat before stopping. The garment now hung precariously from his shoulder.

"Not Lazarus's clinic?"

"Of course, Lazarus's clinic. Everyone passes through there at some point, and Nurse Brand knows them all by name. Wait," I said. "You're not jealous?"

I was tempted to remind Goddard that I'd cut off Lazarus—and the rest of my regulars—for him. Having slammed that door shut behind me, it was preposterous to think that I'd jeopardize my present position by considering that penniless twit Lazarus as anything more than an annoyance to get past.

"Don't be ridiculous." He cleared his throat. "I'm just concerned you not give away our movements to St. Andrews."

"But—"

He turned to me. "Admittedly, it wouldn't be the end of the world if St. Andrews found the statue first. But I shall never forgive him for what happened at Cambridge. I will not work with that man, however common our goal might be."

Well, then.

I'd known, of course, that Goddard had left the university in disgrace. I'd known that St. Andrews had as well, around the same time. But this was the first time he had mentioned that the events were connected. Shooting me a nervous glance, he cleared his throat again and fidgeted with his mustache.

"And I forbid you to do the same with Lazarus," he added, somewhat subdued.

"All right," I said. I searched his face, but he had closed himself off to me.

"And do let Dr. Hendricks examine that bruise before you go. Your ribs—"

"I don't need a doctor," I interrupted.

Truth be told, I should rather have liked for someone to take a peek at the rash on my bollocks. An itch might have only been an itch in Goddard's world, but where I came from it was often a harbinger of something worse. I'd not strayed from Goddard's bed since he took me in. Of course, many a pestilence could sleep for years before thrusting its head through the floor of a perfectly serviceable domestic arrangement. And if that were the case, I'd appreciate hearing it from someone who wouldn't immediately report his findings to the Duke of Dorset Street.

"But I'll have the nurse look at it," I conceded.

Jacket and waistcoat in place with socks firmly gartered, Goddard crossed to the bed and took my hands.

"Forgive me, dear boy," he said. He brushed his fingers across my cheek and pressed me against the footboard with his hips. "The past few days have been most distressing. I'm afraid I'm finding it difficult to be completely rational. And on top of that, the thought of someone doing you harm…Humor me. Please. My physician has been summoned. Don't waste my money or his time, hmm?"

He set his lips to mine with a tenderness that turned my legs to jelly. His kisses became insistent as he leaned me back over the footboard, torso to torso, his hands pinning mine against the cold iron.

"I do love you, you know," he breathed.

I reached for his belt buckle. What should have happened next was interrupted by that meddling manservant. At the sound of the knock, Goddard pulled back with a rueful look and tucked his shirt back into his trousers.

"Come," he called.

The door opened. Collins raised both eyebrows as I self-consciously pulled the edges of my pajama top closed.

"Your carriage is waiting, sir."

"Yes, of course," Goddard said, smoothing his hair back into place. "Thank you, Collins."

As the manservant cleared away the coffee tray, Goddard raised my palm to his lips.

"Later, dear boy. I promise."

"But the meeting isn't until ten," I protested.

I tried to slide my arms around his waist, but he caught my wrists and held them at my sides.

"I've business to attend to."

Then, with a wistful smile, he added, "And I need time to gather my nerve before walking into the lion's den. But when I return, I'll be all yours."

He kissed his fingertips and pressed them against my cock. He turned on his heel, leaving me alone with my face burning, his cologne lingering in the room like a ghost.

After the door swung shut behind him, I wiped the sweat from my upper lip and took a few deep breaths to calm my racing blood. The bed was rumpled, still warm and smelling of him. But I would not resort to self-abuse. It was a waste of time and betrayed an unflattering lack of discipline. After repeating this thought four or five hundred times, the urge subsided. I smoothed down my hair and pajamas and slipped through the door to my own room.

❖

Goddard had set up the blue bedroom for my use when I'd first come to live at York Street. It was a pleasant room, despite its lack of use. The single bed along the south wall was covered with a quilt in complementary shades of azure and sky. There was a desk by the window, outfitted for the confidential secretary I was supposed to be, and a wardrobe that was a three-quarter-sized copy of the one in Goddard's chamber. Next to the wardrobe was a battered trunk, where I kept the few possessions I'd brought with me from Whitechapel. The air always smelled faintly of the lavender water Eileen used to iron the linens, and the fragrant soap Collins used for my morning shave.

As if summoned by the mere thought, the manservant appeared in the doorway, bearing a tray with a basin of steaming water, fresh towels, and a wicked-looking straight razor. Without greeting or preamble, he set the tray down on my desk and then pulled out the chair and laid one of the towels across the back.

I hated being shaved. I hated being shaved by him. But Goddard had made it very clear that in exchange for a roof, fashionable clothing, and all the peaty Islay malt I could bolt down, I was expected to keep my appearance up to his exacting standards. To wit, I'd been clean-shaven when Goddard had met me, and though I sometimes fancied cultivating one of the extravagant beards currently in fashion, clean-shaven I would remain until Goddard grew bored with it.

But that didn't mean I had to be cheerful about it.

Collins cleared his throat.

Ignoring him, I rattled the wardrobe open and looked for the patched, frayed jacket and trousers I'd been wearing when I first came to live at York Street. One couldn't, after all, go poking around Whitechapel dressed like a crime lord's fancy man.

"I've taken the liberty of laying out your brown suit," the manservant said.

"No, not today."

Where the devil were they? When a third inspection of the wardrobe came to naught, I glanced toward the bed. I'd nothing against the chocolate-colored jacket and trousers Collins had arranged there. A canary waistcoat might even have made them attractive. But the immaculate linen would draw pickpockets like flies. The previous night's clothing might have proven adequate. Unfortunately, I'd left it on the floor of the bath, and it was no doubt already below stairs awaiting Eileen's attentions.

"Your shave, Mr. Adler," Collins said impatiently.

"For the love of—oh, fine. Let's get it over with."

I pushed the wardrobe door shut, stalked over to the chair, and offered up my face for the morning ritual. Things could be worse, I thought, as he slapped my face with warm, moist towels. I could still be peddling my arse up and down Dorset Street. I'd have been my own man, but how much was that worth when it meant fighting the rats for a bit of doorway to sleep in? And yet, how long could I stand for the humiliation of being pushed around by a mealy-mouthed manservant? At least I was the one receiving the shave, rather than giving it.

"Doesn't it bother you, Collins," I asked, my words muffled by a damp cloth, "to be butler, footman, and valet to not just one, but two gentlemen?"

To his credit, Collins didn't choke on the idea I fancied myself a gentleman, but merely swiped the razor back and forth across a length of dark leather tied to his apron.

"I'm Professor Goddard's butler," he replied. "It's my job to see to the needs of his guests."

Guests? I started up in my chair. He might fancy himself a butler, but he was not demoting me to "guest"! My face towel flopped into my lap. Collins plucked it up between two fingers, discarded it onto the tray, and pushed me back down.

"Has Dr. Goddard had many *guests* like me?" I asked irritably as he lathered my chin.

"A few."

"But none who have stayed on for two years."

Having buried my face and neck in thick drifts of foam, Collins took the razor by the handle. His hand paused above my throat, as if contemplating the professional repercussions of an unfortunate slip of the fingers. Fortunately, he wasn't the type to throw away decades of service and the extravagant salary that bought his silence for an instant of bloody gratification. He laid the blade against my throat and brought it to my chin in one smooth stroke.

"Your master can afford a proper staff," I continued, while he rinsed the blade in the basin and shook it dry. "He could afford an improperly large staff, for that matter. Surely you must sometimes resent the extra work."

For several long moments, he did not reply, setting himself to his task with a worrying determination. Ultimately my worry came to nothing. Collins's hands were as steady as a surgeon's, and when he wiped the last of the lather from behind my ears, my face was as smooth as it had been the day I was born.

"It's not for me to question our employer's methods," he said, as he toweled the blade clean and folded it. "Speaking for myself, I prefer leading a small, trusted staff to being one of a parade of interchangeable faces, here one day and gone the next without a trace."

Smiling mildly, he set the blade next to the bowl, collected the towels, and piled them onto the tray. With one final glance in my direction, he picked up the tray and turned.

"Breakfast will be served in the morning room," he said.

Parade? Interchangeable? My mind bubbled over with so many retorts that the man's heavy footfall was already sounding on the stairs before I found the wherewithal to speak.

"I've taken breakfast in the dining room for two years!" I shouted.

There was nothing wrong with the morning room. Goddard had given it to me during my first year at York Street, and it was my favorite. All the same, if Goddard had been at home, I'd have been served in the dining room like a member of the household, rather than in the morning room like some unwashed tradesman one was unexpectedly obligated to feed.

But breakfast be damned, and the manservant be damned to hell. I had a statue to find, and to do that I needed to trace my steps back to Whitechapel.

And I was not about to do it in brown linen.

I threw open the trunk next to my wardrobe. I pushed aside a battered hat I'd once thought flash, a cloth stuck through with a surgical needle, and a yellowing, decade-old clip from the *Times:* Limehouse Deaths Recall 1870 Opium Tainting. An acquaintance had told me the picture of one of the 1870 victims looked as if she could have been my mother. The dates were right. There was a resemblance, though since I'd last seen the woman at the door of the workhouse where she'd left me to go chase the lotus, there was no way of knowing for sure. And at the bottom of the trunk, I found my Whitechapel clothes—clean, pressed, and utterly threadbare. Brown suit indeed! I took them out and set them down beside my knee. And when I went to shut my memories back where they belonged, I found the one thing that would have solved the previous night's problems before they began.

My pipe had been a formidable weapon in its day. A section of lead as long as a man's forearm, with one end cut to a sharp angle and the other wrapped in rags, and molded by time and use to the exact contours of my left hand. Even after two years of sitting forgotten in the trunk, it returned to my grasp as if it were part of me. I gave it a swing, relishing the weighty hum as it sang through the air against the somber toll of the Great Westminster bells.

"Fillet of sole," Collins said, behind me once more.

The pipe flew from my fingers and clattered against the legs of the wardrobe.

"Will you stop sneaking up like that?"

Instead of skulking back down the hallway, Collins crossed my chamber. He laid a pile of freshly laundered clothing on the bed, perhaps to reemphasize his belief that being egregiously taken advantage of proved how highly valued he was as an employee.

"Er, I thought the brown suit today," he said as I shook out my old jacket. "With a white shirt and, er…"

He lifted a pair of drawers from the pile. Like the morning room, I had to admit that these drawers were my favorite. Who wouldn't enjoy walking around in cream-colored silk from waist to ankle? But *guest* or not, I'd be damned if I'd let the man dictate the very clothes on my back.

"My old clothing will be better suited to today's activities," I said. "Thanks for the drawers, though."

"Activities? I wasn't informed—"

"Is the *butler* to be informed every time I take a piss?" I snapped.

He considered me for a moment, his upper lip twitching against a snarl. Then a curious serenity descended over his features.

"Of course, Mr. Adler," he said with a short nod. "But might I remind you that Dr. Hendricks is scheduled to arrive within the hour?"

"No doubt I'll meet him along the way. Good day, Collins."

"But your breakfast—"

"Enjoy it with my compliments."

Chapter Five

The Great Westminster Clock was striking half-eleven when I sighted the boarded-up windows of Stepney Clinic. The clinic, where my relationship with Timothy Lazarus had begun and ended, was tucked into a narrow alley off Whitechapel Road in the dour brown shadow of the London Hospital, half a mile northeast of Miller's Court. As I stepped from the hansom onto crumbling pavement, I saw the front step had been recently repaired, and the chipped, dented door hung from new hinges. An angry-looking pair was sharing a bottle against the wall nearby.

Stepney Clinic was one of many infirmaries in the area created by the poor laws. Between the standard of care set by Dr. Lazarus and the relentless advocacy of Nurse Pearl Brand, it was surely the best. All the same, I had never understood why Lazarus chose to squander his talents there. He'd trained with the finest minds at the London Hospital, before going on to serve with Her Majesty's army during the disastrous Siege of the Sherpur Cantonment. I understood mere survival of the latter was a heroic feat—though Lazarus refused to speak of it. Nonetheless, someone with an encyclopedic knowledge of the human condition and distinguished military service should have been soothing the fevered brows of the crowned heads of Europe, not scrubbing some drunk's dinner off the floor of his own surgery. And yet there he was, day after day, as if his salvation depended on it.

As I entered the clinic, my eyes took a moment to adjust to the dim light inside. Out of deference to the heat, or perhaps to save oil, only one lamp had been lit in the waiting room. It stood on the wobbly desk in the far corner where Nurse Brand was sorting the incoming patients according to the severity of their complaints. I glanced around for Lazarus, relieved that he seemed to be elsewhere. The plan was to quietly put a bug in the nurse's ear about the statue, with promise of a substantial reward buying both her best efforts and her silence. The latter hope was scuttled when, with the preternatural perception of one who has spent years surrounded by the worst people at their worst, she looked across the crowded waiting room and met my eyes.

"Mr. Adler!" she exclaimed.

Nurse Brand resembled a draft horse in stature—twelve vigorous stone of fierce compassion in a cap, stained apron, and forearm cuffs—and proved just as effective at clearing a path through the crowd.

"You look terrible," she declared when she reached me.

Of that, I had no doubt. Sweat plastered my hat to my head, my eyes and throat were gritty with soot, the bruise below my sternum was causing me to stoop slightly, and my crotch burned with the fury of hell itself.

"Beastly day," I muttered.

"Well, don't just stand there, you daft boy, come in." She glanced around cautiously. "Don't suppose you're wantin' to run into the doctor."

"Not if I can help it," I said.

She nodded knowingly. It had been two years since Lazarus had slammed the clinic door in my face. I doubted Nurse Brand knew the details, but she'd known how I'd earned my daily bread. Lazarus, despite his best efforts, had made quite a spectacle of himself. Though my reasons for avoiding him that day had nothing to do with our sordid past, there was no harm in allowing the nurse to draw her own conclusions.

"Into the dispensary with you. The doctor ain't stepped out of the surgery for five minutes since we opened the doors. If he ever finishes with the lot of them, he won't think to look in there."

I followed her back through the waiting room, down a short corridor, and into the converted closet that served as a storehouse for the clinic's meager hoard of herbs and potions. A narrow counter ran along one wall, with a series of jars lined up neatly at one end. A crudely made cabinet housed labeled bottles behind locking glass doors just above the counter. The window in the back looked out onto a brick wall.

"Now," said the nurse, folding her arms across her substantial bosom, "What can I do for you, Ira?"

I told her everything—well, *almost* everything. Though she'd only met Goddard once, she'd despised him on sight. If she'd known finding the dog would make his life any easier, she'd have tossed me out on my ear. I also omitted the tussle with Lazarus. The nurse had tried her best not to take sides when things went sour between us, but she hadn't seen me in two years. She worked with him every day.

"A doxy, you say."

"Dressed like one, talked like one, but it was the statue she wanted. I'm certain of it," I said.

She looked up, frowning.

"I had a silver flask in the other pocket, and a handful of coins. She didn't touch those," I continued. "Also, she was Chinese."

"A Chinese? Right there on Dorset Street? Blimey."

She frowned at the long expanse of counter, pulling a rag from the waistband of her apron. I watched as she thoughtfully ran the rag over the cracking white paint, stopping to address a recalcitrant spot with her thumbnail.

"What were so important about that statue, anyway?" she asked, squinting at me through the dim light.

"I'm not at liberty to say. But if you help me get it back, I can assure you that certain parties are prepared to be quite generous."

She narrowed her eyes.

"*Certain parties?* You ain't still with *that man*," she said.

"I don't know what you mean."

She took a step toward me, fist curling around the rag. I stepped back and met wall. Nurse Brand didn't take kindly to interlopers upsetting the apple cart. When Goddard had upset mine, Lazarus's had tipped clean over, in turn causing the nurse's own steady cart to throw a wheel.

"What you does in the dark ain't none of my business, Ira Adler, mortal sin though it be." She pushed a sweaty strand of hair behind her ear, much as a man might roll up his sleeves before a fight. "But when it puts the only surgeon in London who'll work for a chimney sweep's wages so far down in the dumps he don't show for a week, I make it my business."

I swallowed.

"That—that was two years ago, Pearl," I said.

She paused. She looked at the rag in her hand and stuffed it into her apron pocket with a sigh.

"So it was," she conceded. "But it weren't right the way you left with 'im, just walked out as if the doctor weren't even standin' there." She shook her head. "I hope he's treatin' you well, at least. Do you love him?"

I blinked. I certainly loved living at York Street. I was quite fond of my tailored clothes and perpetually full belly. As for Goddard, it wasn't love like in the magazines Eileen liked to read, but it wasn't without affection. It was a shame, of course, that Lazarus had come to depend on our little meetings to the degree that he had. But I'd never promised him anything more.

"Then perhaps," she said, "you think he loves you."

Well, he had said as much just a few hours ago. I opened my mouth to say something clever, when I heard Collins's voice at the back of my mind: *A parade of interchangeable faces, here one day and gone the next without a trace.*

"Er..."

Her hard features softened, and she looked at me with the same expression she'd worn when I'd shown up on the clinic's doorstep for the first time nine years earlier—and eight years before Lazarus had signed on as resident physician.

My first customer had been a brute.

"You daft, daft boy." She sighed. "I don't think you half know what you've got yourself into. No matter." Her eyes went from icy to a warm, sympathetic blue, and she patted my elbow. "I don't forget me boys, Ira. However bad it gets, you always have a home here. Don't forget that. Now," she said, clearing her throat, "I'll put the word out about the Chinese girl and the statue, you can be sure about that. But were there anything else you needed as long as you're here?"

❖

The woman couldn't refrain from chortling as I peeled off my Whitechapel trousers and silk underthings. She dragged in a stool for me to stand on, to better inspect the area, she'd said, but I couldn't help thinking this humiliation was a bit of good-natured revenge on her part. Shivering up there in no more than my shirt and waistcoat, not five steps from a crowded waiting room, the mingled odors of vomit and disinfectant fighting for prominence in the stuffy little dispensary, I felt like a medical school display. Nonetheless, if Nurse Brand could tell me anything about the abominable itch that had settled over my genital region, I'd stand on that stool every day and twice on Sunday for the rest of my life.

"Nothing," she declared, stepping back at last.

"Nothing? How can there be nothing?"

"I'm only telling you what I see, and that's nothing. No sores, no rash, no sign of infestation—"

"But my bollocks are as red as a tomato," I cried.

"Only 'cause you've been scratchin' 'em. Didn't your mother ever tell you… No," she said in a chastened tone. "No, I suppose she didn't. It only makes it worse to scratch."

"Makes what worse?"

She shrugged.

"I don't know what to tell you, Ira. I don't see a thing. Are you havin' other symptoms?"

I frowned. There weren't any other symptoms to speak of, but that didn't mean they wouldn't come later. It wasn't as if it were totally unexpected. In my former line of work, no one went six months without some little burn or drip. But this was different. I could feel it. My palms were suddenly slick with sweat; I wiped them on my shirt.

"God's bollocks, I'm diseased," I muttered.

"Don't be stupid. And don't blaspheme." The nurse tossed me my drawers as I hopped down from the stool. "Are you sure it's not…" She tapped her temple with a long, square finger.

"You think I'm making this up?"

I shook out the drawers and loosened the drawstring. The silk felt cool and smooth between my fingers, but the thought of putting anything over my lower regions filled me with dread.

"It's happened before," she said. "Like that time…no, it were more than once, when you convinced yourself you had consumption…"

"It's not like that, Pearl!"

"Or maybe you're just feeling nostalgic. Remember when you coshed your own noggin with a bottle so's you'd have an excuse to pester the doctor?"

"I did not give myself a malevolent genital pox to get Timothy Lazarus's attention!"

"I'm happy to hear it," said a voice in the doorway.

We both looked over in horror, to where the good doctor stood, looking fresh as a daisy in a crisp shirt and brown trousers, his purple lump of a nose the only indication that he'd spent half the night wrestling on the floor of a Whitechapel dollyshop.

"Medical problems, Adler?" he asked. His voice sounded nasal and tired.

"Nothing that's any business of yours, Tim."

He glanced from the nurse to me. Looking closer, I saw his eyes were as red as mine felt. I derived no small satisfaction from the fact he'd probably stumbled out of bed with an unbelievable opium headache. He circled his left shoulder and winced.

"Come now," he sighed. "If you're having problems below stairs, you could do worse than confiding in an old friend."

"I suppose you'd enjoy going through my pubic hair with a lice comb," I mumbled. Avoiding his eyes, I shimmied into my drawers.

"Or you could let me have a look at your midsection. I worried about that blow you took to the solar plexus last night."

I froze.

"Last night?" asked the nurse.

"Oh, didn't Adler mention that?" Lazarus circled his shoulder again and popped his neck. "We ran into each other, quite literally, 'round Miller's Court."

The nurse narrowed her eyes.

"I'm sure I don't want to know."

"This has been a pleasant reunion," I said, "but I really must be on my way."

"Not so fast." Lazarus scooped up my trousers from the floor with one deft motion. "We have business to discuss."

"Then I'll leave you to it," said the nurse.

"But, Pearl—"

Ignoring me, she bustled past, waving a dismissive hand over her shoulder. Lazarus shut the door behind her and locked it.

"Hey!" I cried.

He tossed me my trousers.

Lazarus well knew I had a horror of enclosed spaces, I realized as he smugly slipped his keys back into his trouser pocket. A cold sweat broke out across my back. I might have tried to take the keys by force, had not my stomach borne a purple-and-black reminder of Lazarus's superiority in a fight. Instead, I shook out my trousers and snarled, "Turn around while I dress."

While I pulled on my trousers and socks, Lazarus rearranged the jars on the counter. He had explained once how working at the clinic helped him to exorcise his demons after he'd returned from Afghanistan. But that had been years ago. Why was he still there? I surreptitiously watched him adjust the collar of his crisp linen shirt. His boots were new, too, and I recognized his citrus and musk cologne as the work of one of London's premier perfumers. What had the nurse said about a chimney sweep's wages? It would seem being kept by Andrew St. Andrews paid quite generously.

"You look well," I muttered as I buttoned my trousers.

Lazarus had moved on to bedpans by that point, stacking and restacking. The increased vehemence of the clatter was the only sign he'd heard me. In the dim light of the dollyshop I'd failed to notice the gray now peppering his neatly trimmed hair. The lines at the corners of his eyes were the same, perhaps a bit deeper. But he wasn't living on tea and biscuits anymore—he'd filled out quite nicely with proper care and feeding.

"Really well," I said.

He turned to me with a withering stare.

"My nose is broken in two places, I'm bruised from top to tail, and my head feels like it was run over by a rickshaw full of opium. Stop lying, Adler. I don't pay for it anymore," he added coldly.

"Well, I don't sell it anymore. May I go now?"

He turned and looked me over, his cool gaze coming to a meaningful stop at the ruby stickpin.

"Not that you have any room to criticize, Mr. 222 Baker Street," I cried. "That's a nice tie, for someone who works in a shithole clinic in Bethnal Green. Is it silk?"

"Same as yours."

I stuffed my shirt into my trousers, shrugged into my jacket, and laced up my shoes. I had to get out of there. But Lazarus wanted to talk, and he had the key.

"Adler, about last night—"

"You didn't have to be so enthusiastic with your elbows. You can kill a man that way, you know."

"I know several ways to kill a man," he said. "A gentle elbow to the gut isn't one of them."

"Gentle?"

He was circling his shoulder again, kneading the muscle with his opposite hand.

"A man your age should avoid fights, not start them," I said.

"You mean this?" He nodded toward his shoulder. "Don't flatter yourself."

He made a pained little noise and stretched his arm across his chest.

I was probably the only man in London, aside from Andrew St. Andrews, who had seen the ugly knot of tissue that bloomed from Lazarus's left shoulder: a souvenir from the Siege of the Sherpur Cantonment. There was a corresponding scar on his shoulder blade where the bullet had entered. Any other man would have worn a bullet wound like a medal, but unlike the hundreds of tossers still dining out on a few bruises sustained in the line of duty, Lazarus did his best to cut off any discussion of Afghanistan before it began.

Lazarus glanced from his shoulder to me and said, "If I didn't want to talk about it when we could tolerate each other's company, you'll understand my reluctance to speak of it now."

"Fine. Open that blasted door, and I'll never mention it again."

"Sit down, Adler."

I sat, but not because he'd told me to. It was getting stuffy in there. Unlike pacing, sitting wouldn't waste precious oxygen.

"I have to know what Goddard has told you about the porcelain dog," he said.

"What has St. Andrews told you?"

"Nothing." He nudged aside a stack of bedpans with his elbow and leaned against the counter. "Nothing, aside from the fact that whatever is inside it will stop the blackmailer cold." He rubbed his eyes and sighed. "Adler, St. Andrews couldn't carry out a case if it had a handle on it. I do most of the work, if you couldn't guess. Even then, his little investigations usually come to nothing. But this time, there's an actual crime with actual consequences—consequences that will affect me, as well. And he's keeping me in the dark."

I let out a long breath. Goddard had put my bollocks in the same vise. Only I was *used* to being in the dark. It was safer that way for Goddard, and for me. On the other hand, none of the other little errands I'd run for Goddard had entailed losing my happy home as a consequence of failure.

"Well," said Lazarus. "Since we're both in the same unenviable situation, wouldn't it make sense to pool our efforts, and—"

"You want to work together?" Goddard's admonishment echoed in my mind. "Absurd."

"Why not?" Lazarus asked, annoyed. "We both want to stop the blackmailer. In wartime, a man often finds himself entrusting his life to someone to whom he'd not deign to—must you chortle so, Adler? To whom he'd not speak two words back on the streets of London. You do trust me, don't you?"

I stopped laughing. Really, it was like asking whether one trusted a St. Bernard. With a cask of brandy. In a snowstorm. Lazarus was an annoyance of the highest order, but he was as reliable as rain. All the same, until one of us found the dog, the point was moot.

"It doesn't matter if I trust you," I said. "I don't have the damned thing anymore."

"What?"

I tugged at my collar. That window was definitely starting to fog over.

"Ask Pearl, if you really must know. Will you please open the door now?"

Lazarus steepled his fingers beneath his chin. He'd no doubt spent the morning mapping out counter-arguments for any objections I might have had to our working together. But clearly he hadn't anticipated my losing the damned statue.

The air was getting thick and the ceiling had definitely gotten lower. I had to get out of there.

"Why are you being so petulant? We'll find the dog, then figure out what it means. It's clearly the most efficient use of our resources. What do you say?" He extended his hand. "Battlefield comrades?"

Lazarus had a workman's hands. They were square and sturdy, though the tapered fingers betrayed an artist's soul. The skin was smooth and pink, the nails clean. The memory of his touch sent a faint shiver through me even two years later. But he was asking me to do something that would send Goddard through the roof, while holding me prisoner in a room no bigger than a rich man's coffin. He had to be out of his sodding mind.

"No," I said.

"No?"

"It's…its impossible. And unethical. Definitely. Now let me out."

"Unethical?" he asked with a bemused smile.

"Let me out. Tim, I'm begging you."

I saw spots. I screwed my eyes shut—which only made my pulse pound louder in my ears. I tried to breathe deeply, but couldn't get more than a few short gasps. Oh God. Oh God.

"Ira?" he asked.

I cocked one eye open, more than a little gratified to see from his guilty expression that he knew he'd taken his little joke too far. And yet he hadn't reached for the key.

We both jumped at the thud of Nurse Brand's fist against the dispensary door.

"Mr. Adler?" she called.

Muttering to himself, Lazarus crossed the room to let her in.

"Thank God," I panted once the door was open. I pushed him aside in my haste to get out of the miserable little room. "You might want to get a building inspector in there, Pearl. I swear the walls are caving in."

I leaned against the doorjamb, reveling in the cool rush of air. I knew it was the same stale clinic air that had been through a thousand sets of consumptive lungs, but in that moment it felt like a clean country breeze. Nurse Brand eyed me as if sizing me up for a straitjacket.

"I meant to tell you," she said warily, "Nate stopped by earlier this week. Asked about you."

"Nate?" I asked.

"Said I ain't seen hide nor hair of you in two years. All the same, he said if you was to turn up, I should tell you he lunches at the Criterion on Thursdays."

"Nate *Turnbull*?"

I'd known Nate almost as long as I'd known myself. He'd been born in the workhouse; I'd come at age three. He'd taught me to pick a pocket, tease open a lock, and charm an orange from a coster's wife. And later, much later, Nate had stumbled upon the knowledge that the money to be made working with one's hands was laughable compared to the price the less noble parts of the body could command. We'd been like salt and pepper, and he'd saved me more times than I could count.

I hadn't meant to cut him off when I left the 'Chapel. But I'd left under the shadow of the gallows. By the time that little misunderstanding was cleared up, we'd both moved on—I to greener pastures, and he to parts unknown. And when your home is whatever bed you can afford that night, it's difficult to receive letters.

Not to mention that Nate was as indiscreet as a tipsy kitchen maid. Not the sort of person one wanted lurking about the front door of the Duke of Dorset Street.

But now the man was lunching at an exclusive Piccadilly

establishmment catering to the most fashionable men's men in London. The mind boggled.

"Thanks, Pearl," I said.

"You'll look him up?"

And that was the question, wasn't it? If I didn't, guilt and curiosity would eat me alive. On the other hand, the man could not be allowed anywhere near York Street.

"Too fine for an old friend, is you?" she sniffed, when I remained silent. "Wasn't so fine when you was beggin' me to check you for the clap. As for you, Doctor," she continued much more cheerfully, "Your...*friend* is here to take you to lunch as well, though I trust that it won't be at the Criterion."

Lazarus didn't even try to hide the pleasure that flushed his usually pasty features. I glanced toward the waiting room to catch a glimpse of St. Andrews. One might think it impossible for someone so conspicuous to lose himself in a room full of indigents, but it seemed he had. I looked closer, but saw only the usual suspects, plus one well-groomed young woman with the earnest air of a missionary.

As the nurse made her way back down the corridor, Lazarus looked out toward the waiting room and sighed happily.

"You're going to have to learn to be more discreet," I said. "If the blackmailer doesn't send you both to prison, your swooning will."

He gave me a look of distaste.

"I can't imagine what you mean by that. Besides, my romantic life is no concern of yours."

"Fine." I turned and started down the corridor. "Just don't say I didn't warn you."

Before I had gone three steps, he added, "You gave up any right to comment when you walked out of my surgery that night with Goddard. You'd never set eyes on him before. But the moment you did, it was as if nothing else existed. Not even the needle and thread I was using to repair the cut above your eyebrow. You didn't even say good-bye."

I whirled, meaning to meet his thoroughly undeserved self-pity with a torrent of harsh, well-chosen words. But there was no self-pity in his expression, only a devilish smirk.

"That was a good, sharp needle," he said. "I miss it."

"You—you're impossible, Lazarus," I sputtered. "Something I'm certain that St. Andrews will discover in time. But for now, allow me to wish the both of you a pleasant luncheon."

His laughter followed me all the way to the waiting room, where every drunk and consumptive in London seemed to have assembled. It wasn't until I was nearly to the door when Lazarus himself emerged. Planting himself in the mouth of the corridor, he called out in a nasal, slightly mocking voice that cut right through the din of the crowd,

"And regarding your little problem below stairs, Adler, you might try a little carbolic in your bath!"

CHAPTER SIX

Carbolic indeed!

The good doctor had effectively announced to half of East London that my bollocks were crawling with lice. I hadn't spent two years recreating myself in Goddard's image only to have some underpaid quacksalver cast aspersions on my hygiene. Emerging onto Whitechapel Road, I glanced in both directions before giving my thigh a desperately needed scratch.

The sun was beating down through the smog hanging over the city like an unwholesome meringue. Through the fog of my snit I heard the sudden sound of a harsh bell, followed by a stream of Italian curses as a scruffy ice-seller swerved his dilapidated cart out of my path at the last moment. He gave me an evil look as he mopped his jowls with a stained handkerchief.

Sweating, even in the relative comfort of my threadbare Whitechapel suit, I made my way through Stepney to Commercial Road. It was four miles back to York Street—plenty of time to gather my thoughts before I'd be expected to present Goddard with a sensible report. Of course, Goddard was at that moment in the chancellor's office, receiving his promotion. He would head straight from there to the tailor for some new clothes befitting his new position. Then to his club for a celebratory port, or, more likely, the London Athletic Club to find a few young men to knock about the boxing ring until his nerves were properly settled. Who knew when the man would actually return home? I certainly didn't fancy waiting for him under Collins's watchful eye—at least not until Collins expelled the bee currently in his bunghole.

On the other hand, there was plenty of time to make it to the Criterion for luncheon.

One thing was certain, though. If I walked another block in that heat and filth, I'd be hacking up lumps of coal for a week. Raising my handkerchief to my face, I set about flagging down a cab from the slow-moving chaos of Commercial Road. Moments later, a hansom nosed horizontally through the wall of carriages and pedestrians, pulling to a stop before me.

"The Criterion, Piccadilly," I told the driver.

As I unfurled myself across the bench, the driver flicked the reins over the horse's back. The cab lurched forward. We merged into the congestion, the horse's steady clip-clop fading into the cacophony of shambling cabs, street hawkers' cries, and the rise and fall of hundreds of shabby boots.

Fewer than twelve hours had separated my first visit to York Street and my last conversation with my friend Nate. It was late December 1887, and I'd just been beaten to within an inch of my life—by a constable, for a change. Trade was winding down for the holidays—sordid back-alley fucks being incompatible with the spirit of Christmas and all. My Friday night assignations with Goddard were regular by that point. Goddard was generous, but not so generous that I could afford to leave him standing, even to sleep off such a beating as that.

When I did finally turn up at our lamppost that night, Goddard didn't raise an eyebrow at my appearance. One might expect an upper-middle-class academic to at least wrinkle his nose at a blood-crusted shirt and one eye swollen shut over a nose smashed all to hell. I should have understood when he simply handed me a bleached handkerchief and packed me into the private hansom he had waiting around the corner that Cain Goddard was more than the mild-mannered teacher he'd portrayed. But I was not in any shape to ask questions, or even to listen to that quiet voice of better judgment reminding me the worst things happen to whores foolish enough to accompany gentlemen home.

Had I been thinking, I might also have questioned the blasé manner in which Goddard's manservant disappeared with my hat, coat, and boots the moment we arrived, meeting us in the bathroom with a tray of surgical implements and a steaming bowl of carbolic. For all of Collins's faults, he had a grasp of propriety that would put the Queen to shame. That he should not vocally protest the intrusion of some lice-bitten renter onto the premises told me he'd at least witnessed such a spectacle before.

"That will be all," Goddard told the manservant, sitting me on the shelf of the mahogany box surrounding his unimaginably large bathtub.

"Very good, sir."

The manservant had taken the liberty of running a bath—a hot one also laced with carbolic. As I sat there, steam puffed up beneath my shirttail, raising a carpet of gooseflesh across my back. Goddard sat down beside me, wetting his fingers in the bowl of antiseptic, and did the same with a bit of cotton.

"Who did this?" he asked, as he swabbed my lacerations with the cotton.

It was his conversational tone I remembered: as if he often passed odd moments sewing people up. When he was satisfied with the cleanliness of the wound, he threaded the needle.

"Come now," he said genially, "Give me a name. He'll pay."

I'd heard of the Duke of Dorset Street. Who hadn't? But to me, the name Goddard meant only ten bob every Friday night. I'd no reason to connect my client with the fearsome crime lord who ruled the East End with an iron fist. All the same, the businesslike way with which the man addressed the constable's grisly work put me on my guard. A loose-tongued rentboy rarely sees his next birthday, though, so despite the insistent questioning that followed—and the half bottle of expensive brandy he poured down my throat after I'd refused laudanum—I held my peace.

"You are a tough little nut," he'd chided as he tied off the last stitch. "But when tough nuts crack, they shatter. Think about it."

I opened my mouth, but he placed a finger over my lips.

"After your bath, come to bed. We'll talk."

I did eventually stumble into someone's empty bed that night. In the morning, Goddard was gone. Collins served my breakfast in the morning room, and told me I was expected for lunch at one sharp.

Then he threw me out.

I eventually stumbled back to the 'Chapel around eleven. I found Nate on Plumber's Row stuffing his face with a baked potato. He blinked at me over his breakfast, all dusky eyes and long lashes, before delicately licking his fingers clean. Not for the first time I marveled at this combination of an angel's face and the table manners of a wild boar.

"Hullo," I said.

I shivered. It was cold as buggery, but someone had slipped four half-crown coins into my trousers, and soon I too would have a potato warming each pocket. But before I could reach for my money, Nate grabbed my arm and pulled me into the shadows.

"Is you out of yer mind showin' yer face 'ere?" he demanded.

"Watch it." I jerked away, rubbing my elbow. "Ol' Wilson wrenched that arm straight to hell and back last night."

Nate's dark eyes had widened, as if with those words I'd somehow made his worst fears come true. He turned his back to the street, pulled his coat tighter around his thin shoulders, and tipped his bowler to a rakish angle. *Sans* potato, he could have them lining up around the block to buy him a drink.

"An' 'e 'ad it comin'," he said. "But, Ira, mate…"

It was a bright winter morning, but dread settled around us like a dark cloak as he related his horrifying tale. Constable Wilson, whose love for the bully club knew the bounds of neither decency nor fairness, had apparently dealt out one beating too many. At some point, while I'd been snoring away in Goddard's lavender-scented sheets, justice had caught up with the constable in the form of an assassin's jagged blade.

"An' they found 'im in that alley next to Crossing'am's," Nate finished. He drew a finger across his throat. "Cut open like a slaugh'er'ouse pig."

My first instinct was to dance a little jig. Wilson had been a menace. Ironically, the East End would be a much safer place short this one copper. But the combination of that quiet inner voice and the way Nate was looking at me made me think. Crossingham's doss-house was right across the street from the lamppost where Goddard and I had met every Friday for the past four months. That alone meant nothing. But Goddard had been both blunt and persistent in his questioning about my attack. When I'd refused to give up Wilson's name, he'd badgered me for other details from which one might identify a man. It had been almost as if he'd taken my beating personally. Who was Cain Goddard, I wondered, that he could divine Wilson's identity from my insensible ramblings in the space of a few short hours, and mete out such decisive justice?

Who was he that he actually *would*?

"Fuck me," I said.

"Fuck you in the arse, mate, half the East End saw him beatin' on yer."

"They fink I done it?"

Nate shushed me, glancing around as if expecting a bevy of blue-bottles to descend any moment.

"I didn't say nuffin'. I won't say nuffin'. But a wise man would disappear for a while, at least until they finds someone to hang for it. Don't yer fink?"

"I s'pose," I said. The day suddenly seemed much colder. I jammed my hands beneath my arms and tried to stomp the numbness from my feet.

"'Ere, take this," he said, slipping me a stack of coins. He smirked. "Last night were a good one."

"Every night's a good one when you look like this." I flicked the brim of his hat.

He smiled, but then his face went serious.

"D'yer have somewhere to go?" he asked.

Did I? God alone only knew. Goddard had given me a bed the night before and invited me back for lunch. If he really was behind the constable's murder, then he'd put me in this position and would bloody well owe me a place to hide until it all went away. And if he wasn't, maybe he could be convinced to offer me shelter for a night or two until

I decided what to do. But I was expected for lunch, and I was quickly coming to the conclusion that whoever Cain Goddard was, he was not to be kept waiting.

I made it back to York Street as the Great Clock was striking one. With the prescience that would prove to be his hallmark, Collins opened the door even before I'd reached the top stair. Once again, he took my coat and hat and ushered me into the morning room.

"Mr. Adler," Goddard said as the manservant closed the doors behind me. He stood before the arched window on the opposite wall, light filtering around him through an artful arrangement of tall, leafy plants. "Right on time."

He crossed the polished wooden parquet with the subdued grace of a predator. He had forgone the formality of a jacket and waistcoat, but his linen shirt and crisp woolen trousers were expensive enough to make the point this was no mere academic.

"I trust that the events of the morning have been to your satisfaction," he said.

"I—ah—the eggs and coffee did go down a treat, sir, thank you, sir," I stammered.

Though my suspicions were growing regarding his role in the constable's murder, there was no profit in sharing them at that point. Cain Goddard held my fate in his hands. If my suspicions were correct, he was an incredibly dangerous individual. If I was wrong, he was still my only hope until the matter of the murdered constable was put to rest. Mentioning I'd suspected his guilt could make an enemy of him.

"Sit, please."

Knees shaking, I lowered myself onto a divan upholstered in olive-colored velvet. Goddard sat beside me and pressed a glass of sherry into my hand.

"It's a dangerous world." He tutted, shaking his head.

"Sir?"

"Drink," he commanded. I did. "I say, if an officer of the law can't even walk his beat without finding himself sliced up like a slaughterhouse pig…"

I choked. He glanced at me out of the corner of his eye. Sweet

Christ, he *had* done it. He refilled my glass. I set it on the floor immediately, lest my shaking hands be the ruin of a piece of furniture worth more than my life.

"I've been giving it some thought," he said. "If a great ox of a constable can't walk the streets at night, what chance does a pretty young thing like you stand out there, hmm?"

I opened my mouth to speak. But it hadn't been an actual question, and he didn't pause for an answer.

"No, Ira—may I call you Ira?—your present circumstances simply will not do."

That was God's own truth. I was in a right spot, and it was his doing. All the same, I knew a deal with the devil when I saw it coming. Unfortunately the devil never seemed to bother unless a person was in no position to refuse. The least I could do was to let him know the seriousness of my position in hopes of a better deal.

"It were bad enough," I said carefully, "wot 'appened to the constable wivout people sayin' it were me wot done it."

His smugness faltered—a tightening of the lips, a short, sharp inhalation, an almost imperceptible widening of the eyes—but he quickly recovered.

"How unexpected." He leaned down to gather up my sherry glass. He placed it back in my hand and closed my fingers around it. "And how undesirable. No matter," he continued. "You were here when the deed occurred. You have two witnesses to that effect."

I laughed. "I don't fink they'd take eiver of us at our word." I tipped the glass back quickly so I wouldn't have to look at his face, which I was certain was flushing with anger at my ungratefulness and temerity. "Well, y-your word is good, I'm sure, sir," I stammered. "But the police won't never take the word of no whore."

"Whore?" His mouth quirked to one side, as if the word somehow amused him. "Whore, my boy? You're my secretary, engaged here last night on business: facts to which I'll testify, should it come to that. But it won't."

"Your…"

"That was what I wanted to talk to you about last night before you fell asleep. I assume you'd have accepted, so, for all intents and purposes, as of last night you were no longer a whore, but my personal and confidential secretary."

I'm rarely speechless, which has often led to no end of misery. But though Goddard's proposition would have got me out of a world of trouble, I had no idea how to respond. I'd heard the word before, but I had no clue regarding the duties of a secretary—save it involved skills laughably out of my ken.

And the regular wearing of suits.

"I'll teach you what you need to know, yes," he said, warming to the subject. He brushed a drop of sherry from the corner of my mouth and touched his finger to his tongue. "You'll live here, of course. And take your meals here. And your clothing—"

"But…"

"And you won't have to worry about the police, not now or ever again. I am, you'll find, a most convenient ally."

"But…"

"And in return, all I ask is your exclusive companionship. Unless, of course, you prefer your current situation," he added.

"But—wot—why—"

He chuckled darkly, his eyes black, smoldering coals—the eyes of the devil himself. Yet, as he laid a warm hand on my thigh, my only thought was of delicious surrender. It would be so easy, and, what did I really have to lose?

"I have people in your world, Ira," he said. "But they serve me out of fear, or out of greed. Which means I can never trust them completely."

"Wot makes you fink you can trust me completely?" I asked.

He frowned, as if actually considering the question. Then he laughed. "You could, I suppose, rob me while I'm away, eh? Murder me in my sleep—or attempt to. But you're not stupid."

His hand on my thigh was solid and warm. Despite the fact Cain Goddard scared the living hell out of me, certain parts of my anatomy were rising to the occasion. I gasped as his fingers moved to the crease of my thigh. When he spoke again, his voice was smoky, his lips brushing against my right ear.

"Only a stupid man, Mr. Adler, would put himself in peril of life and limb for the fleeting comfort a few pawned trinkets would bring, when all he has to do to enjoy a lifetime of ease is simply reach out his hand to accept it."

"Call me Ira," I choked.

Of course I accepted. What else could I have done? If I'd gone back to the 'Chapel, I'd have been in a cell under Bow Street by nightfall. Goddard was offering to make it all go away—and to give me a home.

And such a home! I took in the book-lined walls of the morning room. I allowed myself to imagine, just for a moment, that it was mine. The few, tasteful pieces on the mantel above a blazing fire and the impossible softness of the cushions surrounding me—surely I'd wake soon from this dream?

"I'd be lying," Goddard said, clearing his throat, "if I said that my feelings for you hadn't played some small part in this scheme. Somehow, I find that I've grown quite fond of you, Ira. I trust that if your sentiments don't begin to grow in a similar direction within a reasonable period of time, you'll do the honorable thing."

❖

True to his word, Goddard had seen the matter of the constable's murder wrapped up within the week. I'd been free to return to the streets, but what the devil for? I frittered away the next two years with forceful fucking, expensive whisky, and the occasional burglary. I never gave a second thought to my old life, or to Goddard's exhortation to *do the honorable thing*. Little was I to know how quickly, and with what vengeance, both of these things would come screaming back into my life. But at that moment, I was in the very heart of Sodom and Gomorrah. I had money in my pocket and an old friend to meet. As the driver pulled up before 224 Piccadilly, I flipped him three and sixpence for the fare and a half-crown for his trouble.

Chapter Seven

The Criterion was legendary: a lavish warren of themed rooms, each with its own cuisine. I'd passed by it many times when trade had taken me that way, but it had been beyond my means then. Now that it wasn't, of course, I wasn't allowed. The very idea was abhorrent to Goddard. Considering he was on the cusp of a long-overdue promotion, it simply wouldn't do for us to be seen in a place frequented by, well, men like us. But I stood just in front of the entrance. Inexplicably, Nate was inside. Tossing better judgment aside and a bit of silver to the doorman to turn a blind eye to my shabby clothes, I mounted the stairs and ducked through the door.

The high-ceilinged halls seemed to go on forever, each room more tempting than the last. When I wandered into the American Bar, with its tight-trousered waiters and the mouthwatering aroma of the high-quality beef sizzling away on the grill in the back, I almost surrendered and ordered a steak. Perhaps, I thought, pulling myself reluctantly away from a bar crowded with effete and fashionable men, Goddard could be convinced to take an early luncheon there one day when the place was deserted. He would find the clientele appalling, but he'd nothing against a well-cooked steak.

I eventually found Nate several doors down, in a small chamber with walls covered in gold leaf and hung with Oriental-style depictions of opium dens painted on silk. He still wore his dark hair longer than most, but now it was slicked back and clean. A pair of gold-rimmed spectacles balanced on his nose, and he was sporting the most extraordinary beard. Fine black hairs scissor-trimmed close to the skin and painstakingly shaped to accentuate the angles of his face—a face that now had the studied thinness of an aesthete rather than the hollowness of the street.

As I peered at him through the leaves of a potted palm, my curiosity burned. Someone was keeping him well. Nate always had cash, but would never squander it on restaurants, posh barbers or flash clothing. As often as not, half of what he pulled in a night found its way into other people's pockets—friends, dirty-faced children, and the crawling wretches so beaten down they'd lost the will to even put out their hand and beg. He couldn't turn down a soul. As striking as he was even on the cusp of thirty, it shouldn't have come as a surprise that he'd found a patron. But as long as I'd known him, he'd insisted on holding the reins. It didn't fit somehow.

The small room was cluttered with crowded tables. Nate, of course, had placed himself at the center of it all. While I watched, he sat at the edge of his inlaid chair with his legs crossed tightly, slathering a crumpet with caviar. He gave a devilish glance from beneath his long lashes before bolting the entire disgusting mess and dabbing delicately at his lips with a linen serviette.

As if sensing my presence, he looked up from the table crowded with caviar, oysters, *foie gras*, and champagne—and smiled.

I felt another pang of guilt. I really should have tried to send word once I'd settled in at York Street. Even as I was reveling in newfound luxury, wrapping my new identity around me like a fine cloak, the 'Chapel had never been more than a carriage ride away. But Nate would forgive me, wouldn't he? After all, he had been the one who had told me to leave. Which made it all the more curious that he was seeking me out now.

No matter. He was looking straight at me. Whatever he might think wouldn't be helped by my running away.

I tugged Goddard's ruby-headed tie-pin back into place and stepped into the doorway.

"Adler!" Nate called. He made an affected pass at his face with the serviette before waving it fetchingly.

We clasped hands over the table. Nate was doing a splendid job of pretending not to notice the disappointed faces that greeted my arrival.

But then he'd had three decades to become inured to the effects of his charisma.

"Good to see you again, Nathaniel," I said.

"Wot's yer pleasure? Caviar? A bit of the bubbly? 'S French, you know."

I considered the spread of mismatched delicacies. He had clearly picked the dishes for his luncheon based on price. Whoever was keeping him indulged him, but wasn't bothering to school him in the finer things. And yet the staff smiled and nodded and filled our glasses as if it made no difference to them. His benefactor was wealthy enough, then, to buy the staff's tolerance. At the same time, whoever it was had not been brought up in wealth. Interesting.

"Adler?" Nate asked as I raised my glass to my lips.

"Sorry?"

"I said, 'eard you found a man."

I coughed into my champagne.

"Yes, yes, that's right."

I put the glass down. I glanced around, but Nate seemed to be the only one interested in the details of my domestic arrangement.

"Must be somefing t'keep yer from so much as leavin' word at the clinic," he said.

"I'm sorry, mate, I—"

"No need to explain," he said. "Complicated?"

"To say the least," I said, relieved that he wasn't holding a grudge. At the same time, the evaluating gaze with which he now considered me set me on edge. The degree of discretion that Goddard required had taken a long time to master. A reunion with an old friend, especially someone as perceptive as Nate, would seriously test that mastery.

"Mmm. 'E's rich." Nate nodded as he scrutinized my appearance: trimmed oiled curls, manicured fingernails, black silk cravat. His eyes narrowed as they fell on my careworn jacket and shirt. "'E's rich, but you're pretendin' not to be." He reached out to stroke the ruby-tipped tie-pin. "Might want to put this away, then." He looked up. "So, wot gives?"

I paused. It hadn't occurred to me to enlist Nate's assistance with my search for the dog. I was more curious about what he was going to ask of me. Not to mention that discussing the blackmailer could put Goddard's identity and criminal activities at risk of exposure. However, Nate was even better connected on the East End than Pearl was. He knew everyone, and everyone liked him—or at least liked to look at him. He could charm information out of a doorpost. And I needed all the assistance I could get.

"It's like this," I began.

I gave him a skeleton account of the past day and a half: the loss of the statue, tracing it to the shop in Miller's Court, ultimately failing to retrieve it, and my subsequent return to Whitechapel to chase the thing down. Once I'd laid down a foundation of truth, it was easy to add embellishmments that led away from Goddard himself. I told him the maid had pawned the statue to buy medicine for her ailing mum, not realizing that it had inordinate sentimental value to her master. She threw herself on my mercy, I said, promised never to do it again, and should her entire family suffer because of a single mistake that anyone could have made? This final embroidery made Nate snigger.

"You 'ad me until the end," he said. "I know you ain't that much of a gen'leman. But I'll keep me eyes open for yer ugly statue—for the sake of an old mate, like. An' I won't make you tell me the real reason you're after it."

"You're a friend," I said. "And now that we've gone through my business, perhaps you can tell me why you were really looking for me." I gestured at the delicacy-crammed table. "The Nate I know wouldn't set Pearl on my trail just to wave his money around."

His face clouded over. He opened his mouth to speak, but then hesitated.

"Or maybe you could just tell me how you came to be wearing a silk waistcoat and taking luncheon at the Criterion," I said.

He huffed a short breath of relief, then launched into the slick, rose-tinted pitch of a brothel procurer. I smiled as I fiddled with a piece of smoked salmon. He knew his looks wouldn't last forever. Finding a position in brothel management was a good move. And it sounded like the place on Fitzroy Street was the Athenaeum and a Roman orgy all wrapped into one.

"Gen'lemen only," he went on. "Proper ones, not like them

jumped-up mandrakes wot makes their dosh in trade. They say Prince Eddy's stopped by once or twice. Two crowns for ten minutes' work. Less than ten minutes if you knows wot you're doin', an' you knows better than most," he said with an impish twist of his lips.

"Surely you didn't invite me here to offer me a job," I said.

"You lookin'?"

"Not if I value my life."

Goddard owned a number of brothels. To say he'd pull the trigger himself before seeing me loaned out for another man's pleasure would have been the understatement of the century. Not to mention if I could find myself poxed after two years in the same man's bed, who knew what I'd find crawling around down there if I started spreading myself around again?

"Figured as much." He snorted. "No offense, mate, but your man's got you talkin' like the queen 'erself. Probably even tells you 'ow to scratch your arse," he said, nodding toward my hand, which had been slowly working its way southward to address that pesky itch. "Nuffin' wrong wiv that if you likes that sort of fing…"

I jerked my hand out of my lap.

"Don' worry." Nate laughed as I squirmed on the hard wooden chair. "A bit of mercury'll see you right. Mercury," he repeated, no doubt taking my silence for lack of comprehension. "'A night wiv Venus leads to a life wiv Mercury,' ain't that what they say?" He winked obscenely.

"Venus, indeed," I muttered. "It's the heat, that's all."

Nate shrugged.

"'Appens to the best of us. Your man know?"

It was hard to say which I found more terrifying: the blackmailer's threat or broaching the subject of the French Disease—or whatever this was—with the Duke of Dorset Street. Perhaps it was time to start considering my options. Nate regarded me solemnly.

"I didn't ask you 'ere to offer you a job, Ira," he said. "But if you needs one, it's there. A place to stay when 'e chucks you out. Some money, good money, while you still can. Fink it over."

"You'd do that for me?" I asked.

He straightened and held out his hand over the precariously

stacked plates. His mouth quirked in the half-smile that had signified for most of my life that Nate would take care of everything.

"As assistant to the manager of the Fitzroy Street Gen'lemen-Only Brovel, I 'ereby extend this offer of employment, in the event wot you needs it."

"Assistant to the—not just a whoremonger, then? How'd you manage that?"

He smirked.

"Got me little ways."

I rolled my eyes.

"You mean the manager was sampling the wares and fell under your spell," I said, turning his previous scrutiny back on him. "He couldn't afford to keep you somewhere off the premises, but he couldn't stand the thought of some aristocratic poof sticking his cock in your mouth."

"Somefing like that," he said, smiling into his champagne. His expression went serious. "'E loves me, though, does Nick. Wants to take us bof away. But before that, 'e needs to get some money togever, find us a place where no one'll bover us. I know wot you're finkin'," he said before I could remind him how seldom those sorts of plans work out. "But 'ere, look, 'e give me this."

He withdrew a pocket watch from his waistcoat. He held it out above the remains of his eclectic feast, where it turned slowly on its chain, the intricate engravings along the edges of the case catching the warm glow of the gas jets.

"'S a token, like. A promise."

It was a pretty bit of metal. The delicate latticework on the case was too feminine for my taste, and the metal itself had been hammered too thin. But who was I to tread on his happiness—happiness that would come to a crashing halt the moment this Nick grew bored with him?

"It's lovely," I said, as he tucked the watch back into his waistcoat. "Real nice."

"Yeah," he said, distractedly hooking the clasp through a buttonhole. His gaze wandered over my shoulder toward the potted palms at the entrance.

"Now why don't you tell me the real reason—"

"Don't turn 'round," he whispered. His eyes had gone wide, and he was staring over my shoulder as if Death itself were approaching. Just as I was expecting to feel the scythe at my throat, his shoulders relaxed and he let out a chuff of relief.

"A bit more?" he asked, nodding toward the champagne.

I shook my head.

His fingers trembled as he emptied the last bit into his glass. He drained it, turning to me with a shaky smile.

"What was that about?" I asked.

I twisted around in my seat, but saw only the trickle of patrons in and out of the crowded dining room. When I turned back, he had gone quite pale.

But he was still smiling.

"Is someone following you?" I asked.

A number of possibilities flashed through my mind. Was this Nick unhinged? The last thing I needed was to get between Nate and a jealous pimp. Or perhaps one of Nate's aristocratic admirers had developed a possessive streak. Lunches at the Criterion didn't come cheap. Maybe Nate's man was taking too long putting together their escape, and Nate had decided to hedge his bet with a customer. Maybe Nick had figured it out.

"I been seein' shadows out the corner of me eye all mornin'," Nate said. He swallowed hard, eyes scanning the crowd. "Look, Ira, I need yer 'elp. Pearl said wot you found a rich man, an' the rich, well, they got connections—real connections, not Whitechapel connections. Maybe 'e can 'elp me, like."

I frowned. Bringing Nate and Goddard together was the one thing I was trying to avoid. Yet how many times had he helped me out over the years, whether it was introducing me to my first customer, or taking me to the clinic when that customer turned out to have rough tastes?

"What have you got yourself into?" I asked.

He let out a long sigh.

"'S like this. Nick's the manager over at Fitzroy Street, an' I keep the books."

"They trust you with money?" I joked.

"I keep the books," he said again, "an' that's 'ow I found out fings ain't wot they should be. That's why I needed to talk to you. Even if you can't 'elp me, I wanted to tell you in case somefing 'appen to me."

"In case what? What are you talking about?"

"Shh!" He looked around frantically. But in the crowded lunchroom, no one had noticed us. He pushed aside a plate bearing the remains of a blancmange and leaned in on his elbows. "There's a customer book, see—'o come in, when, 'o 'e sees, an' 'ow much 'e pays—an' an opium book."

"An opium book?" I asked.

"Mr. Sinclair—that's Nick—'e brings the customers to us. 'E takes their money an' give us our share at the end of the week. We gets room an' board, plus if you likes it, you can 'ave opium for cheap. They take it out of our pay. 'Course Nick 'ad me off the stuff before 'e'd let me touch the books. Worst three weeks of me life..."

Goddard ran his own brothels like rooming houses, involving himself only insofar as to collect rent and a percentage of the profits. Fitzroy Street, apparently, employed the young men directly. The opium was an interesting touch. If this Sinclair could get it at a low price, and convince his charges to use it, it would make them a lot easier to manage. He'd also save on food. It was also conceivable if a person's habit got the better of him, he might actually end up in debt to the house with only one way of working it off.

"Then one day Nick tell me to start keepin' two opium books: one to show the owner when 'e come in each month, and one wot's jus' between Nick an' me."

"Is that so?"

A little graft between friends. It made sense. If Sinclair was trying to put aside a little extra so he and Nate could disappear, he could cut the opium with strychnine or sugar or pigeon shit, even, and make himself a tidy profit. With Nate keeping the books, no one would be the wiser.

"Only it's even better, see. There's this new opium wot the owner brings. 'S twice as strong. So Nick cuts it by 'alf, sells it to this bloke down in Lime'ouse, and the bloke don't know no different. 'S brilliant."

"Until the owner gets wind of it," I said.

The fear returned to his face. He looked away.

"You don't know the 'alf of it," he said. "'E might look like Favver Chris'mas, but that bastard'll slit yer throat soon's look at you. I seen it 'appen. Nick tell me wot 'e were a doctor once, in Afghanistan. Done a lot of unnecessary surgery. But that ain't 'ere nor there. Four months ago the old bastard come to me, an' tell me wot 'e want me to start keepin' anover set of books. Customer books, this time."

"Let me guess," I said. "One set for Sinclair's eyes, and one that only you and the owner know about."

"That's right. An' the new one's 'xactly the same, 'cept wiv a few extra customers wot ain't on the books Nick sees. Twice a month the doctor come by when Nick ain't there, wiv a fat sack of money for the safe, and tell me wot to write in the new book. But bugger me if I ever seen them new customers."

"And this started when?"

"March," he said. "Along wiv the 'sturbances."

A brothel is a noisy place—even noisier at night than the Criterion is at luncheon. Had Nate not been off the roster of talent, what he called the "disturbances" might have gone unnoticed forever. But sitting there in his little room, alone with his thoughts on nights otherwise unoccupied, how could he have failed to be awakened by the bumps and bangs in the gray hours? How could he have ignored the snatches of a harsh and unfamiliar language that accompanied them? Having been pulled none too gently from opium's clutches, how could he not have noticed its distinctive odor, wafting inexplicably up from the unoccupied basement long after the last customer had slunk back out onto the darkened streets?

"I fink the owner's movin' more'n opium," he said.

"I think you're right."

The papers were filled with lurid stories of young women, usually blond, wealthy, and virtuous, stolen away and turned to nefarious purpose. In reality, people disappeared all the time on the East End, but their fates, tragic as they often were, didn't sell papers. What didn't make sense was the shouting he described, the muffled crying in a foreign tongue. Anyone who'd grown up on the East End, like Nate, would have no problem distinguishing the sounds of Chinese, Italian, German, Hindoo, Gipsy, and Jewish. If the people being moved through the Fitzroy Street brothel weren't any of these, where had they come from? Wherever it was, the owner must have been getting a pretty price to make it worth the expense of smuggling them.

"You should tell the police," I said.

He laughed.

"Tell 'em wot? That in the course of me work in an 'ouse of buggery—stric'ly as a bookkeeper, mind—I noticed wot look like illegal activ'ty on the part of me employer?"

It was ridiculous when he put it that way.

The weight of this knowledge on his conscience was all too obvious in the heavy set of his delicate features. My introduction to Greek-style love hadn't been gentle, but it had been voluntary. Nate's hadn't. The bruises and lacerations were long healed, but behind his black eyes I could still see the young man sitting up nights in the children's dormitory, a sharpened spoon in his trembling hand, waiting for the warder who had assaulted him to come for someone else.

"'Sides," he said, setting his jaw. "Nick says wot the owner's got connections all the way to Buckin'am Palace. 'E prolly owns the bleedin' p'lice. Naw," he said with quiet determination. "I'm fixin' them bastards meself."

My heart stopped. Nate had been crossing some very powerful people, and he was asking for Goddard's help. Never mind Goddard had troubles of his own—the last thing he needed was to stir up more with people like that.

"Been keepin' me own set of books," Nate continued. "The owner give me the names in code, but I almost got it cracked. I got one name—a member of the bleedin' Royal Family—an' when I get the others I'm gonna make 'em pay. An' when they've paid enough to send these poor…'oever they is back to wherever they come from, I'm gonna drop the books off at Bow Street anyway. But I think someone's found me out. I ain't got much time, Ira."

He looked toward the entrance again and swallowed.

"Have you told this Nick of yours?" I asked.

"'E can't 'elp me. Wouldn't want 'im to. Brought it all on meself. But if your man's connected—"

"Not that kind of connected," I said. "I wish I could help you, but—"

"Then maybe I can stay wiv you. Jus' for a bit, until I get fings sorted out, like."

I let out a long breath. If there were ever a right reason to do the wrong thing, this was it. Nate had saved my skin a thousand times. Not half an hour ago, he'd offered me shelter. Now he'd put his own life in danger trying to help someone else. But Goddard had enough grief with our blackmailer without taking in a second "guest." And while Goddard could keep the police and any number of rival criminals at bay with one manicured hand tied behind his back, I doubted he was a match for the collective wrath of the English monarchy.

"I wish I could," I said. And did I ever.

"But—"

"I'm sorry."

"You mean you can't, or you won't?"

"It's complicated. Let me give you some money for a hotel. How much do you need?" I took out my wallet.

"They'll find me in an 'otel."

"Then leave town. Leave the country."

The solution seemed obvious to me. Goddard had a place outside of Paris for just such contingencies. I wondered whether he'd consider letting Nate stay there.

But Nate shook his head. "Wherever I go, they'll find me," he said. "And when they do…"

His eyes locked onto something beyond the palms. The color drained from his face. I took a handful of coins from my pocket and pressed them into his hand.

"There's close to three quid here," I said. "Take it."

Never taking his eyes from the entrance, he tucked the money into his pocket.

"Take this, too."

His fingers curled around the ruby stickpin, squeezing it as if for luck. I turned again and saw a large man between the potted palms. His face bore a jagged scar from temple to jaw, and his jacket was obviously borrowed.

"Please, Ira," Nate said.

Not a day has gone by since that fateful luncheon that I haven't felt an utter shit for what I failed to do. And yet I couldn't have acted otherwise. Goddard could have made a jealous suitor disappear. But Nate had taken a piss in the corridors of power, and if I dragged Goddard into that, not even Paris would be far enough for us to run.

"I can't take you in," I said. "But if you can make it to the back door, I can give you a good start."

Hurt darkened his features. He lifted his chin, lips pressed together in a tight line, and gave a sharp nod.

"Rat!" I shouted, shooting out of my chair so violently it cracked against the crowded table behind me. "Rat! Great, huge stinking rat!"

I upended that table into the laps of four well-dressed men, clambering over it and barreling toward the man with the scar, still shouting. Scarface tried to step aside, but I shouldered him in the gut and ducked out of his thick arms as he tried to grab me. I sprinted toward the potted palms and looked back to see Nate darting through the crowd toward the kitchen. A strong hand gripped my shoulder as I shot into the hallway, but I twisted free. Giving silent thanks to the fighting arts practice which Goddard insisted upon despite my lack of enthusiasm, I delivered an elbow to a place that would leave the poor bugger thinking twice about doing it again. And then I ran for the street.

CHAPTER EIGHT

I arrived back at York Street near teatime, exhausted. My throat was full of soot, hands and face covered in a gritty film, my sensitive bits burning as if my undergarments were lined with stinging nettles. Giving every farthing in my pocket to a renter-cum-blackmailer fleeing from God alone only knew whom had left me to walk home from the Criterion in the heat. My old shirt was sticking wetly to my body, and there was going to be a nasty blister on the ball of my left foot. The last thing I was in the mood for was the first thing that greeted me when I let myself in.

"Ah, Mr. Adler," said the manservant. He glanced up from the round vestibule table, where he was arranging an armful of fresh flowers in a silver vase. "Dr. Hendricks stopped by. He was inconvenienced by your absence, to put it mildly."

"I'm sure he'll get over it," I said.

I hung my Whitechapel jacket and hat on the rack beside the door before removing my boots and lining them up by the wall. If Goddard had been at home, the manservant would have taken all three, not to mention opened the door for me.

But I had bigger battles to fight.

"I need a bath," I said. "And then I want my tea."

Nate had lit out from the restaurant like a bat out of hell, but that didn't mean he was out of danger. He'd probably head back to the brothel at some point to collect his things or to find his Mr. Sinclair and warn him. Nate could not possibly have stayed under our roof. But

Goddard was the Duke of Dorset Street. There had to be something he could do to help. And that was what I intended to ponder, submerged in hot water and fragrant oil.

When I looked up, Collins had not beaten a hasty path up the stairs to run my bath. He was looking at me, a whisper of a smirk about his mouth.

"The master sent word to remind you about this evening's meeting of the London Society for the Oriental Fighting Arts. It begins in less than an hour."

Sod it. Between the storm in my mind and the inferno between my legs, I was not fit for being slapped about by overenthusiastic amateur pugilists in black pajamas.

"He said there would be a special announcement," Collins continued. "He was most insistent that you be there."

"He always wants me to be there," I said.

"But he told me that tonight, you must not be allowed to talk your way out of it."

I curled my toes against the tiles. The bones in my feet ached. I most decidedly did not want to put my boots back on. On the other hand, Goddard would be bursting to tell me about his new professorship. And there would surely be an excellent supper afterward.

"Fine," I said. "Bring me my *samfu*."

The manservant's smirk became more definite.

"Unfortunately, your fighting garment is being laundered at the moment."

I closed my eyes and counted to five. The only thing worse than the tongue-lashing I'd receive from Zhi Sen, the club's instructor and Goddard's long-time business partner, for showing up unprepared would be for my sharp words to inspire Collins to "accidentally" destroy the garment in some disastrous incident involving hot irons and starch. The manservant couldn't stomach the fact Goddard had scraped me from the gutter and installed me at his right hand, but it had only been in the last few weeks that he'd demonstrated this fact with such boldness. But never in front of Goddard, and never in any way that couldn't be explained away.

Come to think of it, Collins would make a credible blackmailer.

He did have excellent penmanship. Even if he were innocent, seeing him get his comeuppance at Goddard's hands might well be worth the price of a bottle of lavender ink.

"Very well." I sighed, reaching for my hat. "Send for a cab."

Muttering fantasies of revenge under my breath, I pulled my boots back on, lacing them tight against further blisters. I opened the door. As I reached for my jacket, I spied a single-horse vehicle turning onto York Street. It scraped to a stop in front of the house.

"I believe that's a cab approaching now. But considering the importance Dr. Goddard placed on your presence tonight, you'd be well advised to consider a change of clothing. Might I suggest the brown suit?"

❖

It was a short ride to the London Athletic Club in Fulham. As my cab passed through fashionable Mayfair and out of Chelsea, the scrubbed bricks, whitewashed columns, and tree-lined streets gave way to dour gray stone and dark little pubs. Fulham had once been a playground for the debauched rich. The rich had gradually been taking their perversions elsewhere, though, and now the once-festive streets were looking shabby and a little hungover. The area was still neither as colorful nor as vicious as Whitechapel. All the same, I was grateful not to be on foot in my weakened state, especially with the sun hanging low in the sky, casting an evening glow on the taverns and shops.

The club was located at Stamford Bridge: six and a half acres of playing pitches, with a running track and a covered area for spectators. Off to the side stood the modest sports hall where the Fighting Arts Society held its twice-weekly practice. Before his dismissal from Cambridge, Goddard had been a member of the rival Amateur Athletic Association. Had he still been in the university's good graces, he'd have set up the Fighting Arts Society in its lofty halls. However, the L.A.C., which admitted laborers as well as lords, had the advantage of providing Goddard a suitable pool of men from which he had recruited some of his finest nobblers, bodyguards, and bludgers. Goddard's disgrace and exile might have taken its toll on his pride, but it had given him a stunning array of opportunities to build his criminal organization. He had used them all to best advantage.

The sky was warm with the last rays of daylight when I paid the entrance fee and made my way inside the sports hall. The main corridor was quiet and dark. Few lamps had been lit. Most summer sports carried on out of doors, and those that didn't took advantage of the facility's generous windows. The room where Goddard and his students met was at the end of the corridor. I followed the muffled booms, cracks, and squelches of hand-to-hand combat to a door shut fast to preserve the delicate sensibilities of the staff. Cracking it open, I slipped inside.

The students had already worked their way through the forms—the sets of movements that show how strikes, sweeps, and blocks fit together—and were well into their sparring practice. The air was ripe with hard-earned sweat. I hated sparring. I could already fight my way out of most situations, and it seemed pointless to limit the techniques at one's disposal for the sake of aesthetic continuity.

What's more, I always seemed to get paired with some zealot one could just tell had grown up grinding the faces of weaker boys into the mud.

Watching others fight was another matter. When one wasn't personally being pummeled, it was a beautiful dance—and Cain Goddard was a magnificent dancer. I lined my boots up with the others and sat cross-legged against the wall. On the other side of the room, Goddard was working with a ginger-haired man. The other man looked as if he should be all elbows and left feet, but under Goddard's tutelage his movements took on an astonishing fluidity. Goddard had only been to China once, on business. The mark it left on him was plain to anyone who had ever seen the burden rise from his shoulders when he took up his long staff, heard the tenderness with which his tongue caressed the improbable syllables of the language, or witnessed the uncharacteristic patience with which he ministered to his students.

I might have lost myself in watching him, had not my attention been drawn by the stealthy creak of the door. I turned in time to catch a glimpse of dark hair and the rustle of silk skirts before the woman hastily pulled the door back shut. Curious. As far as I knew, the club didn't employ females—and club employees didn't wear silk. I rose and edged toward the door. The woman had been looking for someone, and she'd disappeared when she'd seen me turn toward her. However, she hadn't disappeared completely. The hallway lamp was still casting a woman-shaped shadow against the window on the door. I slid along the wall until my right side met the doorjamb. Soon enough, a face breached the entrance once more. This time I was ready. Before she could slip away, I caught her arm. Her almond-shaped eyes met mine, and the surprise on her porcelain features must have been similar to that which was squeezing the breath from my chest.

To someone not paying attention, one Chinese face might look much like the next. However, I make it my business to pay attention—especially when a whore of preternatural persistence lifts a worthless statue from my pocket.

"Who are you?" I hissed.

Behind us, the sparring continued. Wet slaps as skin met skin, the occasional boom of a muscular body on the floorboards. The woman didn't shrink or struggle as I edged her out into the corridor. Rather, she worked her wrist with subtle motions designed to weaken my grip.

"Where's the porcelain dog?"

There was no response except for an insolent rise of her chin. Her cool stare never wavered, not even when strong fingers suddenly tightened around my collar and jerked me backward just as a foot swept my legs out from under me. My head hit the floorboards with the crack of a cannon, or perhaps that's just how it felt.

"Next time, lift your head before it hits the ground."

The stars cleared, and my eyes focused on Zhi Sen's moon-shaped visage. He scowled down at me. Beneath his long string of a mustache, his upper lip curled in a sneer.

"Better yet, stay away from my daughter, and you won't have to worry about hitting the ground."

Daughter?

The room had gone still. Silence hung heavily in the sweat-humid air. Goddard and the students stared as I rubbed the back of my skull. I opened my mouth to respond when the woman let loose with a volley of livid Mandarin. Goddard might well have been able to translate, but he was busy trying to regain control of the class. While Zhi Sen responded in kind, I crawled past them and found a quiet spot against the wall to contemplate this latest set of developments.

Had Zhi Sen sent his daughter to acquire the statue?

If so, had he done it at Goddard's behest, or was he in league with the blackmailer?

Was he the blackmailer?

That made no sense. He and Goddard had met while Goddard was traveling in China. Zhi Sen was a Wushu master, which was why Goddard had sought him out in the first place. But he had also been instrumental in helping Goddard to expand his opium dealings, so instrumental Goddard had brought him to England and made him his partner. It was an immensely beneficial arrangement for both men. I couldn't imagine either of them wanting to upset the balance. Besides, Goddard had said the blackmailer's threat had to do with "mistakes of youth," and Goddard had been at least thirty when he'd gone to China.

There was no doubt the girl was involved. But when I looked up again, she was gone and Zhi Sen was steaming back into the room, barely concealed fury burning behind his dark eyes.

"Dr. Goddard," Zhi Sen said, pointedly bumping me as he passed. "If your secretary must come to practice unprepared, please ensure he at least has enough work with him to keep him out of trouble."

Goddard gave a deep nod, stepping aside for Zhi Sen to assume control of the class. Disgusted, I stood to retrieve my boots.

"I see that you've managed to impress your Sifu once again," Goddard said, coming up beside me.

"He's not *my* Sifu," I said.

I grunted, tugging my laces loose before shoving my left foot back into its hard, sweaty coffin.

"No, I must correct myself," Goddard continued. "This time you've really outdone yourself. Flirting with the man's own daughter. Tsk, tsk."

His voice was amused, indulgent, but I wasn't in the mood. My head was throbbing, and there was a blister the size of a grape on my right pinkie toe.

"She has the porcelain dog," I said.

"What?"

Goddard was still smiling, but something sharp was in his eyes.

"She was the one who took it from me at Miller's Court after I got it back from Lazarus."

"You must be mistaken."

He took his left hand in right, twisted it to the point where a normal man might scream, repeating the stretch on the other side. When he had demonstrated the unnatural limberness of his wrists, he moved on to elbows.

"No, Cain. I'm sure of it. She was dressed as a whore, spoke like one, too. And she picked my pocket as quick and clean as you please."

"*Mrs.* Wu doesn't speak English, at least not as far as I know."

"She speaks it as well as you or me."

He popped his neck.

"Even if that were true, what would she want with that statue?"

"How should I know?" I leaned closer and lowered my voice. "Listen, do you think that Zhi Sen—"

"No," Goddard said sharply. Then, softening, "No, Ira. I won't hear of it. I trust him as I trust myself."

He shook out his shoulders and stretched his arms above him, bending slowly to each side. To anyone else, it might appear he was merely keeping his muscles warm. However, beneath the movements, I could sense his mind working. The students had paired off behind us to practice their long staff techniques. Bare feet shuffled on the floorboards as they assumed wide-legged stances. Wood knocked gently against wood as they touched the ends of their staves together: a sign that each student respected his partner and was ready to begin.

"Mrs. Wu is a widow," Goddard said. "They pulled her husband out of the Thames a week ago. He ate one lotus too many, they said, walked off a bridge."

"Now, *that* makes no sense," I said. "Someone who eats one lotus too many isn't walking anywhere."

It could only have been a handful of times I had witnessed my mother in an opium-induced stupor. Not even the Salvation Army Band could have roused her.

"Perhaps he had help walking off that bridge," Goddard said. "It's none of our business, at any rate. I offered my assistance, but Zhi Sen was adamant he'd settle the matter himself. As for her, I've no idea why she came, but he certainly didn't seem happy to see her."

I let my eyes wander over to the students clacking their staves together in the eight primary positions. Then I turned back to Goddard.

"If this business about her husband is true, doesn't it bother you?"

"Why should it? I've never met the man."

"Zhi Sen is your friend. Mr. Wu was his son-in-law. You make a lot of money from opium."

"So does Zhi Sen. Besides, I didn't hold him down and put a pipe in his mouth."

"Yes, but—"

He let out a long breath and straightened. Taking the heel of his left foot in his hand, he stretched his left leg out to one side. With a grunt of physical satisfaction, he brought his leg back down and repeated the move on the other side.

"Mr. Wu is an adult, Ira—was an adult. Opium is legal. Are Zhi Sen and I doing anything worse than the man who pours gin at Blue Coat Boy?"

It was a valid argument. And yet the workhouse where I'd spent twelve years of my life had been bursting with children whose parents had chosen gin, or opium, or dice, over them. All of these things were legal, but given the damage they caused, I wondered if they should have been. And though it was arguable that the people like Goddard who pandered to destructive vices were simply fulfilling an economic demand, I couldn't help but feel that they were to some degree responsible for the destruction that ensued.

"It might be legal, but it's not harmless," I said.

Goddard's lips twisted wryly.

"'Harmless' doesn't pay for your eucalyptus baths, dear boy."

He reached out as if to straighten my collar, but let the hand remain for just a moment longer than necessary, the knuckle of his index finger discreetly caressing the hollow of my throat.

"'Harmless' doesn't keep your delicate feet in Italian leather, or fill your lungs with the ambrosial vapors of Egyptian tobacco, hmm?"

He smiled and slowly withdrew his hand, leaving my neck tingling with the traces of his touch. Something stirred deep inside me—and in places not so deep. Goddard and I hadn't touched each other without the taint of foreboding since the first lavender letter arrived. It had been too long.

"Mrs. Wu embroidered the dragon on your new pajamas, you know," he said.

"I'd congratulate her on her handiwork, if I weren't afraid her father would castrate me."

"I'll pass on the compliment. I'm really glad you're here tonight, Ira."

He regarded me with a warmth he rarely allowed himself to demonstrate outside the doors of York Street. Something in my chest clenched. I found myself turning with him as Zhi Sen called the class to attention, reluctant to let go of what had just passed between us.

"Collins said something about an announcement," I said as he stepped back toward the class. He turned.

"I've found a building."

"For the club?"

Goddard had been talking about a separate facility for the Fighting Arts Society for almost a year. Suspended wood floors to minimize injury, brush paintings on the walls, and windows to fill the practice area with natural light—well, as natural as one could find in the heart of London, anyway. To hear him go on about it, one would think he was planning a cathedral. But finding a structure adequate to the task had proven to be a task in itself.

"I found the place a few months ago: a warehouse down by the docks. It's perfect. Nobody knows yet, not even Zhi Sen. I've had workers there for weeks. The opening is Friday night."

"That's wonderful!" I cried.

Zhi Sen cleared his throat impatiently. The students gathered around him looked impatient as well.

"Wait here while I tell them the news," Goddard said with a wink. "Then I have something even better for you."

He padded across to where his motley group of pugilists were anxiously awaiting a word from their mentor. A few of the fresh-faced young men were obviously Goddard's students from King's. There were quite a few others with criminal class accents and oft-broken noses, who would have been at home in Whitechapel. All of them would follow Goddard into the flames of hell itself.

While Goddard shared his news, Zhi Sen stood off to the side, nodding, as if paying rapt attention, but didn't take his eyes off me for a second. I wouldn't have expected anything less from a devoted father protecting his mourning daughter from unwanted attention. But was that all it was? Zhi Sen had no motive for blackmailing Goddard, as far as I could see. His daughter had even less. But she had taken the porcelain dog, and that meant that she was involved. Of this I was certain.

Whether Goddard believed me or not.

It was dark when we emerged from the athletic club. A light rain had fallen. Cool, clean air wafted over the playing fields, raising the wholesome smells of earth and grass. The lights of surrounding Fulham shone from the windows of gambling houses and brothels, but the view from Stamford Bridge had a peaceful, almost homely quality. Goddard and I walked down the path to where our hansom was waiting on Fulham Road. The driver took us back through Chelsea in silence. Goddard's incessant toe-tapping signified something was on his mind. When we reached Kensington Road, Goddard signaled for the driver to stop.

Strolling through Hyde Park at night was one of many pleasures to which Goddard had introduced me. Among those who walked the park after dark, allowing one's fingers to brush those of another man was a misdemeanor beneath notice. And though darkness brought danger even to this refined corner of the city, I was safer at Goddard's side than I ever had been in my life. Most importantly, the shadows and trees and the lapping water of the Serpentine combined to create a deliciously public privacy, the craving for which those whose affections are deemed "decent" and "natural" could never understand.

We left the hansom at the entrance, walked through a forest of ionic columns shining like cold flesh in the moonlight, and passed through the central arch. We ambled along the path at first, but gathered speed as we approached the Serpentine. By the time the city lights disappeared behind us, we were practically running.

Goddard's excitement crackled in the air all around us. There was more to it than the mere opening of an athletic facility. The chancellor must finally have recognized his genius and rewarded him accordingly. There was a moment of panic when I considered Goddard might scale back his criminal operations to the point where his income would be affected. If I fancied living like a church mouse—or a professor at a minor London university—I'd have saved myself the trouble and stayed with Lazarus. But as we came to the weeping beech tree that had been the site of many a stolen kiss, Goddard squeezed my fingers, and I felt instinctively he would let neither harm nor inconvenience befall me.

"You can't know how long I've been waiting for this moment," he said as he led me through the branches into a vast bower.

The full moon cast a blue-gray light over the water and through the leaves. Goddard took my hands in his. When he caught my eyes, there was no sound but the beating of my heart and the wet scrape of branches on the grass.

"They gave it to you, then? The professorship?"

Even as I said it, I could feel his disappointment. Disappointment the university had not rewarded his contributions, and disappointment I'd somehow failed to intuit this. He sucked in a long breath and looked away.

"No," he said. "The chancellor had a different offer for me. One he considers more important than mere advancement. He wanted me to co-chair his Committee for the Promotion of Moral Virtue. 'Bringing honesty and piety back to the working class,' he said. Working for a 'higher authority,' and all that."

"Moral what?" My laughter was part surprise, part outrage. "You told him where to stuff his committee, I hope!"

"Not in so many words. Although I did invite him to the opening of the Fighting Arts Society building on Friday. Can't afford to burn that particular bridge, at least not yet."

I couldn't imagine why Goddard continued to beat the dead dog of his academic career like that. His Cambridge star had risen quickly and burned bright. It was unfair that it all should have ended, as his silence on the matter suggested, in scandal. But he had built a new life for himself, an enviable life by anyone's standards. He had enough money squirreled away in banks across the continent that he could have founded his own university, would he not have considered it cheating. And yet I had the feeling he'd have given it all up for another chance to prove himself to those bastards.

"I've spent twenty-five years of my life in colleges and universities," he said with a resignation that did not suit him at all. "It's about time I realized how little advancement has to do with either effort or qualifications." He squeezed my fingers and withdrew his hands. Smiling tightly, he said, "But I didn't bring you here to talk about my failures."

He reached into the pocket of his coat—the coat that covered his black *samfu*, still slightly damp and redolent with the heady smell of his exertion—and produced a small, wooden box, which he pressed into my hand.

"I've been waiting almost a year to give you this."

The box itself was a work of art in black wood—not stained or lacquered—with brass hinges that looked cast especially for it. No materials wasted, no extraneous frills, and yet everything fit perfectly, beautifully together, so very much like Goddard himself I wanted to laugh.

"Yes, yes," he said with an abashed wave of his hand. "I had it made to specification. Now stop looking at the box and open it."

"Oh," I gasped as I lifted the lid.

The wind stirred the leaves, allowing a thin beam of moonlight to dance over the ring held firmly between rolls of black velvet. It was a golden snake, wound twice around itself, its tail knotted just behind its head. Its body was embellished with engraved scales, and two perfectly matched diamond eyes glittered up at me from an elegant head.

"It represents fidelity, loyalty, and eternity," he said quietly. "The late Prince Albert gave a similar token to Her Majesty, but its eyes were only rubies. Parsimonious bastard," he added with a wink.

I ran my finger over the head. It was the most beautiful piece of jewelry I'd ever seen, and I coveted it with all my heart. But there was a question inherent in the gesture, and I wasn't certain I was prepared to answer it.

"By God," I breathed. "It must have cost—"

He closed my hand around the box.

"It did. So please put it on before Christmas comes early to some light-fingered gutterpup. You'll find it an exact fit for your left pinkie."

Loyalty, fidelity—I had accepted these as conditions of my residence at York Street. An eternity there was something I'd never have dared dream. Two years ago, Goddard had said the day would come when I'd have to tell him whether I could return his affection. That day had arrived, and his expectation hung heavy in the air. There was more at stake, much, much more, than a simple circle of gold.

He pressed my hands between his and leaned his forehead against mine.

"It's unfair to pressure you like this, I know," he said. "But I've made my feelings clear. It's time you did the same."

How I wanted that ring! Loyalty, fidelity, and an eternity of silk sheets and fine tobacco. All I had to do was pledge my heart. At one time it would have been easy to simply say the words and accept the ring, regardless of how I felt. But I had come to respect Goddard, to like him. I wanted to tell him the truth of my feelings. The problem was I hadn't any idea what the truth actually was. I wondered whether Nate had struggled with the same question with his Mr. Sinclair. Oh, Nate! I did hope he had found his way to safety! Goddard deserved the truth. He also deserved to be happy. *Do you love him?* Pearl had asked. Did it matter? In the end, if both people are satisfied with the arrangement, who gets hurt?

And perhaps I did love him after all.

"Do you really have to ask?" I murmured. "How neglectful I must have been, if the answer wasn't perfectly clear."

His face split into a grin as I slid the ring onto my pinkie. It was just as he'd said—a perfect fit. He wasn't a large man, but fighting practice had given his wiry limbs strength and definition. As he pressed me into the trunk of the tree, I felt like no harm could ever come to either of us.

"You should be careful, Dr. Goddard," I mumbled against kisses both ardent and sweet, "under Labouchere's law, one little kiss could bring down your entire empire."

"Then we should make it worth the loss. On second thought, dear boy, you already have."

CHAPTER NINE

We rode home in companionable silence through quiet avenues lined with stately houses and softly glowing street lamps. Though Goddard wouldn't hazard a look in my direction, a gentle smile played about his lips, and his thigh was warm against mine. I had made the right decision. Only a few small twists of fate had placed me at Goddard's side that night rather than in some Whitechapel alley or, like Nate, in a brothel. Even if my affection did not match Goddard's for ardor, it might eventually. Even if it never did, Goddard's happiness, as well as the continuity of my carefully arranged life, was worth this small deception.

Only two things marred the perfection of the evening—my worry for Nate and the fact that our blackmailer was still at large. Nate's plan to pursue the brothel's special customers would shut down the trade, at least temporarily, and provide some relief to the victims. But putting aside the terrible danger he was bringing upon himself—danger which might have found him the moment he left my sight at the Criterion—how did he intend to send those poor people home, when he'd no idea where their home was, nor even how to communicate with them? He had to be working with someone, but he'd mentioned no one. Perhaps Pearl had heard something.

Speaking to Lazarus might also prove fruitful, much as I hated to admit it. Nate had mentioned the owner of the brothel had, like Lazarus, been a surgeon in Afghanistan. No doubt dozens of surgeons had served Her Majesty there. However, a man of advanced age with a reputation for unnecessary cruelty would have stood out like a sore thumb. If Lazarus was able to identify him, I'd only have to point my finger and let Goddard's men do the rest. In fact, Goddard himself could be a greater help than the rest of them put together. Nate couldn't stay at York Street, but he could live almost anywhere else under Goddard's protection. And Goddard had no reason to deny it. It could be my wedding present.

As the driver turned onto York Street, Goddard sighed and shifted on the bench. His fingers brushed against mine. Catching my eye, he allowed them to linger there. Blood pounded in my ears. I closed my eyes, breathing in the faint traces of his cologne and the more insistent smell of his desire. As I followed him out of the hansom and up the stairs, I fingered the golden snake wrapped around my pinkie and allowed my thoughts to dwell on the second cause of worry. The ring would be meaningless if Goddard was in prison, worthless if I had to sell it to support myself, once the house and its contents had been auctioned off for a fraction of their worth. I had to find the porcelain dog. And I had to figure out what Mrs. Wu had to do with it, and how her father fit into the whole mess.

In the vestibule, Collins was already divesting Goddard of his jacket and hat. Goddard turned to me and smiled warmly. I nudged the front door shut behind me, and he reached out his hand. He took my fingers in his, and I worried no more.

❖

The peace did not last the night. For the first time in much too long, we'd consummated our passion without a thought to our blackmailer. After, we drifted off to sleep, loose-boned and sated in one another's arms. But when the clock in the vestibule chimed me awake at two, my mind was abuzz with morbid thoughts, and the insides of my thighs were burning. As I turned over once again, Goddard's hand closed around my arm.

"Sorry," I whispered.

He pulled himself against my back with a sleepy mumble. The air was fragrant with passion, humid with sweat. It was all I could do to not leap to my feet and pace. If that weren't enough, that crawling sensation was making its way across my most tender bits and making steady progress toward the back passage. I was grateful for the sudden distraction of furtive noises coming from downstairs.

City nights are filled with curious sounds, but some are more curious than others. When one has done his fair share of sneaking about, the stealthy creaks and shuffles of someone who doesn't want to be heard announce themselves as distinctly as the bells of the Great Westminster Clock. There was an intruder at York Street—someone with the nerve to rob the Duke of Dorset Street in his very lair, and the unparalleled brilliance to get past the modified self-locking Chubb detector locks with which Goddard had fitted the doors—locks which had proven, to Goddard's glee, impervious even to my deft fingers and trusty tools.

Approaching the matter alone, clad only in velvet slippers and a silk *robe d'interieur* was unutterably stupid. How different my life would be now, had I but asked Goddard to accompany me! But the more time that elapses without constant threats to life and health, the more lax one's judgment becomes. And with the diamond eyes of my precious token glittering reassuringly in the light of my lamp as I crept down the stairs, I was determined to assume my rightful place as one of two masters of the house.

The vestibule was deserted. I took a cautious step onto the checkerboard tiles and cursed the slippers' wooden heels. The runner on the stairs had swallowed my footfall, but the slippers seemed to echo infinitely on the bare floor. I jumped when the grandfather clock clanged the quarter-hour. I'd have bolted back up the stairs, if not for the little golden snake. The privilege of a home meant the responsibility for it. One way or another, I would see the problem through.

I left the slippers at the foot of the stairs and tiptoed across the vestibule to the hallway. The door of Goddard's *sanctum sanctorum* was locked, and no light showed through the crack between it and the tiles. The noises began again, and were coming from below stairs. I padded back across the vestibule to the servants' door. It, too, was locked. Another curious thing—one of the cardinal rules of Goddard's house was that the servants' door always remain open. But the lock was a silly thing. I made quick work of it.

Without my slippers, my descent down the servants' staircase was silent. I stopped halfway down and peered over the railing into the kitchen. Knife in hand, the manservant was hunched over the broad kitchen table with his back to me. To his left was a pile of shiny red seed pods. With quick, efficient movements, he grasped a pod, slit it open, and squeezed the insides into a bowl before carefully scraping out the husk. It was the scrapings that seemed to interest him. These he carefully wiped off the knife onto a plate to his right.

I took another step.

Collins was, of course, within his rights to potter about below stairs at any hour. On the other hand, cooking was Eileen's job. Moreover, it was far too early for anyone to be preparing breakfast. But he wasn't preparing food. I'd never seen raw opium being processed, but everyone knew that the first step was to slit the pods and extract the nectar. My heart quickened. Was Collins stealing from Goddard's stores? I'd thought Goddard only worked with processed opium—powder, syrup, brown paste dried into bricks—but he had kept me largely ignorant of the details of his doings. He could have had his own poppy field out in the country, for all I knew.

I held my lamp over the railing and leaned in for a closer look. The metal groaned under my weight.

"If the master knew about that," Collins said without looking up, "he would have the railing replaced, and thus deprive me of a most effective warning system."

"What on earth do you think you're doing?" I demanded.

I stalked down the staircase, trying my best to look imperious. He didn't turn when I came up behind him, but merely sighed, his beefy shoulders drooping as if my presence were the last straw.

"I'm doing my duty," he said. "Can you say the same?"

"I heard a noise."

He was still wearing his day clothes. Either he'd put them back on, or he'd never gone to bed. His usually crisp white shirt was soft with the day's grime. The sleeves were rolled up past his elbows, and he wore Eileen's stained apron. Whatever he was doing, he didn't want the evidence ending up all over him.

"Does your duty include stealing your employer's poppies?" I went on. "You're wasting your time. There's not enough there for a rat to fill its pipe."

Even the dimmest thug knew it took a lot more than a soup dish full of opium pods to extract anything of use. What Collins hoped to gain from such a small yield was beyond me. But now I had an excuse to be rid of the man once and for all. However, instead of panicking, Collins just laughed.

"My God, you're a stupid boy. To think I actually worried when I heard your footsteps."

"I'll tell him," I said.

He hadn't bothered to look at me before that, but he stopped laughing. He turned slowly on his stool and considered me, twirling the knife idly in his right hand.

"You'll be dismissed without a reference, you thieving swine."

"A bit rich, coming from you," he said.

"Is that why you can't stand me? Because I'm not rich like Goddard?"

I wasn't Goddard's equal. I wasn't even Collins's equal. Only Goddard's esteem stood between me and the streets. But that night, Goddard had made his esteem manifest in gold: loyalty, fidelity, and eternity.

It didn't matter what the manservant thought.

"That's part of it," he said.

"What's the rest?"

He cocked his heavy, closely cropped head, examining me as if for the first time. Though he held himself as befitting a gentleman's confidential servant, spoke the Queen's English, and had Eileen press his garments twice daily, the manservant had a boxer's nose and the hands of a strangler. His eyes were small and mean. His disdain for me did not change as he considered my question. In the end, though, he shrugged, as if figuring there was nothing I could do to him regardless of his answer.

"How long have you been in Dr. Goddard's employ, Mr. Adler? Two years? A bit longer than the others, that's true. But I've served Dr. Goddard for twenty. I've seen your like come and go."

I wasn't Goddard's first, of course. The night of our first

assignation, he'd taught me things I hadn't learned in my years whoring myself on the streets. But he'd never mentioned anyone else coming to York Street to live. I glanced at my ring.

"I was with him at Cambridge, when his troubles began," the manservant continued. "I was here when he carried each of you boys back from the East End like half-drowned kittens, and I'll be here when Dr. Goddard realizes the futility of his misguided charity *again*."

My head snapped up at the mention of Cambridge.

After the promising start of a brilliant career, Goddard had been dismissed from his post. The door of the ivory tower was locked so firmly behind him that more than a decade later, he still couldn't do better than an occasional evening class in basic composition. He might have made an enemy of the wrong person, found himself on the wrong side of some political struggle. But Goddard preferred persuasion to confrontation, and avoided politics of all sorts. I suspected a scandal—something shaming him into a lifetime of silence.

Something that would ruin his career forever.

And St. Andrews had been at the center of it.

A nauseating picture began to form in my mind.

"What happened at Cambridge?" I asked.

Collins regarded me evenly.

"That's for Dr. Goddard to reveal, should he see fit to do so."

Which he wouldn't bloody well do, and we both knew it. No matter.

"I'm not leaving," I said.

Collins turned the knife over in his hands, watching the blade catch the light from the lamp I'd set on the edge of the table. He suddenly gripped the knife by the handle and stabbed it into the thick wood of the kitchen table, where it quivered beside the pile of empty red seed pods.

"For a while I thought you were different," he said. "You didn't throw the master's money around as if it were your own. You didn't bring your filthy friends by when he was gone. You genuinely seemed to appreciate that he wanted to improve your mind. But you don't care for him. Not like you should."

"But I said I wasn't leaving," I argued.

My tone was unconvincing. I'd been mindful of Goddard's unusual generosity and careful not to abuse it. But I couldn't help feeling that Collins was right on some level. I had definitely been taking advantage of Goddard's affection. I did enjoy Goddard's company. I respected and liked him. But was that enough to merit that evening's grand gesture?

"He asked me to stay, and I intend to," I said.

"In the end, your kind always leave. And it always takes its toll. Dr. Goddard is a very busy and very important man, Mr. Adler. He can really do without this kind of abuse."

Enraged, I thrust my hand in his face. The golden snake's diamond eyes glittered in the gaslight. Collins's eyes narrowed as he examined it. One corner of his mouth lifted in a sad half-smile.

"He gave you that, did he?"

"He said he had it made specially."

"Especially for you? Oh, yes," he continued. "I've seen that ring before. I keep trying to tell him that it's useless, but he never listens. Forgive me, Mr. Adler. I was taken in by the first few of your predecessors as surely as Dr. Goddard was, but it always ends the same way. This time, I'm not taking any chances."

"But—"

"Tell me, is Dr. Goddard aware of the little problem between your legs?"

For a moment, there was no sound save for the pounding of my heart. Though it was cooler below stairs, the air suddenly felt hot and thick. Needless to say, the crawling sensation that had been merely irritating earlier an hour ago, now raged and burned with the fury of hell.

"What do you know of it?" I asked.

"Oh, I've seen it before."

He leaned over to pick up the dustbin. He held the bin below the lip of the table, and used his hand to sweep the empty seed pods into it. He reached for the bowl of pulp and tipped it in as well.

"It starts with an itch," he said, taking the bowl to the sink. I watched him rinse it, give it a shake, and set it on the rack to dry. "You begin a bathing regimen, but it only seems to aggravate the situation. You scratch, it gets worse. You do nothing; it becomes unbearable. You try every manner of pharmacopoeia—one of your predecessors even sought the services of a spiritualist—but nothing seems to help."

He crossed back, removing the apron and using it to brush the remaining traces of his activity from the table.

"All the while you keep the secret festering inside you, terrified to broach the subject with the master, because you're not sure which would trigger a more violent response, his supposition that your misery was a result of your own infidelity, or your implied accusation of a dalliance on his part."

He met my eyes, his own like two cold pebbles.

"Of all the reasons for leaving, Mr. Adler, a shameful disease is the most disappointing, wouldn't you agree?"

I swallowed. Goddard credited my recent fondness for oil rubs and herbal baths to a newfound hedonistic streak. But though the oil provided a pleasant enough distraction when Goddard applied it, even my favorite herbs now seemed to irritate. Nurse Brand had sworn up and down there was no evidence of disease, and yet Nate had spotted the problem immediately. From Collins's unerring description of the progression of symptoms, he knew the truth as well. Whether Goddard had brought the infection to our bed or whether it was my souvenir from earlier days was immaterial. Sooner or later, we would both have to face the truth. And if Goddard thought I had disrespected him in this way, his justice would be swift and merciless.

And, I thought, Collins's words echoing in my mind, perhaps I deserved it.

Two floors up, there was a faint thump. I'd been gone too long for a simple call of nature. Was Goddard getting up to investigate? I snatched my lamp from the table.

"I could be wrong, of course," Collins said, glancing toward the ceiling. "Your problem might clear up on its own before Dr. Goddard becomes suspicious enough to take action. The question is, how much are you willing to risk on such a hope, Mr. Adler, when you know in your heart that it's futile?"

I opened my mouth to speak, but there were simply no words. So this was how it was to end? On the very night that it began? The lamp began to tremble in my hand, and I had the sudden sense the entire basement was closing in around me. Collins said nothing, merely picking up the dustbin in one hand and the plate of scrapings in another.

"Sooner or later, the truth will out, Mr. Adler. Do him a favor. Do yourself a favor." He glanced up again. "He's always so disappointed when you boys just vanish, but eventually he picks himself up and moves on."

"Vanish?" I swallowed. His tone and his expression suggested the others hadn't simply abandoned the big house on York Street in favor of some Whitechapel doorway. "What do you mean? What happened to them?"

His mouth quirked into a sleepy smirk. "I'm rather curious about that myself. I have no idea what became of the other young men who wore that ring. Good night, Mr. Adler."

He turned toward the corridor where his room and Eileen's lay. I watched him pad away, the bin in one hand, the plate of scrapings in the other. When he got to the corridor, he paused briefly to turn out the kitchen light.

The truth will out. Did he intend to share his suspicions with Goddard? A few pilfered opium pods seemed silly compared to a venereal disease. I absently stroked the head of the golden snake, but the metal felt cold against my finger, and the band felt more like a prisoner's shackle than the symbol of commitment it was meant to be.

With the wall lights extinguished, I became aware I was in a small, dark basement, with the weight of two well-furnished stories bearing down above me, and only the lamp in my hand for protection. I felt sick. And yet I couldn't go back to bed, not just now, not like this. And I couldn't stay in the basement. I had to get outside, just for a moment, and clear my head.

Back in the vestibule, I retrieved my slippers from the foot of the stairs. I considered dashing upstairs to dress properly. But I was only going out onto the front steps for a smoke. I clacked into the morning room and retrieved one of my cigarettes from the gilded box on the mantel. Ignoring the brush of the lavender letters against the backs of my fingers, I lit the cigarette with the barrel-shaped lighter beside the box. I inhaled deeply: Nile mud, dry desert air, and pyramid dust. On my life, there were few more things more salutary than a lungful of Egyptian tobacco when one most needed it.

In retrospect, the rectangular back garden, where Goddard grew his prized roses, would have made a much better choice. I might have stayed there for the rest of the night, the spicy smell of my tobacco mingling with the sweetness of the roses, until I'd either figured out how to tell him about my condition, and about Collins's treachery, or until I'd fallen asleep on the ornate iron bench. But I was in too much of a panic to think clearly. All I wanted was out. Leaving my lamp on the mantel, I went back to the vestibule and snatched, for decency's sake, the obnoxious tweed coat from the rack by the door. I slipped out the front, pulling the door shut behind me.

The very door, I realized, as the tumblers of the Chubb detector lock clicked into place, which had time and again proven impervious to my persuasion and the picklocks jingling in the pocket of that hated coat.

Chapter Ten

The Great Westminster Clock tolled three. The sun would be up in a few hours, but so would the neighbors' servants. One just didn't encounter half-naked men with kiss-swollen lips and love bites on the doorsteps of middle-class bachelors. In broad daylight, it wouldn't take five minutes for someone to twig to the idea my presence and state meant exactly what they did mean, and to rob our blackmailer of the opportunity to turn us over to the police. That fragrant breath of Egypt went foul in my mouth, and I expelled a sour plume of smoke into the early morning air.

The obvious solution was to let myself back in through a window. I'd have done it, too, had Goddard not nailed the ones below the second floor shut. I might have put a rock through one of them, but the sound of breaking glass would have attracted the attention of the legions of constables wandering the streets around Regent's Park instead of patrolling places where they might encounter actual crime. Eileen's room had no windows to scratch at, and the hope the girl would rise before her peers to scrub the front step was uncertain at best. The only thing for it was to wake either Collins or Goddard.

The cigarette was turning to ash in my fingers. I ground it out on the landing, leaving a black smudge, which I spat on and rubbed with the toe of my slipper until it became a long, ugly smear.

"Sorry, Eileen," I said under my breath.

I glanced toward our bedroom window. Goddard had excellent hearing, and was normally a light sleeper. However, after a night of vigorous exercise, even more vigorous sex, and half a bottle of expensive brandy, I doubted anything would have awakened him.

"Cain!" I hissed.

Silence.

I looked around for a pebble to toss, but of course both street and landing had been swept clean.

"Goddard!"

Suddenly, I heard approaching footsteps.

I almost cried out when I saw the unmistakable form of a bobby in his tall hat, silhouetted against the street lamp on the corner. I flattened myself against the doorway just in time to avoid his sweeping gaze, and drew in a long, cautious breath. That I should be skulking around my own doorway like a common housebreaker was outrageous. And it was all Collins's fault. Somehow, I'd have to convince Goddard that Collins was a thief before Collins convinced him I was a disease-bearing whore. I'd start the moment I found a way back into the house.

Eventually, the constable grew bored of searching a quiet street for imaginary criminals, and stepped out of the light. I waited until his footsteps faded away before letting out my breath and turning my attention back to the problem at hand. There had to be something I could use to get Goddard's attention—a stone, some acorns, a light piece of rubbish. I glanced around again, but York Street was as bare as a pauper's plate.

A lazy breeze billowed my robe up around my knees, reminding me I was as naked as a Scotsman beneath it. It wasn't cold enough for the brown tweed coat, and God knew, there was never a right time to wear such a revolting garment. But if the constable did double back and surprise me, and didn't bother to look at the bare shins and slippers sticking out beneath the tattered hem, he might just be prevented from jumping to unfortunate conclusions. Muttering to myself, I pulled it on.

I really could have used another cigarette. Unfortunately, the box and lighter were both back on the mantel in the morning room, sod it all. I listened to the hollow echo of my slippers on the landing. And then it came to me. A wood-soled velvet slipper would surely shatter the bedroom window, wake the neighbors, and bring the coppers running.

But thrown carefully against the wall, the same might well rouse Goddard alone from his slumber and bring him to the window.

Stepping out of the beautiful, beaded house shoes that cost more than an entire night at Nate's brothel, I picked one up, took aim, and flung it. The slipper landed true, right beside the window—fabric side down, unfortunately. I watched it slide down the wall, landing with an insipid slap near the gated well that led to the neighbors' servants' entrance. I considered vaulting over the waist-high row of iron spikes to retrieve it, but no sooner had I balanced my one shod foot on the spikes than the neighbors' light came on below stairs.

The next-door butler was a sour-tempered fellow, a teetotaler, a God-botherer, and a vegetarian.

He and Collins were the best of friends.

"Cain!" I hissed again.

A light switched on in the main house next door, another below stairs on the other side, and again across the street. Our own under-stairs remained deliberately, stubbornly dark. Footsteps rang out.

In daylight, it would have been easy to explain myself. I was Goddard's secretary. I lived on the premises, a fact to which the neighbors would all attest. But in daylight, I would have been clothed and shod, washed of sweat and musk, the unmistakable marks of passion—of which Goddard bore a similar set—hidden beneath high collar and cravat.

Before my appearance could send us both to prison, I wrapped my coat around me and ran.

Regent's Park wasn't more than a few blocks away. I sprinted down Baker Street, and, before the constable could have made his way back to the lamppost, I was through the gate. Ignoring the pebbles bruising my feet, I ran past the lake, darted up the canal, and threw myself into the hollow beneath Clarence Bridge. Gasping and panting, I forced myself to take long, deep breaths.

There was a commotion beginning down on York Street. God only knew what people were saying. By now there were too many police about for me to return. If I somehow convinced them to wake Goddard, he would have a lot to explain. He'd do it without question, of course, but even if the police believed whatever story he came up with, he would forevermore carry the taint of suspicion. No, I would not do the blackmailer's work for him. At the same time, I couldn't very well wait until daylight to make my way back. Goddard might forgive me for prowling the streets of London in nothing but a robe, but the scandal of my return, in full daylight, in such a disreputable state, before God and the neighbors? Even the Duke of Dorset Street had his limits.

No, I would have to find a friendly place to sit out the rest of the night, and hopefully get my hands on some trousers. The clinic came to mind. Pearl always kept a few boxes of donated clothing for just such contingencies. But the clinic was five miles of rough road away, and my feet were already stinging. On the other hand, Nate's Fitzroy Street brothel wasn't more than a mile away, and I could stick to the park for most of it.

The question was, of course, whether Nate would be there. He had lit out of the Criterion with a scar-faced devil on his heels. But was that particular devil a minion of the brothel owner, whom Nate had so feared? If so, then Nate would be long gone from the place. On the other hand, if Scar-Face had been sent by someone else, Nate might well be holed up at the brothel, waiting for the smoke to clear. Either way, I thought, fingering the picklocks in my pocket, it was a roof for a few hours, even if I had to hide in a closet. Moreover, in a house full of men, there were bound to be trousers.

Slowly, painfully, I emerged from under the bridge. I picked my way along the banks of the canal, sticking to the shadows and trees. Thankfully, after dark, the park was peopled only by those who couldn't be bothered with my state of dress, once they'd determined I carried nothing of value. Eventually I came to York Bridge, and then the Outer Circle. I exited the park at York Terrace and turned left onto Marylebone. Gray had begun to creep into the edges of the night. As I turned onto Fitzroy Street, I was relieved to see the windows of the houses were still dark behind their lace curtains and aspidistras.

Number 19 was quiet as the rest. The last of the clients appeared to have left the somber brown brick house. The young men who serviced them were now allowed to close their black shutters and sleep. The teachers, merchants, and tradesmen who made their homes nearby were genuinely ignorant of what went on under their very noses. The power of the human mind to ignore what it didn't want to see was nothing short of miraculous.

I let my gaze follow the plane of the façade, lighting briefly on each of the second-story windows. There was no way of knowing which was Nate's. And even if I had known, the copious pebbles on the sidewalk and street would make no noise at all against the shutters. Pity I hadn't my slippers with me. My eyes fell on the servants' stairwell. The houses on Fitzroy Street also had two entrances. Family and visitors naturally used the front door. Servants and tradesmen descended a gated stairwell to the left of the entrance. Mindful of the spikes, I carefully climbed over the gate and made my way down the stairs, while palming my picklocks.

The door gave way easily. I locked it behind me. Blinking, I gave my eyes a moment to adjust to the dim light from the street above. In Goddard's house, this would have been the kitchen. A male brothel wouldn't retain a cook or any other kind of servant. They might have a girl in now and then to clean, but anything more would have been too much of a risk. Past the unused kitchen table, there was a doorway on the opposite wall. I assumed beyond it were one or two small rooms that in another house would have been servants' quarters. Nate had said the "disturbances" he'd heard—muffled cries, bangs, crashes, words in an unrecognizable tongue—had come from the basement. But though I strained my ears listening, I perceived nothing but the stillness of a place left vacant for some time and the faint whiff of opium.

I followed the smell across the room to a hallway. Light from a small window at the end revealed a single door to my left. The door had once latched from the outside, but the latch had been forced. It now swung from the door on a single, twisted screw. Dents in the doorjamb and a black gash in the wood testified to the violence with which the job had been done. The smell of opium was stronger there, but no sound proceeded from the room—no crying, no one stirring in the arms of Morpheus. Cautiously, I turned the knob.

The hair stood up on the back of my neck as I opened the door. That the noises Nate had described had so spooked him—Nate, who had always been the one to comfort the younger children through the dark workhouse nights—gave me pause. But nothing rushed at me from the darkness. I was quite alone, save for the overpowering smell suffusing the mounds of clothes and bedding on the floor. I quickly crossed to the window and pulled down the blanket hung over it. The dim light creeping in made it easier to see, but the window had been nailed shut—there would be no relief from the smell.

Under the opium, the room smelt strongly of urine, sweat, and despair. My stomach rose. I rushed for the door, gulping air from the hallway until I was certain I would neither vomit nor pass out. There was no doubt now people had been brought here against their will and held. But who were they? Where had they gone?

In the corner a slop bucket lay on its side in a pool of filth. The largest opium lamp I had ever seen sat in pieces on the floor near the window. The chamber-pot sized base bore a dent that matched a long scratch on the wall above it. Before the glass bulb had shattered, it had been as big as my head. Opium lamps were usually no larger than my fist—the volume of smoke this one emitted could have kept an entire room of captives helpless and docile. There was a dark, spattered line from one end of the far wall to the other. A struggle had taken place—from the coppery note of blood mingled with the other smells, it hadn't been that long ago.

I stepped over a pile of limp, grimy sheets. Flashes of bright fabric caught my eye. A few garments were tangled in the sheets—eccentric in design, absurd in color, but anything had to be better than my current state of indecency. Kneeling, I began sifting through it all. The first thing I pulled out was an embroidered tunic with billowing sleeves, which I immediately discarded. It would have been too small, even for Eileen. There was a lovely piece woven from rough, colorful strands. I considered it for quite a while until I realized it was a skirt, and slim as my hips were, it wouldn't have fit over them. I eventually found a pair of pink drawstring trousers that only came down to my knees but just might hold if I didn't bend over. I shimmied into them, trying to ignore the delight of a regiment of lice, who wasted no time tucking into my sensitive flesh.

The lice and the constriction of my bits might have been tolerable, if not for the lump of something now attempting to dig its way through the small of my back. I prodded it gingerly at first. Soft. A wad of fabric balled into a pocket. Yes, there was a pocket—my fingers felt the edges of the pouch. But there was no opening. Frowning, I felt around the edges again. My fingers eventually found a bit of stitching that was slightly coarser than the rest. Not a pocket, then, but something sewn into the garment—something hidden. A chill swept over me as I ripped open the stitching. When I pulled out the object that someone had gone to such great trouble to conceal, I wanted to vomit.

It was a doll: a child's doll, no bigger than my palm. The eyes and mouth were black stitches on a face made from faded cloth that had probably come from a parent's worn-out garment. A bit of multicolored silk had been wrapped around the doll's body for a tunic. Its hands and feet were knots. A simple urchin's doll, such as I'd seen a hundred times, fashioned from scraps for the comfort of a small child. Someone had loved this doll. And someone had loved its owner enough to sew what was quite probably her only toy into her undergarments before sending her to meet her fate.

I ripped off the pantaloons and flung them away. Someone was moving children through a brothel. My stomach was empty but my throat was burning with bile. Shaking, I sat back on the pile of sheets. It wasn't unknown, even in London, for parents to sell their children—or their children's favors—to settle a debt. I suppose I was fortunate my own mother had put me in the workhouse when my upkeep became too much of a burden. Part of me liked to think even when up to the eyes in her opium habit, she wanted to make sure I'd be cared for. Where were the parents of these children? What sort of debt could have amassed that they would have sold their little ones to bondage in a foreign land?

And judging from the clothes, England was very foreign, and very far away…

I pushed back the flood of thoughts that followed. I had to keep my head. Nate hadn't mentioned anything about children during our luncheon, which meant he hadn't known then. Had he figured it out? I glanced at the broken opium lamp, the trail of blood, the ruined latch swinging from the door. He must have. And the moment he did, he'd marched down to the basement with a crowbar, ready to smash in the door—or the skull of anyone who tried to stop him. But whose blood was on the wall? And where were the children now?

I drew a shaky breath, looked stupidly at the doll in my hand, and shoved it into my coat pocket with the picklocks. Above me, the house was still silent, though morning's light was beginning to push through the dirty glass of the windows. The shuttered rooms upstairs and the late hours kept by their occupants would buy me some time. I had to find the extra set of books Nate kept. If I was too late to help him—it was certainly too late to help the last group of children who had been through here—at least I could finish what Nate had started and turn his records over to the police. Shivering, I wiped my mouth with my sleeve.

Leaving that miserable little room, my foot struck something hard hidden beneath a wad of bedding. I kicked it free of the sheets, and it skidded across the floor with a metallic hiss, coming to rest near the door. It was a watch, I realized, bending to pick it up. Attractive but inexpensive, hammered too thin, and much the worse for wear, I recognized it immediately. It was the token given to Nate by his Mr. Sinclair. I was certain Nate would have sooner died than been parted from it.

I bolted out of the miserable little cell, found the servants' stairs, and lit upstairs as fast as my bare feet could carry me. I was certain Nate had come back to the brothel after our luncheon. There had been a struggle, and he'd lost his watch. But when had the struggle taken place? Who had been there? And where were Nate and the occupants of that room now? I had to find Nate's room, and I had to get my hands on those ledgers before someone else did.

Eight seconds later, I was standing in the vestibule of a very posh brothel. So posh, they hadn't turned off the lights to save gas, as Goddard insisted we do at York Street. As a result, the ground floor was cast in perpetual twilight, unrelieved by the rising sun pushing at the thick curtains of the front window. The black and white floor tiles were exactly the ones Goddard had chosen for his own vestibule, and there was a hat rack beside the front door. The similarities to our home stopped there. The decorator's flamboyant taste would have sent

Goddard fleeing, from the curvaceous vase of black ostrich plumes on the spindly table to the gilded lamp in the form of an angel with the wings of real doves to the intricate scarlet and gold wallpaper and the framed sketches on the wall.

Like the vase and wallpaper, the sketches reflected an Oriental style and predictably depicted various sex acts between men. Were I to have encountered the arrangement in someone's home—straight rows of evenly spaced pictures, two across and three down—I'd have taken it as lack of imagination on the part of the owner. In this context, it was clearly a map. If the rest of the house resembled ours, there would be three rooms on each of the top two floors. One could assume from this that if one were seeking a particular service, he could find it in the room corresponding to the picture.

Nate's specialty was unique. I found it quickly. Though he hadn't been offering his favors for several months, they probably hadn't bothered to move him to a different room. Composing a mental picture of the second floor, I crept up the stairs. The layout was exactly as I had imagined. A heavy cloud of fatigue and inebriation sat over the house. Not a creature would be stirring for at least an hour. Nonetheless, there was no reason to tempt fate. With a glance in either direction, I darted down the corridor to the room at the end, shutting the door behind me.

I wasn't sure what I was expecting. Perhaps a bed built for three and billowing velvet canopies? Persian rugs, silk sheets, and fat pillows arranged carelessly around a hookah. But Nate's room was clean and spare, containing a single bed, wardrobe, and a tidy desk before the window. A Persian rug lay under the bed, and it had seen better days. There were no signs of struggle, no indications anything untoward had happened there. Everything was neatly put together, as if the owner had stepped out with every intention of returning. Or, I thought, considering the uncharacteristic precision with which everything had been arranged, as if he suspected he might not be.

I tried to imagine the last few moments Nate had spent in the room. Daring rescue attempts weren't normally his style. His blackmail plan would accomplish both punishmment and restitution from a distance. Some sound, some event, some exchange of words must have revealed the true nature of the brothel owner's basement trade. And that knowledge had caused Nate to abandon his carefully laid plans and go downstairs.

Which meant the ledgers were still in this room.

The desk was the natural place to start. It stood to reason he'd keep the doctored books somewhere obvious so they'd be close at hand when either Sinclair or the owner demanded to inspect them. Reason didn't fail me. When I jimmied open the top drawer, two identical fabric-bound ledgers stared back at me. I flipped through them. Nate had used the same system to encode both the opium book and the client book. Between this and his workhouse scrawl, he was probably the only one who could make heads or tails of either set of records. I glanced around the tidy room once more. The second set of books, reflecting the owner's special transactions and Sinclair's embezzlement, would be hidden somewhere—as would Nate's documentation of it all.

I set the ledgers on top of the desk and lifted out the drawer. The bottom and sides were solid, and nothing was secreted beneath it. I carefully replaced the contents and put it back as it had been. There was nothing underneath or behind the desk, or under the chair. The wardrobe was unlocked, and though it too was free of secret panels, I did find a pair of trousers and a silk shirt that would fit me. I folded them and set them on the ground next to the wardrobe.

As I rose, something about the lay of the rug beneath the bed caught my eye. Crossing to the bed, I knelt down beside it and lifted the fringe. A little more than an arm's length away, a floorboard had warped. A corner was sticking up…or had it been purposely left up, perhaps for someone to find in the event of Nate's sudden departure? Glancing over my shoulder, I slid beneath the bed and pried the board loose. It came up easily enough, and I reached inside.

Two books—the true ledgers—were there, along with a stack of papers tied with string. I stuffed the ledgers into the pocket of the brown coat. There would be plenty of time to examine them later. I was more interested in the papers. I slid out from under the bed and sat on the rug. Holding the letters in one hand, I picked the knot apart. A flurry of handmade envelopes fell into my lap. About a dozen letters, penned on ordinary white stationery and addressed in Nate's sloppy hand, in a most extraordinary lavender ink.

Bugger me.

The letters were addressed to *The Times*, *The Morning Mammoth*, *The Daily Telegraph*, Scotland Yard, and a few individuals whose names I recognized from the gossip pages. None were destined for either Goddard or St. Andrews. Had Nate been our blackmailer all along? It didn't make sense. Back at the Criterion, he had said he was going after the clients purchasing the services of the children from the basement—or purchasing the children themselves. While Goddard was a criminal, there was a limit to the sordidness in which he would personally involve himself—at least I'd thought so. I couldn't speak for St. Andrews. I slipped a trembling finger beneath the corner of the one addressed to a prominent MP, unfolded the paper and read:

> *Yer gon rot in hell for what you done but first im gon make yer life hell. im gon tell em all startin wiv the times dont fink i wont you filthy bastard. bring 100 quid to the old east india warehouse on friday july 5 at 8 oclock. come alone an dont tell noone.*

I let the paper fall into my lap with the others. The coincidence was uncanny—blackmail letters written on plain white stationery in lavender ink. But it was all wrong. Goddard's letters had been written by an educated man with excellent penmanship. What's more—though Goddard seemed to know what his blackmailer wanted, the letters coming to York Street had never stated a demand. Could Nate have been working with Goddard's blackmailer? Or perhaps Goddard's blackmailer was someone Nate knew, someone from whom Nate had borrowed the idea—if not the very ink and paper. I thought again about his Mr. Sinclair. Sinclair and Goddard both ran brothels. They were both in the opium trade. It was very likely that at least they were aware of each other. Nate had described Sinclair as older, and Goddard kept talking about the "mistakes of youth."

Could they have known one another in the past?

Sunlight was trying to stream through the bare window, hindered by the thick clouds and the proximity of the brick wall comprising Nate's view. Morning had arrived, and Goddard would soon be sitting down for breakfast, wondering where I was. I bundled the letters back together, shoved them in my pocket, and was about to make my escape when a voice behind me said,

"'O the devil are you?"

I scrambled to my feet. A barefoot, robe-clad man stood in the doorway. He was pale of hair and eye, wan of complexion, and just a little younger than I. His eyes were red, hair tousled, and he was blinking more than one might expect in muted light.

"I might ask you the same question," I said.

"This is me room."

"This is Nate's room."

"Nate's gone."

I straightened my coat with as much dignity as one could while barefoot and half-naked in a strange place. Nate couldn't have been gone more than a day, and someone was already moving in to take his place. I wondered whether Sinclair had fled with Nate, or whether Nate's replacement had been his choice.

"Since when?" I asked.

He shrugged a thin shoulder.

"Where did he go?"

"Ain't me business to know where. And ain't nuffin' in this room wot's your business, neither. Now ge' out."

I was taller than him. I also had two years of solid nutrition behind me, and the muscle earned from a year with the London Society for the Oriental Fighting Arts. I took a step forward. He took a step back, but to his credit didn't look away while I held his eyes. His fingers twitched as he picked at the frayed edge of his robe.

"I'm a friend of Nate's," I said, breaking the gaze to pick up the shirt and trousers from the floor.

"If you're 'is friend, why you stealing 'is togs?"

"If this is your room, why are Nate's clothes in the wardrobe? And why did you sleep in a different room last night?"

He frowned. I watched his eyes dart from me to the desk, the wardrobe, to the rug where I'd been sitting. His nervousness crackled in the air. Given the probable circumstances of Nate's disappearance,

I'd have been anxious, too, were I in his position. But I suspected there was more to it.

"Where's Sinclair?" I asked, moving closer.

The young man hugged his elbows to him, his expression remaining defiant.

"Takin' out the trash. Which is my job now, too, come to fink of it."

"Is that so?"

I took another step toward him. I noticed red welts in the crease of his arm. Sinclair had made Nate get off opium before working with the books. Injecting cocaine was a quick way of ridding oneself of the habit. But these injection sites had been there long enough to become infected.

How long had someone been grooming this little shit to take Nate's place?

I tried stepping around him. He'd spent the last ten minutes trying to throw me out, but now he seemed determined to block the door with his skinny frame.

"On second thought, the doctor'll be 'ere soon. Quite a fevver in me cap to catch a burglar in the act."

"Oh, for crying—"

"Tell me why I shouldn't."

One good uppercut would have answered the question. Yet something in his dogged defiance touched me. Perhaps it was just a reluctance to deface what would have been a countenance of angelic beauty.

Or at least it would have been, after a long bath and a week of good meals.

"First," I said, planting a hand on his sternum and giving him a gentle push back through the doorway. "You couldn't detain a mouse in your condition. Second, you don't know who you're dealing with. And third…"

He really was pitiful. Malnourished, scared shitless, and caught between one nasty drug habit and the next. He might not have known the circumstances of Nate's disappearance but he was clever enough to recognize he'd signed a deal with the devil when he'd accepted Nate's mantle. He was in over his head and knew it. But what else could he have done?

"Third," I said gently. "Cocaine is no better a mistress than opium in the long run. They both lead to the same place."

He knew this place. I saw it in his eyes. Years from now, his face prematurely creased, poisons having coarsened what was once supple and delicate, he would find himself back on the street with nothing to show for it but a pox and a costly drug habit.

"I have friends in powerful places," I said. "One day, you might be grateful for their assistance."

When he met my eyes, his were full of a fear so deep and familiar it made me shiver. If fate had twisted a different way two years ago, it might have been me standing in his place. It might still be if I didn't rid myself of the little problem between my legs before Collins went skipping off to Goddard with tales of syphilis and indiscretion.

"The name's Adler," I said, reaching out my hand.

"'Arrington. Marcus 'Arring—"

A great crash cut off the rest of his words. The building shook with the sound of breaking glass and splintering wood.

"Police!" someone shouted.

"It's a raid," 'Arrington whispered.

He looked terrified. I'm certain my own expression was similar. I was half-naked in a brothel with another man, covered in love bites, with Goddard's ring still snug around my finger. I didn't fancy explaining myself to either a judge or Goddard.

Footsteps thundered up the stairs. Grasping young Mr. 'Arrington by the wrist, I tried to lunge back into the room—but a heavy hand caught my shoulder.

"Well," said a voice with the smug ring of a Whitechapel bobby, "Look what we've got 'ere."

CHAPTER ELEVEN

The constables apprehended eight men at the brothel that Friday morning—five gorgeous young things whose profession would have been written on their sleeves had they been wearing clothing, 'Arrington, myself, and a very embarrassed second son of a marquis. The earl's son negotiated his immediate release through that easy application of cash and implied threats that must be taught in boarding school. A few of the constables had stayed behind to close up the brothel, while the rest loaded us into the back of a Black Maria headed for Bow Street Station.

My bowels began to clench before they had even locked the door. As the prison van rolled away, I closed my eyes, pretending I was somewhere else. The dispensary at Lazarus's clinic, perhaps. Or somewhere roomy like a kitchen cupboard. At least they hadn't chained us. My imagination wasn't good enough to ignore that.

All around me, my fellow prisoners chatted amiably. The easy life they had enjoyed was disappearing behind us, but these young men had seen too much milk spilt in their few years to cry over it. It was fortunate the raid had occurred in the morning. Only one client had been present, and he'd been asleep. Without actual proof of penetration, the worst any of us faced was two years—and two years of a guaranteed bed and three meals a day was better than what most of these young men would get on the street. As we trundled along, the carriage fairly hummed with jokes and speculations about being locked away with labor-hardened men, and what was really meant by "turning the crank."

I tried not to think of the dark, windowless room where I'd live out my sentence. I tried not to wonder how small it would be.

In contrast to our fellow travelers, 'Arrington sat beside me, silent and grim. His sentence would be no worse than anyone else's, but it would begin with simultaneous withdrawal from cocaine and opium.

"I meant what I said," I told him. "When this is all over, come and see me. Ira Adler."

He nodded and hugged his arms tighter around his chest as if he were actually cold despite the sweltering darkness inside the carriage.

"You'll be fine," I said without conviction.

The truth was I was unlikely to be in a position to help myself in two years, less so someone else. Some dangerously optimistic part of me was convinced Goddard was already at Bow Street, pulling strings and calling in favors on my behalf. But even if this were true, he wouldn't be sweeping me into his arms the moment we were alone. He had made me a very serious proposal last night, and I had accepted his ring before disappearing. Whatever lies Collins had been whispering into his ear since would only be amplified by the fact I had been arrested in a brothel.

I gave my ring a twist and shifted on the splintering bench. My muscles ached, my feet were torn and bruised, and my eyes burned from lack of sleep. Yet even if I'd been in my own bed, my racing thoughts would have kept me awake. One pocket of my horrible brown coat bulged with documents that could send the brothel owner to the scaffold. Through the scratchy fabric of the other pocket, I could make out my picklocks and the sad little doll. I'd finish Nate's work if I died doing it. It was bad enough destitution forced children into that situation now and then—for people to deliberately put them there was unconscionable. I'd see someone hang for it, if it was the last thing I did.

The prison van lurched suddenly as the horse stumbled over a rough bit of pavement. I opened my eyes, then squeezed them shut again, forcing myself to breathe.

A lifetime ago, another carriage had been taking me to the Stepney Street clinic, though in truth no more than twenty-four hours had passed. I wondered whether Pearl's sources had turned up any information about the porcelain dog. It would have been fast, but Pearl knew everyone. Someone might well have heard something. I also wondered whether Goddard had someone else standing ready to take up the search, now that I had proven incapable of this simple task. Goddard seemed to know what his blackmailer wanted, which meant he knew who it was. I wondered again about the brothel's manager, Mr. Sinclair. Goddard and Sinclair were in some of the same circles, and they were likely close in age. And Nate had to have got the idea for the lavender letters from somewhere. If I ever saw Goddard again, I'd ask him about it.

When he was finished shouting, that is.

At last the carriage pulled to the side and stopped. The back door opened. A constable led us, blinking, out onto the street. London's first police station loomed over us: gray, ominous, and possessive. One of the peelers took me by the elbow and attempted to lead me toward the massive stone façade. There's a network of cells below Bow Street Station, where prisoners are housed until they can be tried. Depending upon where the judge is in his circuit of the courts, a case could take up to a month to come to trial.

Thirty days. No windows. A door of solid steel.

Goddard speculates my dread of enclosed spaces stems from the day my mother left me at the workhouse. After they ripped me from her arms, I screamed for six hours straight, alone in a dark closet set aside for that purpose. Though I've no recollection of it, several of the warders recounted the story exactly that way.

Which is probably why I sank to the ground, insensible and immovable, instead of meekly following the constables through the big wooden door.

I could see people milling about, mouths moving and arms waving as they tried to figure out what to do with me. Why they couldn't just pick me up was a mystery. I wasn't particularly heavy, and finally they did give it their best. My body simply wasn't going anywhere. Quite a crowd gathered round. Marcus was looking at me dolefully, when a voice cried out,

"Constables, move aside!"

The voice sounded tinny, faraway, and yet I could make out a certain impatience that made my heart leap. Someone said *Ira*, and a hand closed over my shoulder, so strong, so full of concern, that just as I'd been powerless against my body's urge to collapse into a boneless heap, I was powerless to keep myself from turning into those familiar, linen-clad arms.

"I'm sorry, I'm sorry, by God I'm so sorry," I whispered into a freshly shaven jaw. My throat tightened around the words. I didn't trust my voice not to crack. "Please take me home. I'll never so much as look out the window again."

He was freshly bathed as well, his warm, clean skin redolent with musk and citrus—the work of M. Piesse, if I wasn't mistaken. The new fragrance was not unpleasant, especially when accompanied by discreet, comforting caresses at the back of my neck.

"You smell good, Cain. Is that a new cologne?" I asked.

The arms around me suddenly stiffened and pushed me away. There before me stood the last person I wanted to see, wearing a dour brown jacket, trousers creased to a razor's edge, mustache twitching as if caught between irritation and smug amusement.

"I suppose I should be grateful to get any sort of apology out of you," Lazarus sniffed. "Even one meant for someone else. But considering the circumstances of your arrest, and the fact our blackmailer is still at large, you might reconsider how you choose to express your gratitude. And yes," he said, smirking at my consternation. "The cologne is new."

"It's not that I'm not happy to see you," I said as Lazarus packed me into a luxuriously appointed brougham.

The carriage was miles better than Goddard's. To be fair, Goddard preferred an unadorned black hansom. One didn't advertise ill-gotten gains, after all. On the other hand, St. Andrews's carriage was a gold-touched masterpiece of overstatement. While he chatted with the driver outside, I melted into the velvet-upholstered bench beneath a pair of gilded angels and closed my eyes. The inside smelled like old money and new paint. Lazarus folded down the hard little seat in the corner and perched on it. He and his earnest beau weren't my first choice for saviors, but they weren't going to leave me bleeding in a ditch, either.

"To what do I owe this eleventh-hour rescue?" I asked. "I'd think that you'd be happier with me out of the way."

"It would make things easier," Lazarus admitted. "But when St. Andrews learned you were caught up in the raid, he figured you'd be of more use to us as a free man."

I cracked an eye open.

"What do you mean 'of more use'? To *you*? And how the devil—"

"'O d'yer fink tipped off the rozzers, old chap? Eh?"

Wood squealed, and for one horrifying moment the carriage tipped onto two wheels as St. Andrews swung his long body through the door. He landed beside me in a heap of knees and elbows. His imitation cockney was appalling, but it was hard to be properly irritated with someone who resembled nothing so much as an overgrown puppy—soft of middle, floppy of limb, and grinning. St. Andrews's age was somewhere between Lazarus's and Goddard's—late thirties was my guess. Despite his lack of decorum, his enthusiasm did lend him a certain charm. Sitting shoulder to shoulder with the enemy only seemed to delight him.

"My old coat!" he exclaimed, looking me over with evident pleasure. He thumped a merry fist on the roof, and the cab began rolling. "You wear it well, Mr. Adler."

"I might have known you'd be at the center of it all," I said.

"Now, is that any way to speak to someone who's just pulled your crumpet out of the fire?"

"If I'd known there were strings attached, I'd have preferred my crumpet to remain where it was."

St. Andrews laughed and rubbed his enormous hands together, relishing a bout of witty repartee. My head throbbed. I yanked down the window shade.

"In case you were curious," he began.

"I wasn't."

"I told the police that you were our man inside. A special operative."

"Bet that didn't raise eyebrows," I muttered.

"We can take you back to prison, if you prefer," said Lazarus. The swelling had gone down on his broken nose, but it had turned a beautiful shade of purple.

"The way I see it," St. Andrews said, "Everyone benefits from our current situation. Mr. Adler, you're now a free man. Just say the word, and I'll have my driver deliver you to York Street, with no further 'strings.'"

"Right now, please," I said.

"But," he carried on, as if he hadn't heard, "considering we've just extricated you from a very sticky legal situation, an honorable man would at least hear my request."

Sighing, I opened my bleary eyes and shifted in my corner to face him. His sandy hair seemed to disappear against the amber velvet covering the walls.

"I knew you'd see reason." He grinned.

Lazarus rolled his eyes. Curious. One doesn't expect a man to display such undisguised contempt for someone he cares about, especially not in that person's presence. I remembered the look of rapture that came over Lazarus's face the other day at the clinic, when Nurse Brand had announced his luncheon companion had arrived. That rapture certainly didn't square with Lazarus's current posture, nor with his derogatory remarks about St. Andrews's abilities Wednesday night at the dollyshop. His present attitude was more befitting a long-suffering employee, which he might have been.

I'd just never pictured old Tim as a kept man.

"First point," St. Andrews said, cutting through my uncharitable speculation. "Goddard and I are enemies, as you know."

"I know."

"Second point: we're being blackmailed by the same person."

"Nick Sinclair," I said.

It was a guess, and I wasn't disappointed when it hit the mark. St. Andrews stopped mid-blather, mouth open, eyes wide.

"How—what—how—"

"No," I said. "You tell me. Who is this bastard? What does he want? And what the devil were you thinking, raiding his brothel this morning?"

The carriage swayed and creaked as we made our way across the evenly paved streets of Westminster. The trees cast dappled shadows on the window shade. With any luck St. Andrews would stutter out an answer that would mollify Goddard by the time we reached Regent's Park—at which point I would leap out and sprint down York Street before he could start asking his own questions. Lazarus turned on his little seat and was watching us with a combination of curiosity and envy.

"I had understood from our real operative that Sinclair would be at the brothel last night," St. Andrews said. "Since neither you nor Lazarus had managed to get hold of the porcelain dog, Goddard and I thought we might take care of the matter this way."

"What the—Goddard was in on this?"

"He certainly didn't expect *you* to be there," St. Andrews said. "The raid was an act of good faith: my idea undertaken with Goddard's blessing."

"I don't understand."

St. Andrews looked me over with an evaluative eye. He might have been a bumbler, but he wasn't stupid. I wondered what he had read at Cambridge, and what he might have ended up doing had he not been expelled so early on in his studies.

"That was me at York Street, Wednesday night, in disguise," he said.

"That was a disguise?"

He pursed his lips.

"I was hoping Goddard would work with me until this nasty business was over, or at least agree to a temporary truce."

"Let me guess: he wouldn't."

St. Andrews shook his head.

"He's a bitter, bitter man."

"He has a right to be after what happened at Cambridge," I said.

Of course I didn't know what happened at Cambridge. Unfortunately, St. Andrews was disinclined to enlighten me.

"That was over ten years ago," he said. "And I didn't leave Cambridge unscathed either."

"It's easy to be sanguine when you've got the family fortune to fall back on."

St. Andrews glared for a moment, then chuckled. "'Sanguine.' You've quite a vocabulary for a hustler."

"I have a good teacher."

"You have the best," he said. "But we've wandered far enough from the topic at hand. I have nothing to say about Cambridge. That's Cain's story to tell, if he chooses."

He might not have said anything outright, but his unexpected intimacy in referring to Goddard by his Christian name gave me more information than he would ever have willingly revealed. Goddard and St. Andrews had been at Cambridge around the same time—Goddard as a lecturer, and St. Andrews as a student. A little more than ten years ago, they were both dismissed with the ruinous finality that follows a scandal. Goddard held St. Andrews responsible, and from what he had said, the sentiment was mutual.

The more I thought about it, the more I realized the intensity and duration of their grudge reminded me of the undying resentment reserved for lovers parted unpleasantly.

My nausea returned. On the other side of the cab, Lazarus looked away.

The carriage slowed. On either side, I could hear the scrapes and creaks of neighboring vehicles, hear the singsong voices of the drivers as they called back and forth to one another. We'd left Westminster, merging onto a major thoroughfare, and yet we hadn't made the series of sharp, close turns to take us to York Street. Perhaps St. Andrews had told the driver to take the scenic route around the park.

"For a long time, I blamed Cain for my troubles," St. Andrews mused. "I know he still blames me. But perhaps it's time to put the past behind us."

"Who's Sinclair?" I interrupted. "I mean, who is he to you?"

St. Andrews blinked at me. I cocked an eyebrow.

"I'll answer your question, but first you'll tell me how you came up with that name," he said.

Wordlessly I handed over Nate's letter to Scotland Yard. St. Andrews frowned at the lavender ink, but as he took in the handwriting, and then the rough language, I saw the same understanding come over him that had come over me. He handed the letter to Lazarus, whose eyes widened as he read, but otherwise he hid his shock admirably.

"That letter was written by Nate Turnbull," I said. "Sinclair's assistant, his lover, and…"

"And?" St. Andrews asked.

"An old friend of mine."

"An old friend." He smiled ruefully. "I might say the same of Nick Sinclair."

Lazarus folded the letter and handed it back to me.

"He, Goddard, and I knew each other at Cambridge," St. Andrews said.

"So what does he want now?"

St. Andrews looked pensive. It was an uncomfortable expression on a face that preferred to arrange itself around an easy smile. He ran a hand through his hair.

"What he wants from Goddard, I can't say. From me, though, he wants silence," St. Andrews said. "That's what he's always wanted: silence about his misdeeds. For ten years he had it, too, as long as Zhi Sen had the porcelain dog."

"Why? What's inside the dog?"

His face went stony. "If I'm not going to tell you about Cambridge, Mr. Adler, I'm certainly not going to tell you that. But I will tell you that the statue houses a piece of evidence that, if released to the world, would send me, Goddard, and Sinclair to prison for a very long time."

"And now Sinclair has it," I said.

He nodded solemnly.

"In neutral hands, the evidence acted as a balance for our hostilities. It kept Goddard and Sinclair from going after one another once their business dealings went sour, and it kept me from blowing the whistle on their illegal activities."

"I'd hardly call Zhi Sen neutral," I said.

St. Andrews cocked his head. "I wasn't asked for my input, of course. But as far as the other two went, Zhi Sen seemed ideal. He, Goddard, and Sinclair were equal partners in a highly lucrative opium venture. And none of them were the type to allow friendship to get in the way of business."

This was news to me. I'd known Goddard and Zhi Sen were partners, but Goddard had never mentioned a third. If St. Andrews was telling the truth, something had gone wrong and Sinclair had been pushed out at some point. But what had prevented Goddard from simply asking Zhi Sen for the statue and using it against Sinclair—or against St. Andrews, for that matter? Unless Zhi Sen wasn't as good a friend as Goddard thought.

Unless Sinclair was holding something over Zhi Sen.

And what about Zhi Sen's daughter, Mrs. Wu? She'd taken the statue from me. One would expect her to have returned it to her father forthwith. But if she'd done that, the balance would have been restored. St. Andrews and I wouldn't have been having this conversation. She might have been working for Sinclair, though that seemed a stretch. But if Zhi Sen and Sinclair were conspiring behind Goddard's back, it was entirely possible they'd hired her to guard the statue. There was also the possibility she herself had some interest in the statue or its contents, though I couldn't fathom what it might be.

One thing was for certain, though: I was not about to loose Lazarus and his puppy on the daughter of Goddard's business partner until I had spoken to Goddard himself about it.

"Sinclair had access to a cheap opium supply," St. Andrews explained. "Zhi Sen's connections allowed them to import the drug to China as well as England. The whole operation was Goddard's idea. He brought everything together, made it work."

"Wait," I said. "Import the drug *to* China? Doesn't opium come *from* China?"

"A common misconception," St. Andrews said with a wave of

his hand. "Opium comes from India and Afghanistan. The Chinese managed to ban it for more than a century, but the East India Company went to war with them, twice, so that people like Goddard would have the right to push the poison through their ports. A lot of people have made a lot of money in the intervening years, Cain Goddard not least of all."

"Why did Goddard and Sinclair part ways?" I asked.

"No idea."

"Where's Goddard getting his opium now?"

"You'd have to ask him that."

"What do you want from me?" I asked.

St. Andrews nodded toward the letter in my hand.

"You've already given me more than I expected. But you say Sinclair is your friend's lover. Any idea why he wasn't at Fitzroy Street last night?"

It was surreal to be discussing the case so nonchalantly with Goddard's nemesis. Didn't someone once say the enemy of an enemy is a friend? It made sense for Goddard and St. Andrews to combine forces against Sinclair, no matter how they felt about each other. But I wouldn't put it past Goddard to face prison with his head held high, if it meant St. Andrews would be there as well. One might argue I was doing this for Goddard's own good.

"Do you trust your operative?" I asked.

"With my life."

"Then I'd guess Sinclair and Nate are together somewhere. Also, Nate disappeared from the brothel sometime yesterday, and I have reason to believe that he didn't go willingly."

St. Andrews nodded and leaned back in his corner, his thick eyebrows beetling together over the bridge of his nose. He steepled his long fingers beneath his chin. "You think that your friend took it upon himself to put a stop to…"

"They were keeping those children in the basement," I said. "The children were gone when I arrived. It looks like someone got them out of there in a hurry. I found this."

I hesitated for a moment before handing the little doll across the bench to St. Andrews. He held it out to Lazarus, who shrank back into his corner, making a superstitious gesture with his hands.

"I also found Nate's watch under a pile of discarded clothing. It was his most prized possession."

"Your friend rescued them, perhaps?" St. Andrews suggested, laying the doll reverently on the bench between us.

"There was also a lot of blood."

"Ah."

"I don't know or care what Sinclair's role is regarding the children," I said. "But I want my friend back safely, and if Sinclair is our blackmailer, then I want him dead."

"That makes four of us, then, Mr. Adler," he said. "Including Cain."

The rest of our journey proceeded in silence—St. Andrews thoughtfully looking out the window. Lazarus was just sulking, though whether that was because my embrace had been for Goddard and not him, or because St. Andrews was showering me with information he'd withheld from his grouchier half, was anyone's guess. It didn't matter, though. I'd repaid their favor and now was going home to square things with Goddard. I settled back against the overstuffed cushion and closed my eyes.

I woke sometime later when the horse stumbled. Rubbing my eyes, I sat up. The road had grown considerably rougher beneath the wheels, and there was a familiar stink in the air. I pushed the shade back from the window, just as the driver pulled up to the curb before the clinic.

"You'll forgive me for leaving you off here, Mr. Adler," St. Andrews said. "I'm needed on urgent business elsewhere. After I signed the papers for your release at Bow Street, I took the liberty of sending word to Cain, informing him you were safe. When you return home, I'd appreciate it if you'd ask him to consider once again what I proposed."

"A truce?" I yawned.

"Yes, but also leaving the opium trade. He's aligned himself with some extraordinarily dangerous people, and these alliances are not as stable as he thinks they are. Cain may have come from humble beginnings, but he has more money now than he'll ever need, every penny wisely invested, if I know him."

And St. Andrews did know. From his expression, he knew him well.

"I'll see what I can do."

Lazarus sprang out of the carriage as soon as it stopped. He stood impatiently by the door.

"Thank you, Mr. Adler," St. Andrews said as I stepped out. "And Lazarus, old chap, do look after your shoulder. It's been giving him nothing but trouble lately," he explained.

Lazarus rubbed at his left shoulder self-consciously. The driver flicked the reins over the back of the dappled mare, and the carriage rolled away down Dorset Street. I watched it disappear into the midday traffic, and a long-suffering voice behind me asked, "Well? Are you coming?"

CHAPTER TWELVE

Inside the clinic, the air was heavy and hot. The paraffin lamp at the nurse's station gave just enough light for her to inspect the arm of a young woman who seemed to be the morning's only patient. The darkness seemed like an accident waiting to happen. But it was rather soothing in the face of the unremitting heat already seeping through the walls. Hell wouldn't really start to break loose until that night—when people had a chance to spread their pay around the pubs and gambling houses. The place would be bursting at the seams by dawn.

"I've been meaning to ask you about that shoulder, Tim," I said, following him through the gloom toward the back corridor.

"Shh. How has it been today?" he asked the nurse.

"About like this. Care to have a look?"

Lazarus angled the patient's arm into the light. The dressing was gray and tattered on its surface, but when he unwrapped it, the cloth below was clean. Beneath the dressing the wound showed no sign of infection.

"It's healing well," he said with a reassuring smile to the patient. "Good work, Nurse. Anything urgent that I should know about?"

"Nothing what can't wait."

"Thank you. Adler," he said, without giving me a second glance, "The surgery, if you please."

I waited until he disappeared through the doorway and came around to the nurse's side of the table. She looked me up and down, taking in St. Andrews's old coat, the rumpled silk robe, and my bare, dirty feet. That brought a smirk.

"Not sure as I should ask what you've been up to," she said.

"Whatever you're thinking, it's got to be more fun than what actually happened."

"I'm almost sorry to hear that."

The nurse unwound the rest of the bandage from the woman's arm and tossed it into a bin at her feet. She took a clean flannel from the pile on her table, dipped the corner into a bowl of carbolic, and dabbed at the wound.

"Any news about the porcelain dog?" I asked over the patient's sharp hiss of pain.

"Not a whisper."

"But you did mention it?"

She looked up. The lamp caught her face from the left, softening the curves and lines, bringing sharp contrast to her starched cap and cuffs.

"Nurse's honor, Ira, but it's only been a day. These things take time."

Time I didn't have—time enough for our blackmailer to land Goddard and St. Andrews in prison. Lazarus and myself as well, if the police were really diligent. She didn't know that—and didn't need to.

"Thank you," I said, making my way toward the surgery.

Compared to the waiting room, the surgery was almost cheerful. The walls and floors had been scrubbed that morning. The sweet, tarry odor of antiseptic hung in the air. The large window opposite the door had been carefully rubbed dry to allow in as much natural light as possible. When I entered, Lazarus was looking out onto the brick backside of the neighboring warehouse. While he'd been waiting for me, he had found a pair of trousers and a shirt in the charity box. They sat neatly folded on the stool by the door. On the floor beside the stool sat a pair of boots that looked my size, and socks I was hoping were not. The thoughtfulness of the gesture took me by surprise.

"Thanks," I said.

"Can't have you walking up the front steps of York Street looking like you just fled a whorehouse."

He didn't turn around, but continued to gaze out the window, massaging his bad shoulder with the opposite hand. It had been months before Lazarus had allowed me to see him without his shirt, and even longer for him to speak of the ugly rosette of flesh the bullet had left behind. He had eventually taught me to work out the knots in his back. Some part of me wanted to go to him and lay hands on that one spot near the bottom of his shoulder blade he never could quite reach on his own.

But he would never have allowed it.

With a vague noise of dissatisfaction, he stopped massaging the shoulder and turned. A small spot of red peeked out from beneath the edge of his waistcoat.

"Is that the bullet wound?" I demanded. "You came back from Afghanistan nine years ago. What on earth kind of wound still bleeds after nine years?"

"You really don't want to know."

He looked away while I slipped into the trousers and shirt. I laid St. Andrews's coat over the stool and folded the silk robe on top of it. I picked up the socks and looked at them dubiously.

"They've been washed with lye soap and carbolic," Lazarus said.

"Thank God for that."

The socks weren't that bad, and the shoes fit as if made for me. Lazarus allowed himself a small smile. The wheeled operating table stood against one wall. Next to it stood a smaller table with a pile of clean cloths and an autoclave. Lazarus took a cloth from a pile, unfolded it next to the autoclave, and began unpacking the clean surgical instruments onto it.

"St. Andrews thinks he's protecting me by keeping me in the dark," Lazarus said.

"That sounds familiar."

"But I know more than he thinks. And he has no idea what he's up against."

"And you do?" I asked.

The soft clinking of the instruments stopped. He considered me for a moment, his intelligent brown eyes searching and evaluating.

"Sinclair has connections to a cheap source of opium—opium,

which he once supplied to Goddard, and which I suspect is being used to facilitate the exploitation of the children mentioned in that letter you showed me."

"Nate and Sinclair were close," I said. "If Sinclair had been involved with that business with the children, Nate wouldn't have stood for it."

"I'm talking about the opium," he said. "Do you know the name of the brothel owner?"

"Nate never said. I'm not even sure that he knew."

"I have my suspicions," he said.

I wondered how he had come by those suspicions. The instruments began clinking again. He pretended to rearrange them to hide his shaking fingers.

"He did say the man was a doctor," I continued. "Or he had been one in Afghanistan. Said he was as old as Father Christmas and had a reputation for performing unnecessary surgeries. I've been meaning to ask—"

The instruments clattered to the ground. Lazarus hissed a curse, then knelt down to pick them up. For several moments there was no sound, save for a soft clink-clink as he stood and carefully laid the instruments once more on the cloth.

"Show me the doll again," he said when he finished.

The sad little doll was at the bottom of a pocket in the tweed coat. I handed it to him across the table. He turned it over in his hands. I watched dread turn first to suspicion, and then to professional distance.

"This came from Afghanistan," he said, handing it back to me. "This pattern, these colors, I recognize them." He reached for the instruments again, then, sighing, laid his hands on the table. "I think I know who is importing those children, and who is behind the dissemination of the strongest strain of opium this city has seen since 1870. Of course, it would be suicide to proceed without being certain."

He exhaled heavily, then winced. A drop of red beaded below one nostril then ran down his face.

"Damn, blast, hell." He took a cloth from the pile and pressed it to his nose. A red blotch formed on the cloth, spreading until the cloth was more red than gray. Lazarus dropped it and quickly reached for another. "Oh, hell!" he swore again.

"Should I go?" I asked.

He shook his head, wincing again.

"Call the nurse?"

He waved an irritated hand.

"Because you're bleeding from two places that I can see, and it's starting to frighten me."

"You and St. Andrews, that big ninny," he said through the cloth. "The shoulder is just something that happens from time to time. As for the nose, that was your work. I'm not an invalid, Adler, I just need a moment."

I gave it to him.

The surgery had been the site of the most significant events in the saga of Lazarus and Adler. We'd met there, for starters. I'd admired the confidence with which he wielded his instruments despite the fact he couldn't meet my eyes. Later, he'd fumbled through what had to be his first solicitation. There had been a few stolen kisses in that room, though the one time he'd allowed anything more serious to happen on the premises, it transpired in the dispensary. It was also in the surgery, two years ago, where I saw Goddard for the first time. He had been touring the facility with a group of prospective donors, and though Lazarus and I had had a standing date for a year and a half, somehow that night it completely slipped my mind.

When I glanced up, the good doctor had his hemorrhage under control and was regarding me with the strangest expression. I opened my mouth to say something, but he cut me off.

"Ira, I wouldn't drag my worst enemy into this." He dabbed his face with the cloth, then discarded it, and the other, into a bin. "I hope you know that I include you when I say that."

"I'm your worst enemy?"

He smiled wryly.

"Far from it. In fact, I'd say that right now, you're one of the only people I can trust. I can trust you, can't I?"

"With what?" I asked.

"And therein lies the question."

He ran a hand through his freshly trimmed hair. There was quite a bit more gray than there had been a mere two years ago, and the light from the window accentuated it. "This has been a long time coming. It should be a relief, I suppose. Nine years is too long to carry something like this."

"Now you've completely lost me," I said.

If I was the only one Lazarus could trust, he must have been in a right spot indeed. But wasn't I in the very same spot?

"Yeah," I said. "You can trust me."

He gave a solemn nod.

"Then that will have to do."

Chapter Thirteen

Having never been outside of London, it was difficult for me to imagine any place not walled in by dark, teeming tenements and blanketed with a layer of yellow fog half the year. But as Lazarus spoke unblinkingly about the worst period of his life, an alien landscape took shape in my mind's eye. A country with a vast, unforgiving wasteland of treacherous mountains and desolate, rocky plains with hostile, turban-wearing denizens as cunning as they were difficult to subdue. The year was 1879; the place, Afghanistan. Lazarus, a newly commissioned army surgeon, hadn't been much older than I was now.

"My division had set up camp at the Sherpur Cantonment," Lazarus said. "A godforsaken sprawl of trenches dug into the rocky hills outside of Caboul. Between the barren plains and the blizzards that would come thundering down the mountains without warning, it was bleak, but at least it was away from the fighting. The peace, however, was not to last.

"On December fifteenth, rebel forces attacked, led by Mohammed Jan. I was certain that we were done for, but somehow we managed to hold them off until General Gough arrived with reinforcements on the twenty-third. By midday, the rebel forces had been crushed. It was then that Edward Acton came to my attention. I don't suppose you've heard of him."

I shook my head.

"He was the general's personal physician, and something of a legend. Acton had been the sole survivor of the massacre at Gandamak Pass during the first Afghan war. Sixteen thousand souls perished, all except for Acton, who rode hell for leather all the way to the garrison at Jalalabad, dodging bullets from long-range Jezail rifles the entire way."

Lazarus went on to describe the man's immaculate coat, the lamb's wool hat perched atop his long head, his pointed white beard, and the fat mustache, impeccably waxed and curled at the edges even on that fateful day. I thought how the besieged troops must have caught their breath when he and the general rode into the valley.

"After the uprising had been put down, we received orders to scour the area for surviving rebels. No prisoners were to be taken. Any Afghan found in possession of a weapon was to be summarily executed. Medical personnel were exempt from this duty, but Acton volunteered. He seemed to relish the idea, and always returned from the searches glowing with an unseemly radiance. It was then that I began to watch him out of the corner of my eye, for though I had no evidence to support my immediate distrust of the man, I knew that sooner or later my suspicions would be borne out.

"It happened the night before Christmas. The valley had been quiet, the weather bearable, though snow clouds had been hanging over the mountains for several days. I had been enjoying my first good night's sleep in weeks, when I was awakened by a cry. I lay there for a bit, wondering whether one of the men was having a nightmare, when it came again. The sound of suffering was unmistakable, and it was coming from outside the camp."

I wondered whether Lazarus allowed himself a second thought that night as he pulled on his boots and tucked his pistol into his pocket. I wondered whether he'd permitted himself to question the sanity of sprinting across the rubble-strewn plain, darting from bush to rock to crumbling shed, for the sake of someone he'd never met. Probably not—Lazarus took his physician's oath more seriously than he did his own life.

Eventually his investigation led him to the base of a far hill, his tent barely visible on the horizon. When the next cry came, there was no doubt as to where it originated: in an ancient fortress rising from the top of the hill.

"Bala Hissar," Lazarus said. "It was grand, once, Adler, at least until the rebels blew the armory to hell. When I arrived at the top, I was disappointed to find that fully half the complex had been reduced to ruins, though it would make it easier to continue my search undetected."

Following his instincts, and the low moans of several voices now, Lazarus picked his way across the wreckage. It was a windless night, and this saved him. Just as Lazarus was about to round the corner of the first unbroken section of building, his senses were overtaken by the aroma of a very expensive tobacco. He pressed himself to the wall. Inching along the smooth, cold stone, he peered around the corner. A lone guard stood near a wooden door, his rifle carelessly propped against the wall next to him. A cigarette burned in his fingers, gray smoke curling lazily upward.

"I'd no idea what I'd stumbled onto," Lazarus said, stopping mid-pace and looking up. "But I knew that if it had to be undertaken in the dead of night, far removed from the danger of scrutiny, it couldn't be right. I found a rock and hurled it toward a broken wall some distance away, to distract the guard. It took two more rocks, but eventually, the guard jogged off to investigate.

"The moon had been descending for some time, but enough of its light still shone through the slit windows of the fortress to provide a dim view of the corridor. I followed the sounds until I came to what appeared to be a battlefield hospital."

Inside a small chamber bathed in light, several Afghan men lay on pallets on the floor. Along one wall stood a table with stoppered bottles Lazarus took to be medicines, a lamp, and some sort of logbook. Acton stood on the other side of the room, his back to the door.

"He was standing over one of the men, taking notes," Lazarus said. "I'll never forget that." He met my eyes and held them. "The patient was writhing in pain and bleeding from every orifice. He was crying for mercy—one didn't need to understand Dari to understand that—and Acton was calmly taking notes."

"What did you do?" I asked.

He let out a long breath and turned back toward the window. The sun had gone behind a cloud, casting the alley behind the clinic in deep shadow. When Lazarus spoke again, his voice was heavy with regret.

"Nothing. I…was too busy trying to make sense of what I was seeing. We had a hospital in the cantonment, so there was no reason for another, especially one so far removed. Also, we'd had orders not to take prisoners. I'd treated the odd villager before the uprising, but at that time, there was no reason for an entire Afghan ward."

Unless it wasn't a hospital, I thought. Medicines needed to be tested, treatments proved. I'd known more than one London workhouse to make ends meet by providing subjects and facilities to enterprising chemists. Battlefield prisoners would be an ideal test population.

"A laboratory," I said. "They were subjecting the prisoners to some sort of experiment."

"Indeed," said Lazarus. "The patients were the men that Acton had apprehended during that day's search. The ones he was meant to have summarily executed."

"But what was he testing?" I asked.

Lazarus turned. He twisted the edges of his waistcoat nervously, and I could tell it was costing him to keep his voice steady.

"Acton developed several particularly nasty poisons while in Her Majesty's service, most notably a concoction based on the venom of specific Asian vipers. For military use, you understand."

He rubbed his shoulder absently. The bleeding had stopped, and the stain on his shirt had mellowed to a rust color. He began to pace then, his measured steps reflecting his methodical thought processes as he chose the words to describe the events that would alter the course of his life forever.

"I don't know how long I stood there before he turned around. Felt like ages. I'd been so careful to be quiet. Perhaps he heard my heart pounding.

"'The venom of certain elapids,' he said as he turned, 'has the most spectacular effect on the human body, wouldn't you agree, Doctor?' He was so calm," Lazarus marveled. "The prisoner was shuddering through his death throes, spattered with so much blood that it was impossible to tell where, specifically, it had come from, and Acton was waxing poetical about the virtues of hemotoxins over neurotoxins. I was horrified, of course, but I was also paralyzed with fear.

"'The bite of some species,' he went on, 'causes spontaneous bleeding from every orifice, sometimes even from wounds long healed. This particular venom takes three hours to produce noticeable effects, which makes it ideal for assassinations. The only problem is that snake venom is generally harmless when ingested. It can, however, be effectively delivered by means of an injection.'

"He went on for quite some time, so enraptured by the subject that he didn't see me reach into the pocket where I'd stashed my pistol. My hands were shaking so, Adler. It's a miracle they didn't shake the gun right out onto the floor. I'd never shot anyone. But the short time that I'd served with Edward Acton had shown him to be prudent to a fault. The carefree manner in which he went on to describe his most vile and unlawful experiments left no doubt that he did not intend for me to leave that room alive—a conclusion that was verified when the hammer of another pistol clicked into place behind my head."

Lazarus outstrips me handily in speed of thought and action. I'd have already been lying on the floor in a pool of my own brains at that point. But Lazarus ducked and whirled, and before the guard or Acton could register what was happening, he'd knocked the guard's pistol out of his hand and disappeared into the corridor.

Bullets ricocheted off the stone walls of the corridor as Lazarus fled. As he reached the door through which he had entered, he felt a hammer blow to his back. The impact pitched him forward through the door, where he lay, dazed for a moment, until the ring of footsteps in the corridor behind him brought him back to himself. He scrambled to his feet and ran headlong into the deafening wall of storm that had thundered down from the mountain while he and Acton had been debating wartime ethics, still clutching the pistol to his chest.

❖

"I cannot tell you how fortunate I was that night," Lazarus said. "A shepherd I had once treated found me before I perished from my wounds. His family hid me and nursed me back to health, after which I found my way to a distant regiment, gave a false name, and was invalided out forthwith."

It took a moment for the last bit to register, but when it did, I had to stifle a highly inappropriate snigger.

"Wait," I said. "Do you mean to tell me that for all these years, you, Timothy Lazarus, the most tediously law-abiding person in all of London, have been drawing a fraudulent pension?"

"Only the name is fraudulent," he said irritably. "My injuries are quite real. I'd have been receiving the same pension, had I gone back to my own unit and somehow avoided an accident of Acton's making."

"And how does Acton fit into this again?" I asked.

He sighed.

"Opium. While serving with the East India Company, Acton was working on medical-grade opium derivatives. He spent some time experimenting with varieties of poppy, trying to increase the concentration of alkaloids in the resin. Some people believe that Acton harvested and secretly distributed opium made from the new poppies, and that this was the cause of those deaths in 1870, and in Limehouse ten years later."

I looked up sharply. I'd last seen my mother in 1866, when she'd left me at the workhouse in Bethnal Green. Though I'd only a grainy photo in a crumbling newspaper clipping to back it up, I'd always suspected that she'd been among the 1870 victims.

"Nate mentioned something like that," I said. "The brothel owner provides it on credit to the young men in his employ."

"Mmm." Lazarus nodded. "The opium was what made me think of Acton. When you said that the brothel owner had been a surgeon in Afghanistan, it confirmed my suspicions. I believe that Edward Acton is the owner of the Fitzroy Street brothel, and that he's bringing those children, along with opium, from Afghanistan. But to make an accusation like that, I need more evidence."

"*You* need?" I asked.

Lazarus was a force to be reckoned with on many levels, but he'd been hiding from Acton for almost a decade. If he failed, at the very least, he'd find himself up on charges of desertion and fraud. He would certainly never practice medicine again. More likely, though, if Acton was as powerful and well connected as the personal physician of a decorated general would have to be, then Timothy Lazarus—or whatever his name was—would find himself at the bottom of the Thames before he could say "elapid venom." Lazarus was an irritant and a prig, but he didn't deserve that.

"You might as well ring the man's doorbell and say 'here I am,'" I said.

Lazarus exhaled heavily and ran his hands through his hair. When he looked up, his face was that of a much older man.

"You've no idea how stressful it is, living like this," he said. "Sitting up at night, wondering whether you might have said or done something to inadvertently give yourself away. Waking every morning, thinking that this might be the day that it all comes crashing down around you—"

"Then stop," I said. "Let St. Andrews take care of you. Why do you do *this*, anyway?" I demanded, gesturing around the inadequate surgery where Lazarus spent his days. "You live in the lap of luxury. You did your bit in the army, you've spent nine years in this shithole—"

"I built this shithole," he said quietly.

"So you've done your bit for humanity as well. There's no need to throw it all away. We know who Acton is, and we have Nate's documentation to show what he's done. I'll deliver it to Bow Street, and you'll never have to think about it again. Just walk away and leave the drunks and the whores to Pearl. Doesn't St. Andrews have a country house or something, where you could retire?"

"Retire?" He laughed, miserably at first. As his mind came to some hysterical realization to which I was not privy, misery turned to confusion, to glee, and laughter shook his entire body until his eyes were moist with mirth.

"Wait," he said. He dabbed at his face with his shirt sleeve. "You think that St. Andrews…and I…" He sniggered. "Oh, Adler, that's revolting."

"I always thought so," I said.

"Repugnant," he chortled. "Oh, the very thought of it."

"I suppose you're going to tell me that you're 'just friends,'" I said. Really, if this was the thanks I got for showing a little concern, it was little wonder the good doctor had to rent company from time to time.

"Well, yes. St. Andrews is a member of the Piccadilly set, to be sure, but our arrangement is purely professional. We met a year and a half ago. I needed an affordable set of rooms *sans* rats, and he needed someone to keep his cases organized. In that respect, I definitely earn my keep," he added.

"But surely, between his money and his connections, he could help you nonetheless."

"Not if he's breaking rocks at Pentonville because we failed to recover that blasted statue."

"Right," I muttered. "Bugger."

"But even if we didn't have the blackmailer to worry about…"

He began pacing again, stroking his chin thoughtfully. Behind me, I heard the front door of the clinic open and close. There was an exchange of voices, shuffling feet—the first casualties of the weekend trickling in.

"The truth is," Lazarus said, "I've wanted to clear my name for some time. But I could never find the courage to do it. One lie led to another, then another, until one day I looked around to find that Timothy Lazarus wasn't just an alias; he was me. I was him. Which is fine when you're spending your days among people that no one cares to know. But Adler, there's no birth record for Tim Lazarus. No baptism, no education. The less said of his military service, the better. Frankly, I never expected that particular lie to hold up as well as it did. But without any of these things to prove who he is, Adler, Timothy Lazarus cannot marry."

Chapter Fourteen

Marry?" I blinked. "To a woman?"

"Elizabeth Campbell," he said. "Bess. She's American. The daughter of missionaries. Nurse Brand introduced us a year ago."

Of course.

The daughter of missionaries.

My thoughts flashed back to the scrubbed woman who had been in the waiting room when I'd left the clinic that day. She'd looked so out of place, and yet perfectly at ease.

It explained the lovesick look on Lazarus's face when Pearl announced his luncheon companion had arrived, when I'd searched the waiting room for St. Andrews that day and not found him. It explained the utter lack of sexual charge between Lazarus and St. Andrews inside the brougham. And yet…

A blush crept across his cheeks. He reached into his waistcoat and produced a folding metal tintype case a little smaller than the palm of his hand. He opened the case, and I immediately recognized the broad-featured brunette. She had an impish glint in her eye, and was unsuccessfully suppressing a smile. She was older than what I understood to be the desirable age for women—maybe twenty-eight or twenty-nine, and not classically pretty. Still, if she possessed in person a fraction of the warmth conveyed by her portrait, her charm would have been irresistible.

"She's beautiful," I said honestly.

"Yes, she is." He gave his lady-love one final look before

reluctantly tucking the portrait back into his waistcoat pocket. "I don't expect you to understand."

But I did understand. Love is mysterious, unfathomable. It can bring the most unlikely people together. And it was plastered all over his face. Instinctively, I felt for the golden snake on my pinkie. As my fingers traced its curves and ridges I felt…as if I should be feeling something more.

"What's that?" Lazarus asked, nodding toward my hand.

"Nothing."

Before I could tug the ring off and bury it in my pocket, he was across the room. He lifted my hand to his face. His breath was hot against my knuckles.

"By God." He looked from the ring to me. "That looks like— Is it? It couldn't be!"

"It's not Her Majesty's ring." I snatched my hand away. Really, even Goddard had some scruples. "Same design, better materials."

"Do you mind?" he asked.

Not waiting for an answer, he took my hand again, this time angling it into the light until the diamonds projected twin fields of stars onto the ceiling and walls of the surgery.

"Good Lord," he said. "They're real."

"Goddard told me it represents loyalty, fidelity, and eternity," I said.

"Did he now?"

"I just wish I was the only one to have worn it."

Part of me had been desperate to hash through the string of coincidences, misunderstandings, and just plain bad luck leading to my arrest. Lazarus's frown and the furrows of concern at the bridge of his nose were all the encouragement I needed. I sank down onto the stool and opened the floodgates, releasing a tide of nonsense involving genital irritation, perfidious butlers, disappearing predecessors and impossible Chubb locks. When I was finished, I looked up to find him leaning against the doorjamb, arms crossed over his chest, gazing thoughtfully down at me.

"Well," he said. "At least you don't have syphilis."

"I don't?"

It had been my morbid fear of the disease, coupled with the itch that had plagued my private parts, that had made Collins's tales about my predecessors seem so plausible. Had I not been terrified of how Goddard would respond when he learned I'd brought the French Disease to his bed, I'd never have gone out onto the front steps for a smoke.

And I wouldn't have locked myself out in a blind panic.

"Syphilis doesn't itch, for one thing," Lazarus said. "There are also distinct lesions. You don't have sores down there, do you?"

I shook my head.

"It could still be any number of things. Do you have any discharge from your—"

"No," I said.

"Painful urination?"

"No."

"My money would be on a fungus, then, perhaps a skin irritation. Is Goddard's laundress using a new soap? Or perhaps you're putting something different in your bath?"

"You mean besides carbolic?" I asked.

He chuckled.

"If it had been a parasite, carbolic would have taken care of it. The important thing is, from what you've said and from what I saw, we can rule out a venereal disease."

It's impossible to express the relief those seven simple words produced. I felt weightless, boneless, and in sudden danger of melting into a puddle of relief.

"Tim, I could kiss you."

He cleared his throat.

"Actually," he said, "While you were ranting about the manservant, I was developing a theory. Will you indulge me?"

I gestured for him to continue. He fixed his eyes on the brick wall on the other side of the window and paused dramatically, his square fingers steepled beneath his chin.

"The last time I saw you, you were so bedeviled by your little problem you could hardly stand still." He turned. "But today I've yet to see you so much as wiggle. When was the last time your nether regions troubled you?"

I thought for a moment. The last time I'd given the matter any thought at all had been on the way to the London Athletic Club. My encounter with Mrs. Wu had distracted me considerably, even more so Goddard's proposal. The itch had provided a minor annoyance while arguing with Collins in the kitchen. However, after fleeing York Street, I was too busy stumbling upon possible murder scenes and being arrested for gross indecency to worry about it overly. Looking back, I couldn't remember the last time I'd thought about the little matter between my legs.

"It was at least before I left York Street," I said.

"What were you wearing?"

I stood and flourished a hand at my robe and St. Andrews's coat still draped over the stool. Lazarus smiled triumphantly.

"Then it's my professional opinion that whatever is troubling John Thomas is somehow tied to Ira Adler's undergarments."

"To my…"

By God!

And who was it who folded my underthings, brought them to my room, and hand-picked them every morning? And who had had it in for me from the moment I stepped over the threshold at York Street?

"That filthy, conniving—"

"Laundress?" Lazarus finished.

"Butler," I seethed. "Manservant. Weasel-of-all-work. The under-house girl washes the clothes, but Collins lays them out for me in the morning."

"And you think he has a grudge?"

"Doesn't think I'm good enough for his precious master. Doesn't think I care as much as I ought to."

"Do you care?" Lazarus asked.

"Whose side are you on?" I demanded.

He shrugged. "Not the butler's, surely. But let's just say that I have a certain sympathy for Goddard's position in all this."

My face went hot—not in the least because I was aware of how shabbily I had treated Lazarus at the end. I liked to think it was different with Goddard. I had consented to stay with him. I'd accepted his terms. But when it came to where my affections truly lay, I'd evaded the question. I exhaled, threw my hands up, and began to pace.

"It's not the *manservant*'s job to question my affections," I said. "It's his job to shave my chin and shine my damned shoes."

Lazarus folded his arms over his chest and sighed.

"Well, has he shown any signs of insolence before now?" he asked.

"Little things. Calls me 'Mr. Adler,' like I'm an employee, serves my meals in the morning room when Goddard's not there." I stopped at the little table and flipped the lid of the autoclave shut with a bang. "I know he never liked me, but he really seems to be ratcheting it up lately."

"I see." Lazarus said. "Any idea why?"

"He's stealing Goddard's poppies."

Lazarus's carefully groomed eyebrows shot upward.

"I caught him at it last night," I went on. "Strange noises below stairs woke me up. I thought someone had broken in, so I went to investigate. Caught him red-handed, scraping the insides out of a pile of shiny red seed pods. What?" I demanded.

Lazarus had been following my words like a diligent schoolboy, but now he was looking at me as if I were speaking Swahili.

"Adler, opium pods are green. Moreover, one doesn't scrape out the insides; one scores the outside with a special tool, and collects the resin when it oozes out."

"Then what the devil—"

Lazarus frowned.

"Does Goddard keep roses?" he asked after a moment.

"In the back garden. But what...why...what on earth do you find so amusing?" I demanded.

Suppressed laughter hissed from his nose. He bit his lip. He looked away, darting a glance at me, let a rude laugh escape.

"Oh, that's brilliant," he chortled.

I cleared my throat.

"Evil, but brilliant," he said. "Let me explain. Rose hips—the fruits of the plant, which are red and shiny, as you described—make a delicious and healthful tea. The fine hairs inside the fruit, however, when dried, make a devastating itching powder."

That son of a bitch.

No wonder Collins had known my symptoms. He had caused them. He'd used my insecurity regarding my position in the household to keep me from discussing the issue with Goddard—who would have got to the bottom of it immediately—subtly manipulated my neuroses until the only conclusion I could arrive at was that I needed to leave immediately.

Genius, really.

"I'll kill him," I said.

"Let's not say anything we might—"

"I mean it, Tim, I'll stick my hand up his arse, pull out his intestines, and strangle him with them."

The look on my face must have indicated how serious I was because Lazarus stopped laughing and took a step back.

"Well, perhaps you should consider washing your own knickers from now on, at any rate," he said, hazarding a little laugh.

"I do not wear knickers."

An errant curl flopped across my forehead. I spat on my fingers and pushed it back. I had to tell Goddard immediately. If Collins really had been with Goddard for twenty years, getting Goddard to dismiss the man might be tricky, but it had to be done. I could not remain at York Street if I was expected to endure disrespect and outright sabotage from the staff.

"The worst part," I said, sinking back down onto the stool, "is when Goddard gave me the ring, I thought it meant something. I'm not stupid, Tim. I know I'm not the only man Goddard has ever taken to bed. But Collins made it sound like I'm the latest in a long line of pretentious guttersnipes who fell for Goddard's line about 'loyalty, fidelity, and eternity,' and then walked right into the old false-venereal-disease trap."

Lazarus was silent for a few moments. Then he said,

"And you believed him?"

Of course I had, but why? After months of trying to dislodge me, he'd said the one thing he'd known would push me over the edge. And I'd jumped.

"Tim, what have I done?"

I should have gone to Goddard last night, shoved a handful of rose hips under his nose, and demanded Collins's immediate dismissal. Instead, I'd taken the manservant's word at face value and panicked just as intended. I hung my head. For a moment there was no sound, save for my shaking, drawn-out breaths as I tried to keep myself from hyperventilating. Lazarus came up beside me and put a hand on my shoulder.

"I want to take a rubbing," he said.

"Two quid, no less."

"Of the ring, Adler. Don't be a jackass. A ring like this was bound to have made a stir when it was cast. If I can find the jeweler who made it, he can tell me when, and under what circumstances. Perhaps Goddard did commission it for you."

I nodded and held out my hand. Taking a pencil stub and scrap of paper from his waistcoat pocket, he laid the paper over the ring and rubbed the pencil back and forth across it. A rough approximation of the snake appeared on the paper. When Lazarus was satisfied, he slipped the paper back into his pocket.

"There," he said. "Hopefully the jeweler will be able to put your mind at ease. I'd like to take that watch you found as well."

"Get stuffed," I said.

The watch was my only connection to Nate. It was his most prized possession, and wasn't leaving my custody until either I gave it back to him or tucked it into the pocket of his burial suit.

"There's gratitude," Lazarus muttered. "May I see it at least?"

I rummaged through the pockets of St. Andrews's coat. I held it out for his inspection, keeping the chain wrapped tightly around one finger.

"Nice," Lazarus said, taking in the ornate case. "Not too nice, though. Sinclair gave it to him, you say?"

I nodded.

"I promise I won't let anything happen to it."

"Can't you just take a rubbing?" I asked.

He shrugged.

"The ring, I've no doubt, is one of a kind. The watch isn't. It's likely whoever sold it has sold a dozen others just like it. You're right. It's probably meaningless."

That hurt more than the idea of losing the watch. But before I could dwell on that particular barb, a terrible commotion erupted in the front of the clinic.

"Doctor!" cried the nurse. "Come quickly!"

With a rueful look in my direction, Lazarus rolled up his sleeves, pulled a white coat from the hook on the back of the surgery door, and ran to the waiting room.

CHAPTER FIFTEEN

"Nate!" I cried.

The last time I'd seen my friend before the previous day was in the wake of the worst thrashing I'd thought a man capable of surviving. But the beating Nate had suffered made my ordeal look minor. In his current condition, he couldn't have stumbled one block under his own power—which meant someone had brought him to the clinic and dumped him on the doorstep.

"Get me the stretcher!" Lazarus barked. "Nurse, clear this room!"

While Pearl chased away the gathering crowd, I dashed to the surgery. The stretcher was a faded canvas litter, which had probably seen action in the American insurrection. I pulled it out of its corner and ran. We unfurled the stretcher on the floor and eased Nate onto it.

"It's all right, mate," I said. "You're going to be fine."

Lazarus shot me a look, which I ignored. Every inch of Nate's skin appeared either split, scraped, lacerated, or covered in blackish stains. His left arm lay at an unnatural angle across his stomach, a shard of bone protruding from the elbow of his shirt. Someone had been very thorough in his work.

Someone had *enjoyed* this.

"Adler," Nate rasped, blinking up at me through his one remaining eye.

"Don't try to speak," I said. "Save your energy."

"What…for?"

His split lips twitched in what might have been a cheeky grin had his face not been caved in like a rotten squash. The beginnings of a sob stirred deep inside me, but I fought it back down.

"On three," Lazarus said from near Nate's feet. "One…two…"

We heaved him up and wrangled him into the surgery, laying him out on the operating table. I removed the poles from the stretcher and placed them carefully back in the corner. I turned around to find Lazarus shaking off his gore-spattered white coat. He carefully folded the coat before placing it beneath Nate's blood-caked head.

"Who did this, Nate?" I asked, as Lazarus checked out the damage. "Was it Acton?" Realizing that he might not know the name of the brothel owner, I added, "The doctor. The old man."

"'E…were…there."

"He brought another group of children through the brothel," I said. "You tried to help them."

His ruined brow furrowed.

"'Ow'd yer…"

"I went looking for you last night. I found the room in the basement. I saw the clothes, the opium lamp. I have the letters you wrote, and the true books. You tried to help, didn't you? But Acton wasn't working alone. Don't worry, mate," I said. "I'll turn the books over to the police. I'll send the letters. Then I'll track down that bastard and kill him myself."

His good eye closed and he exhaled. Lazarus, having finished his inspection, caught my eye and shook his head.

"Nick," Nate breathed.

"Was he there? I'll kill him, too."

"Brung me…"

"Where's Sinclair now?" I asked.

Nate's eye fluttered and rolled back into his skull.

"Nate! Where's Sinclair?"

"Ware'ouse," he rasped. "Kids…Tell 'er…"

"Who? Tell who?"

He swallowed and forced his eye to focus on me.

"Mrs. Wu," he whispered around a swollen, split lip. "Lime'ouse…"

"Mrs. Wu is in Limehouse?"

Or did he mean the warehouse was there? Were the children in the warehouse, or somewhere else? Was Sinclair with them?

"Are Mrs. Wu and Sinclair working together?" I demanded.

But Nate wasn't listening anymore. His body shuddered. The spark faded from his eye, and his last breath left him with a dry rattle.

"Nate!"

He was gone. Nothing remained but broken teeth, splintered bone, and fine, tailored clothing never meant to be soaked in blood. My legs wobbled beneath me. A gray mist formed at the periphery of my vision as the room began to sway.

"Not now, Adler," Lazarus snapped.

He waved a little bottle in front of my face, and the smell of *sal volatile* hit me like a mallet between the eyes.

"Thanks," I muttered as Lazarus put the vinaigrette back in his pocket.

"Think nothing of it. I'll find this Mrs. Wu," he said.

"You what? Do you know how many warehouses there are in London?"

"I'll find her," he said again. "If only to show you that you don't have to be on the wrong side of the law to get things done on the East End."

I nodded, wiping my hands on my charity-box trousers. Lazarus had treated damn near everyone in East London. He could call in a lot of favors.

"Her father is Zhi Sen," I said. "He's an importer and a fighting arts master."

Lazarus frowned.

"Goddard's business partner?"

"And she has the porcelain dog," I finished. "But she's not acting on Zhi Sen's orders. Or if she is, Zhi Sen is no longer the impartial guardian of the statue."

"Are they working for Sinclair?" Lazarus asked.

"Maybe. Or maybe only Mrs. Wu is. Or perhaps she has her own interest in the statue. I don't know. But you can't tell St. Andrews any of this until I've spoken to Goddard."

He drew in a sharp breath.

"I'm not going to just hand St. Andrews the dog, not with so much bad blood between him and Goddard," I explained.

Lazarus glared so hard his eyebrows nearly met in the middle. I think I actually heard his teeth grind. Then his features smoothed, and a thoughtful expression came over his face.

"So you do trust me, after all."

The words caught me up short. Lazarus was sneaky, too clever for his own good, and I wouldn't put it past him to manipulate our situation to put me in my place. But he was fundamentally honorable. He wouldn't *intentionally* cause injury.

"I trust you to do the decent thing," I said. "I trust you to do what you can to help those children without sending Goddard and me to Pentonville."

He rolled his blood-flecked sleeves back down over his forearms and fished a pair of gold cufflinks from his pocket.

"A gift when I finished my training at the London Hospital," he said as he tacked his cuffs shut. "They remind me of happier times."

"I really do trust you, Tim," I said.

"I suppose I'm forced to trust you as well."

His tone said it was only because he didn't have a better choice.

"Ira, if you do find the dog, don't let Goddard use it to punish St. Andrews. He's a good man, and he was serious about letting bygones be bygones."

I believed him. I had believed St. Andrews when he'd said as much in the brougham. And after everything Lazarus had told me, I didn't think I could live with myself if Goddard's revenge sent old Tim to prison, too.

I held out my hand.

"Battlefield comrades?"

Lazarus clasped it with a grim smile.

"You have twenty-four hours," he said. "Leave the watch and the documents you took from Fitzroy Street. If you're not back here by noon tomorrow, I'll go to the police as well as to St. Andrews."

"You wouldn't!" I cried.

"If I want to clear my name," he said, "I have to deal with Acton. I intend to do this by handing over evidence of his crimes to the police and letting them do the dirty work. If the watch can give us any additional information about Acton, Sinclair, or Mr. Turnbull, all the better. But, Adler, if you double-cross me, I'll have no compunction about turning you over to them as well. And if Goddard isn't as happy to see you as he ought to be," he added, "you might appreciate a constable popping by to check on your welfare."

I swallowed. That was one angle I hadn't considered. As far as Goddard was concerned, I had accepted his ring before disappearing and turning up in his blackmailer's brothel. God only knew how St. Andrews had presented the situation in his message.

"Fair enough," I said.

Lazarus gave my fingers a squeeze and withdrew his hand.

"As for your friend," he said with a nod toward Nate, "Pearl will send for the coffin maker. It'll have to be St. Bride's, unless you can pay for something else. Now go home. You haven't slept, and you need to speak to Goddard. I'm sure he's itching to know how on earth you came to be arrested in a brothel raid."

Itching. I winced at the reminder of my affliction. Goddard and I would discuss the future of the *soi-disant* butler as well. But first I needed a cab. I patted the pockets of the loaned trousers. Empty, of course.

"Don't suppose you've got cab fare?" I asked.

Lazarus rolled his eyes, fishing the requested coins from his pocket.

"I'll owe you," I said, reluctantly handing over the watch.

"I'll put it on your tab."

CHAPTER SIXTEEN

It took forever to find a cab. So when the dilapidated two-seater pulled up the curb outside the clinic, I fell on it. The roof and walls gave small relief from the heat, but the upholstery was soft with wear. As I leaned back onto it, the tall wooden wheels creaking on either side as the driver navigated us back into the flow of vehicles, I wished for all the world that I could switch off my thoughts and have a kip.

But of course it was not to be.

Two days ago, Goddard had sent me to retrieve a porcelain dog containing evidence incriminating him, Andrew St. Andrews, and Nick Sinclair—evidence to do with certain mistakes of Goddard's youth, possibly dating back to the three men's association at Cambridge. After Goddard's and St. Andrews's ignoble expulsion from the university, Goddard and Sinclair had gone into the opium business together with Zhi Sen. Goddard and Sinclair had fallen out, and Zhi Sen had been given custody of the dog by mutual agreement. Sometime in the past few months, Sinclair had got his hands on it, and was using the evidence inside to blackmail Goddard and St. Andrews—for what reason, Goddard had not seen fit to reveal. Mrs. Wu had the dog now, and whether she was working with Sinclair or on her own was unknown.

On the other side of the equation, there was my old friend Nate, currently laid out on a table in Lazarus's surgery waiting for the coffin maker. It had been chance he had contacted me again after years of separation. Perhaps our history allowed him to trust me with the details of his dire situation, and the fact I moved in higher circles now had given him the impression I was in a position to help him. His murder had been inevitable, though. When he chose to go up against Edward Acton, brothel owner, opium importer, and personal physician to kings and generals, he'd taken on the politicians and aristocrats for whom Acton was procuring Afghan children. Not even Goddard himself could have saved him.

Chance had crossed Nate's path once more with mine, but the more I thought about it, the more evident it became that Goddard's blackmail and Nate's murder were connected. Goddard's erstwhile business partner Sinclair had also been the manager of Acton's brothel—the brothel where Nate had worked.

And there was Mrs. Wu.

Two days ago Mrs. Wu had lifted the porcelain dog off me in Miller's Court. Nate asked me on his deathbed to deliver a message to her. But how on earth had he known her?

It had to be opium. Acton imported it, Zhi Sen distributed it, and Nate kept track of the opium transactions for Acton's brothel. Nate might have run messages between the brothel and Zhi Sen. Perhaps this was how he and Mrs. Wu had met. But Zhi Sen was Goddard's partner, not Acton's. He distributed the opium Goddard imported. And Acton supplied the brothel with his own high-alkaloid opium and didn't need what Zhi Sen could provide. So the brothel wasn't getting its opium *from* Zhi Sen, but perhaps it was supplying the new, stronger drug *to* him. This would make sense if Zhi Sen and Sinclair—Acton's distributor—were going into business together again with the intention of driving Goddard out.

But why go to the bother of blackmailing Goddard and St. Andrews if he and Zhi Sen had a superior product in sufficient quantity? They could easily put Goddard out of business—and St. Andrews had nothing to do with any of it.

Unless he and Goddard had something that Sinclair wanted. Information? Evidence of a greater crime? Or perhaps St. Andrews wasn't selling his silence so easily anymore…

The road smoothed out as we came to the well-groomed streets around Regent's Park—yet every stumble and creak rang in my bones. My eyes burned from lack of sleep. My head pounded. I could have murdered a rack of lamb right then. Or even a crust of bread and rind of cheese. But first I had to set things right with Goddard. The sun crept out from behind the clouds and danced for a moment across my ring. Goddard had to know I hadn't deserted him on the very night he had offered me loyalty, fidelity, and eternity. And if it was the last thing I did, I had to see that manservant sacked.

The cab pulled up in front of the house as the Great Clock struck one. I paid the driver and sent him on his way. The red brick structure had come to mean so much more than a place to hang my hat. It was security, permanence, a life I'd experienced only in vicarious bits and snatches through my clients' clean clothes, their soap-scented skin, their endearments and blasphemies murmured in apologetic middle-class tones. A feeling of foreboding descended as I put my hand to the iron railing. I'd only been gone a day—a day Collins had no doubt spent whispering all manner of slander into Goddard's ear. And, if that weren't enough, I hadn't my keys. Sighing, I rang the bell.

"I'm not going to ask your permission to enter," I said when Collins opened the door.

How fortunate the stained glass had obscured the manservant's view of me until it was too late. It was interesting to watch recognition dawn on his doughy face as he took in the threadbare shirt, rough pants, and worn boots from the clinic's charity box. In addition to recognition, his expression also betrayed surprise, and though he'd better control of his emotions than to let me scent fear, I could see him calculating furiously how best to be rid of me.

"Thought you'd frightened me off, did you? Clever business with the rose hips. It's almost a shame to spoil it by telling your master. Though I can't see how you'll remain in his employ after this."

The manservant lifted his chin slightly, but showed no intention of moving his massive frame aside. I might have been able to squeeze past, if he were distracted by a swift kick to the testicles. Of course, that might only have made the gorilla irate. There was a brief commotion in the background followed by footsteps on the stairs. My heart leaped when I heard Goddard call,

"Collins, who's there?"

"The master is not at home to salesmen," Collins said loudly.

"And for future reference, you'd be well advised to present yourself at the tradesmen's entrance next time."

He moved to slam the door, but I'd a foot in by that point. He glanced back at Goddard. I slid in my leg. By the time Goddard came into view—burgundy smoking jacket, dark trousers, Chinese slippers, and a tumbler of whisky in one hand—I had half my body in.

"Cain, it's me!" I called.

"He came for his things," Collins said through clenched teeth.

He struggled to push the door closed, but I slid past him, pulling my left leg through just as the door crashed shut behind me. I managed one step toward the staircase before the manservant jerked me around by the shoulder.

I instinctively spun into the turn as all of the rage and panic of the past day came back to me. It burned a path down my left arm and my fingers came together in one magnificent punch. There was a crunch as my fist met the manservant's jaw. Collins stumbled back half a step and blinked. Then he lifted me by my shirt collar and heaved me into the door.

"Stop it, both of you," Goddard said as I slid toward the floor. There was a pause, and he added, "Have you any idea how much that stained glass cost?"

He stepped onto the checkerboard tile, sipping his whisky and frowning down at me. His clothing was clean and pressed but he hadn't been shaved that morning, and the shadow beneath his eyes told of his own sleepless night. Perhaps that was why he was indulging in a midday whisky—which he normally would have eschewed.

"Have you come for your things, then, Ira?" he asked.

"Can we talk about this alone?"

I rubbed at the back of my skull with my good hand. Goddard took another sip of whisky, rolling it around his mouth for what seemed like an hour before he said, "I don't see why not."

"But, sir," Collins began.

"Leave us," said Goddard.

The manservant made a show of straightening his shirt, shooting me a black glare as he made his way to the servants' stairs. Goddard shut the door behind him and helped me to my feet.

"The morning room?" I asked. My hands were trembling as I hung up St. Andrews's coat. Goddard didn't seem to have noticed.

"After you."

As he pulled the double doors closed behind us, I was overcome by a sense of déjà vu. Despite the flourishes I'd added here and there, the décor was essentially the same as the day when Goddard had asked me to stay. The olive sofa still sat along one edge of the Chinese rug. The deep leather armchair before the fire had become two, but they were identical. Books lined the shelves. A desk sat before a tall window. The sill was set about with green plants in such a way so the light filtered through them, rather than flooding the room. And beyond the window, Goddard's prized roses basked in the summer heat, a mocking reminder of how I had come to be a visitor in my own morning room.

"Ira," he began.

"Your manservant," I said, turning from the window, "has been sabotaging my undergarments."

"I beg your pardon? Whisky?"

I nodded. Goddard topped off his whisky from a cut glass decanter on a cart beside the sofa. When he was finished, he prepared a second glass for me.

"He made an itching powder from rose hips and put it inside my drawers," I continued. "It's invisible and uncomfortable as the very devil. Rather like the symptoms of a venereal disease, though I wouldn't know from personal experience."

"You don't say."

He crossed the carpet to press a glass into my hand. He leaned against the back of his armchair, gesturing for me to continue.

"He's been doing it for at least a month, and the entire time, I've been worrying myself stupid about what you'd do if I turned out to be diseased. He's done it before. He didn't admit it, of course. He spoke of the legions of young men that you'd taken under your wing, who had subsequently developed similar symptoms, then vanished without a trace."

Goddard tapped his fingers on the rim of his glass. A vituperative diatribe against his manservant was probably the last thing he'd thought he'd be entertaining that afternoon. I could see him weighing my words against whatever lies Collins had been putting forth to explain my disappearance.

"Well?" I demanded. "Is it true?"

"That there have been others? Yes," he said cautiously. "And they did leave unexpectedly after experiencing complaints similar to your own. I'd hardly call two a 'legion,' though," he added to himself. "Ira, this is quite an accusation. Do you have any evidence?"

I let out a long breath. There was no doubt Collins had disposed of the rose hips and scrubbed the knife and plate clean. All the same, it was plain from the way Goddard's eyes kept darting between my face and the ring on my finger he wanted to believe me.

"Strange noises woke me last night," I said. "I went to investigate and caught him up to his elbows in rose hips, with a paring knife in his hand. If you examine your rose bushes, I'm quite certain that you'll find that their fruits have been harvested recently."

There was no point in revealing it was Lazarus who had made the connection between Goddard's roses and my affliction. Once Goddard heard another man had had my trousers down, he wouldn't have listened to another word.

"I see. Assuming you're correct, why would he do such a thing?"

I opened my mouth to answer, but thought better of it. The last thing I wanted was for him to think I'd accepted his offer on false pretenses. Was there such a thing as undecided pretenses?

"He seems to think that you'd be better off without the distraction," I said instead.

"Hmm."

Put like that, it *did* sound hollow. But the man's transgressions spoke for themselves. His motive was unimportant.

"I'm not making this up," I said.

"No. I don't believe that you are. But, Ira, why didn't you wake me immediately to tell me what you saw?"

It was a question I'd been asking myself since the lock had clicked shut behind me the night before. The answer was true, and as pathetic as Collins's excuse for his sabotage. I tossed back my whisky and set the glass on the desk.

"Between the blackmailer and wondering whether some ill-conceived coupling in my past was coming back to haunt me," I said, "I was so panicked I could hardly breathe. I had actually thought to speak to you, but I wanted a cigarette first to calm my nerves. I took one out onto the front step, and then…"

I paused. He was looking at me with an expectancy that made me loath to disappoint.

"I locked myself out."

A hint of a smile twitched at one corner of his mouth.

"Blasted Chubb lock," I said.

Goddard's smile widened until it eventually reached his eyes. Chuckling, he stepped forward and straightened my collar. He shook his head indulgently, running a finger down my jaw.

"I don't suppose you had your picklocks with you," he said.

"I did, but they're no bloody good against that thing, and you know it."

He laughed loudly. Then his expression became serious.

"It still doesn't explain how you came to be arrested at a brothel. St. Andrews informed me of your narrow escape, but you'll forgive me if I find the idea of you clandestinely working for him to be a little far-fetched."

I blew out a long breath.

"It's a long, embarrassing story," I said.

"I'd very much like to hear it."

I picked up my empty glass and gave it a shake. Goddard refilled it while I lowered myself into one of the armchairs that faced the cold fireplace. The chair was deep, but the leather was firm and I couldn't suppress a sigh of satisfaction as I sank into it. Goddard set my glass on the table near my elbow and claimed the other chair for himself. Once the whisky was burning its way down my gullet, I related the whole wretched chain of events—my barefoot run through the park, the gruesome discovery in Acton's basement, the raid, and my last-minute rescue by Goddard's nemesis and my own. When I came to Nate's death, my voice cracked unexpectedly, and I had to fortify myself with another belt of Goddard's finest before finishing.

There was a long silence.

"As much as it pains me," he finally said, "I suppose I owe St.

Andrews a debt of gratitude. If you'd gone down for gross indecency, neither one of us would have fared well."

"Is that all you have to say?" I asked.

"I am sorry about your friend. Will you allow me to see to his killer?"

I'd have paid to see that, actually. But as much as I respected Goddard's ruthlessness and his dedication to whatever task he set himself, I wasn't at all certain of his ability to take on someone who pimped children to aristocrats and come out of it intact.

"St. Andrews requested that you reconsider his offer of a truce," I said instead.

"Over my dead body."

"He seemed sincere."

Goddard rolled his eyes. "If nothing else, the man is sincere."

"No, it makes sense," I said, turning in my seat to face him. "The enemy of my enemy is my friend, and all that."

Goddard looked amused. "You're quoting Chinese philosophy now?" he asked.

"I'm quoting you. Look, I don't know what happened in Cambridge—"

"No," he said. "You don't."

"Then why don't you tell me? No one else will," I added.

His fingers tightened around his glass. His mouth became a hard line. For a moment I was certain that he would chuck me out. But he turned away and let out a long breath. When he finally started to speak, he kept his eyes fixed firmly on the gilded cigarette box on the mantel, hands circling the whisky glass that now sat on the chair between his knees.

"I met Andrew St. Andrews and Nicholas Sinclair during my first, and, sadly, last year at a position that I'd thought would be my life's work. The year was 1872. I was a fellow in classics at Trinity."

He smiled ruefully, reciting the facts as if he'd made this speech to himself many, many times before.

"I had distinguished myself early on. However, I hadn't the background necessary to truly fit in with my colleagues. The less said of my origins the better, but suffice it to say that my lack of connections ensured that even after having fought tooth and nail for my position, I'd always be regarded as an outsider. I suppose this was the reason I took up my, shall we say, extracurricular pursuits as an undergraduate. Don't let the popular claptrap about heredity fool you, Ira. I chose the criminal path, and by the time I began at Trinity, it had made me very wealthy. Of course, at that time, there had been no way to enjoy it without arousing the suspicion of a faculty already uneasy about accepting me into their ranks, and yet, in light of my superior qualifications, unable to turn me away."

He set the glass back on the table before standing and walking to the mantel for a cigarette. He conjured a flame from the round lighter beside the cigarette box and took a long pull. I noticed the lavender letters had disappeared. He exhaled as he turned back to contemplate me through a fragrant haze.

"They were my students, as you might have guessed. St. Andrews was just eighteen, and brilliant. If not for his inability to settle into a single course of study, he'd have ended up one of those odd but much-loved birds renowned for his genius yet incapable of tying his own shoes. Sinclair was different. He was intelligent enough but, like myself, a businessman. And even if he had harbored academic ambitions, his impending marriage would have put a stop to them. Upon his graduation, Sinclair was to go to work for his father-in-law. No, Sinclair was never going to amount to anything as a scholar," he concluded. "But his business acumen was second only to my own."

I shifted in my seat. The boldness the whisky had lent me was dissipating, and my head felt like lead. I rested it against the cool leather. Movement in the window caught my eye. Eileen was in the garden, carefully shoveling manure onto the ground at the bases of Goddard's rose bushes. Goddard continued.

"When he came to me one day, bearing a rough diagram of my organization, my first thought was that he was about to try his hand at blackmail. My second thought was what a shame it would be to have to kill him. It was embarrassing, really. I'd thought myself so discreet. I lived in rooms appropriate to my station and always comported myself with the self-consciousness expected from one of my humble origins. Yet somehow Sinclair had managed to get a good handle on my enterprises. Not everything, of course, but enough.

"He'd been losing interest in his studies for some time, and it showed. It was only a matter of time before he tried to extricate himself. Given his lack of subtlety, I'd have expected him to use the information he'd gathered to coerce me into brokering some sort of honorable exit. But, as it turned out, he was interested in continuing his education in a different direction. After I recovered from the shock of being so unceremoniously exposed, he showed me some of his own ideas and offered me a cut if I helped him get started."

"Did you?" I asked.

Goddard's mouth went hard, his regret at the decision more evident in his expression than in anything he might have said.

"Of course I did. I was flattered, and his plans, though clumsy, had merit. Moreover, I thought that it might be useful to have a protégé, especially one who was bright, but not too bright, ambitious, and grateful for my assistance."

I sat up abruptly. *Protégé* was how Goddard sometimes introduced me to those who knew that he had no use for a private secretary.

"Protégé?" I asked suspiciously. "You mean like me?"

Goddard made a moue of distaste.

"A rat-faced little upstart like that? Never. Besides, he seemed quite taken with his future bride. No, my interest laid not so much with Nicholas Sinclair as with his connections."

"Like Edward Acton?" I asked.

The times when I'd caught Cain Goddard off his guard were few and precious. I savored his sharp inhalation, the flare of his nostrils, and the way his left eyelid twitched.

"It's his brothel on Fitzroy Street," I said. "And Sinclair, our blackmailer, is the manager. You can't tell me you didn't know."

He cleared his throat. All that remained of his cigarette was a brown-edged twist of paper. He narrowed his eyes before tossing the butt into the cold fireplace. I could sense him trying to figure out how much more of the story I knew, and how much more he should admit.

"How I came upon this knowledge is another long story," I said.

"Suffice it to say St. Andrews confirmed it. He also said you've made alliances with some very dangerous people in the opium trade, and those alliances aren't as stable as you think they are. Are you doing business with Acton, Cain?"

He exhaled heavily.

"What if I am?"

"High-alkaloid opium?"

Goddard wasn't comfortable with this line of inquiry coming from me. He tried to keep me out of the inner workings of his organization, for his own safety as well as mine. But the situation was getting more complicated and perverse by the minute. Sinclair was siphoning off high-alkaloid opium from the brothel and re-selling it to Zhi Sen. Goddard was getting the same from Acton, but cutting Zhi Sen out of the loop. Zhi Sen and Sinclair were going into business with the goal of driving Goddard out. But why was Acton selling to Goddard and not to Sinclair? Was he playing them off against each other? As tight a rein as Goddard kept on his criminal network, it didn't take a Trinity professor to see that it would soon be spinning even out of Goddard's control.

"You need to stop," I said.

Goddard laughed and reached for another cigarette.

"I'm serious, Cain. Acton is unspeakably dangerous."

He looked up. "So am I."

"Not like this. He's…he's evil."

Goddard's eyebrows shot up, and he forced back another laugh.

"And I'm Father Christmas?" he asked.

"St. Andrews says—"

"St. Andrews can be such an old woman sometimes," Goddard scoffed.

"I think he's right."

Goddard popped his cigarette between his lips and held it to the lighter, inhaling until the end glowed.

"What do you know of it?" he asked, leaning back against the mantel.

I couldn't tell Goddard what Lazarus had told me. It was Tim's story to tell. More importantly, if things started to go bad, Goddard might try to curry Acton's favor by handing him Lazarus.

I couldn't allow that to happen.

"What went wrong between you and Sinclair?" I asked instead.

Goddard made an impatient noise, but having already begun the story seemed resigned to finishing it. He took a quick drag from his cigarette, flourishing it in a professorial gesture.

"I'd been trying to protect you, Ira. But since you already seem to know everything about the situation…"

He paused to blow a fragrant plume toward the ceiling. The smoke spread out, swirling lazily above his head.

"After the three of us left Cambridge, Sinclair of his own volition, and St. Andrews and myself against ours, Sinclair and I became partners. Sinclair had married Acton's daughter, so Acton was anxious to see him get along in the business. Acton was highly placed in the East India Company at the time, though the company would be dissolved some two years later. He was heavily involved in the company's opium importation operations. Sinclair worked in company records, and found that he could skim quite a bit from the company's stores without being noticed. He brought me in as a distributor, and that's how I entered the opium trade.

"Sinclair and I carried on like that for some time, until one day, the old man approached me. He'd known that we were up to something for some time, but instead of being angry, he suggested that I look into distributing in China. Opium had been legal there since Britain had forced that treaty down Prince Gong's throat, and demand was at an all-time high. He even offered to help me, provided I not tell Sinclair."

"Why not? I asked.

"He regarded Sinclair as something of an amateur. He was also deeply disappointed in him as a son-in-law. It turned out that Sinclair preferred the beds of certain male acquaintances to his wife's bed. Though Acton would never humiliate his daughter by bringing her husband's peccadilloes to the attention of the police, he did want to punish him. He did this by promoting me. The profits allowed me to expand my organization beyond my wildest dreams: brothels, gambling houses, opium dens—"

"Is that how you met Zhi Sen?" I interrupted.

He nodded.

"And now you're cutting him out, just like you did Sinclair."

"It's nothing personal," Goddard said.

I laughed. "More than ten years later, Sinclair's still out for revenge. Is that why he's blackmailing you?"

"In part," he said. "But what he really wants is revenge against Acton. Emily Sinclair is Acton's only child. According to Sinclair, Acton put a special directive in his will, stating that, in the event of his death or incapacitation, all of his property would revert to her. I have information that Sinclair has discovered some aspect of Acton's business that would send Acton to the scaffold. If that happens, then everything Acton owns—and it's quite a bit—would come to Sinclair's wife, thus, indirectly to him."

I knew exactly what Sinclair had discovered—but did Goddard? Was he ignorant of the nature of Acton's basement business, or just trying to protect me? I wondered, had Sinclair known how much Nate had discovered, or had he had been surprised when Nate had shown up last night in the basement intent on putting a stop to it all?

"Zhi Sen won't be happy when he finds you've left him out," I said.

"Zhi Sen is making too much money running my opium dens to care," Goddard replied.

"That's what you think. Acton has been supplying high-alkaloid opium to the young men at the Fitzroy Street brothel for some time. Sinclair has been cutting the opium with the regular stuff and selling the difference to Zhi Sen behind your back."

There was another flummoxed moment while Goddard puffed away on his cigarette and processed this information. That the information had come from someone purposefully kept ignorant did not sit well with him. If I had figured it out, he must have been reasoning, others had as well.

"I trusted him," he said after a moment.

"He trusted you."

Goddard began to pace.

"So you were correct when you said that his daughter took the dog from you. She and her father are working for Sinclair now."

"Maybe," I said.

He stopped. Frowned.

"Or maybe she has some other reason to want the thing," I said.

"I can't imagine what."

I thought about Nate and Mrs. Wu. It wasn't as if men and women mingled freely on the streets of London. Or English and Chinese. Or rentboys and respectable widows. Yet Nate had named her on his deathbed. Perhaps Nate's plan had consisted of more than breaking the Afghan children out of the basement. With her father's connections, Mrs. Wu might even have been in a position to get them out of the country. If Sinclair was on Acton's side in the matter, she could have used the dog to command his silence and his assistance.

"Cain," I asked, "Did you know about the children in Acton's basement?"

The subsequent pause lasted too long. He glanced at me furtively before looking away.

"I knew," he said. He pinched out his cigarette and threw the butt into the fireplace.

"And you were all right with that?"

"It's none of my business," he replied.

"How can you say that?"

He turned and looked me in the eye. "Acton imports opium. He sells it to me. Whatever else he buys or sells is his affair, not mine."

A cold and ominous dread gathered in my stomach.

"Did he offer you a stake in that part of the operation?" I asked.

"He did." Goddard shrugged. "I turned him down. With his connections, he can operate with impunity. For me, it wouldn't be worth the risk."

I opened my mouth to speak, but couldn't find the words.

"Profit and risk," I said after a moment. "That's all it comes down to for you."

He crossed the room and sat down on the arm of my chair. With a patronizing smile, he cupped my cheek in his hand—hard muscle under smooth skin fragrant with bergamot and jasmine.

"That's all anything comes down to," he said.

And that included me, I supposed. A gamble, a calculated risk, judged to be worth the effort, at least for now. I jerked away.

"They're throwaways, Ira," he said as I pushed up out of the deep chair and stalked over to the window.

My heart pounding, I rested my damp palms on the mahogany desk, as familiar as my own boots, with inkwell and blotter lined up so precisely, the ivy snaking up from the pot on the corner the only bit of wildness Goddard would allow. And yet, as I ran my fingers over the thick pad of paper in its leather-cornered holder, I was struck for the first time since I'd settled in at York Street by the knowledge I didn't really belong there. Goddard wasn't trafficking children, and yet I couldn't reconcile myself that to him it was the moral equivalent of importing textiles. How could I trust my life to someone for whom life was just another commodity to be bought and sold?

"Their own parents sold them to pay off their debts," he continued. "No one misses them."

"Someone misses them," I said, thinking of the doll in the pocket of the tweed coat hanging in the vestibule.

"It's not like the same thing doesn't happen in London."

I turned.

I rarely talked about my childhood. Goddard knew my mother had abandoned me at the workhouse, but it was a common story and I couldn't imagine he'd given it much thought. He certainly had made the connection between me and the children in the basement of the brothel. And he didn't care.

"You don't have to tell me that," I spat. "My mother gave up everything for opium, including me. I could just as easily have ended up in some brothel basement myself."

"But you didn't," Goddard said. "You're here."

I shoved my hands into the pockets of my charity-box trousers and took a deep breath. Dust motes floated, suspended in a ray of light from the window.

"You can run the world, Ira," he said as I stared at the rack of unused rifles above the doorway. "Or you can try to save it. Saving it is a losing battle, and not nearly as much fun. But that's not for you to worry about." He narrowed his eyes. "Is it?"

"I don't know anymore."

Until St. Andrews had taken him on, Lazarus had lived on tea, stale biscuits, and the kindness of strangers—kindness he had freely shared with me. It couldn't have been easy living in hiding, and yet he not only managed, but thrived—not only thrived, but found a way to help people. I used to sneer at the fact he wasn't living much better than some of his patients. Yet, knowing what I had come to know about how Goddard made our living, the thought of going back to my cushy life made me want to vomit.

"Ira."

"She died in 1870, you know. That tainted opium nobody was ever able to trace back to its source."

Lazarus suspected Acton had been behind that, but as much as I wanted to pin it on him, there would never be conclusive evidence. Everyone had stopped looking a long time ago.

Goddard crossed the room. His hand on my back, his breath was warm against my cheek.

"You must be exhausted," he murmured. "Why don't you go upstairs and lie down? I'll join you in a bit. Then we can wander down to Piccadilly to find something to eat. The trip is long overdue, don't you think?"

Goddard in Piccadilly? Of his own free will? He *must* have been worried. Every fiber of my being screamed "yes"—but for the cold, hard lump of conscience at the pit of my stomach. He knew about those children. He knew how easily I could have ended up in a similar situation.

And it didn't bother him a whit.

"What's inside the dog?" I demanded.

"What?"

"The porcelain dog, Cain," I said. "That damned statue over which I've been beaten, jailed, and very nearly driven out of my home. What the devil is inside it? You could at least tell me that."

"I..." he stammered. "I'm...sorry, Ira. I...I can't."

"Right," I said. I unclasped his hands from around my waist and pulled away. I didn't know where I was going, but I wasn't staying there.

"You're not leaving, surely?" he asked as I gave the double doors a violent shove with my good hand.

Was I? I didn't know. All I knew was I couldn't be there right then. I didn't know if I'd ever be able to be there again—at least not in the same way. Whether this surprised him or me more was impossible to say. I pulled the tweed coat from the coat rack.

"If it's about Collins," he called, "consider him sacked."

"I just need to think," I said. Collins was a significant olive branch.

Goddard came to the morning room door and leaned against the doorjamb.

"As you wish. But don't forget the opening of the Fighting Society building tonight. Eight o'clock sharp, at the warehouse on Narrow Street in Limehouse."

He couldn't be serious.

"Zhi Sen is scheming with Sinclair to put you out of business," I said. "You can't mean to spend the evening congratulating each other as if he weren't stabbing you in the back with your own dagger."

"There will be more than enough time to deal with him and Sinclair both," he said. "But tonight is about the Fighting Society. Ten years' hard work is finally coming to fruition."

Unlike his academic career, which was dead in the water, or his criminal enterprises, now mired in revenge and betrayal.

Or his personal life, which looked as if it were crumbling around his ears.

"It would really mean a lot to me if you were there," he said.

The arrogance was gone from his voice. Standing there amid the subtle splendor of his house, he looked diminished somehow—deflated, sad, and tired.

"Of course," I said gently.

I reached for the doorknob.

"And Ira?"

I looked back.

"It may be easier to love a poor man than a rich one, but life is much more comfortable with a rich one."

I felt a right bastard. But with the little Afghan doll a solid lump against my thigh, I knew if I didn't leave at that moment I'd have said something that I couldn't have taken back.

"I'll bear that in mind," I said.

I took my set of keys from the hook near the coat rack and shoved them into the pocket of St. Andrews's coat. I perched my bowler on top of my head. Mumbling something about cab fare, I pinched a handful of coins from Goddard's pocket. With one last backward glance, I pulled the front door shut behind me and descended the stairs to York Street, wondering whether it would be for the last time.

CHAPTER SEVENTEEN

The afternoon was as hot and miserable as it had been the day before. A sickly yellow haze filled the sky. The air was humid, laden with grit. Blisters sprouted across my feet like mushrooms as I wandered the city streets. I was light-headed from fatigue. Yet once I'd walked off my anger, an unaccustomed elation came over me. Two years ago, my choice had been between sleeping in alleys and being someone's pet. But now that my paralyzing fear of syphilis had come to nothing, I realized this was no longer the case. I no longer had to leave York Street to avoid Goddard's wrath. If I chose to leave on my own accord, Goddard had equipped me with the skills to carve out a respectable life. He'd taught me to read, write, and speak as someone born to the educated middle class. I now understood how to run a household and could manage basic bookkeeping. I had no references, but the right employer might overlook that. I was also still an accomplished housebreaker. I wasn't planning to leave York Street—not yet, at any rate. But it was quite a revelation to realize I could, and it wouldn't necessarily mean a return to hiring out my arse for six shillings a go.

On the other hand, I wasn't ready to go back to Goddard's house. Doing so would have been tantamount to declaring the matter of the brothel children closed, which it certainly was not. Though I was no longer bubbling over with rage at Goddard's indifference to a grievous wrong so close to my heart, I knew ignoring the problem wouldn't make it go away. One way or another, Goddard would have to end his involvement with Edward Acton if he wanted me to stay. And it was the realization I could actually entertain such conditionality, that I had the luxury of considering my own scruples, which buoyed me along as I wandered the streets of London, frittering away in daring contemplation the time remaining before I was expected in Limehouse.

At half-seven I found myself on the far side of Regent's Park, near the Royal College of Physicians. Well-shod horses clip-clopped past through the lengthening shadows while I made my way through the throngs of well-heeled Londoners stepping out in search of evening entertainments. In the gathering dusk, the combination of St. Andrews's coat and my expensive hat allowed me to pass through them unnoticed, though scrutiny would have quickly revealed my charity-box clothing beneath the tweed. What I really wanted was supper. Unfortunately there was no time for a proper restaurant meal, and no street vendor would dare sully these posh avenues with his humble spring-barrow. So though my stomach was protesting loudly, I found a cab instead.

"Narrow Street," I told the driver. "Limehouse docks."

There turned out to be as many warehouses in the area as there were green carnations in Piccadilly. However the one Goddard meant was impossible to miss. It was smaller than its neighbors, but was sporting a fresh coat of white paint, and the door was painted bright red. There was new glass in the windows. Red scrolls with gold lettering hung on either side of the door. Behind the building, a wide canal joined the Limehouse Basin with the Thames. A row of red paper lanterns hung from the roof, rising one by one on the foul, fishy breeze.

A small crowd had gathered. I recognized several students from the Fighting Society as well as a few rough-knuckled men—bodyguards—who greeted me with a businesslike nod. There was a reporter leaning against a lamppost scribbling notes, and a photographer setting up his tripod. Goddard himself was attempting to find a comfortable position at the lectern in front of the building. He looked sharp in a black suit and topper, chin freshly shaven and mustache waxed. A subtle relief crossed his face as his eyes met mine, and giving the pile of notes upon the lectern a final pat, he abandoned his position to meet me.

"Thank you for coming, Mr. Adler," he said, addressing me with a handshake and the professional distance one would expect between a man and his secretary. Despite his formal words, his voice betrayed a nervousness few who hadn't been on intimate terms with the man would have comprehended. "I trust that you'll do your best to document this occasion accurately."

His eyes darted from side to side. He licked his lips. It wasn't simply the fruition of a long-cherished dream upsetting his nerves. He was no doubt trying to reconcile Zhi Sen's invaluable contributions to the Fighting Arts Society with the fact the man was double-dealing with our blackmailer. And there was me. I still wore my ring, but it was obvious my departure had left him as shaken as I had been with regard to the future we'd both thought secure.

"You can rely on me, Dr. Goddard," I said.

He searched my face. "Good, good," he finally said. He gave my back an avuncular pat, the most intimate gesture of affection he dared in public, and then directed his scrutiny to our surroundings.

Turning his back to the building, he surveyed the nearby ship works, the warehouses that lined the Limehouse basin, and the people milling about the docks. His attention finally came to rest on the black hansom parked on Narrow Street. I'd never before seen Goddard's horse this well turned out. The usual driver was in fresh livery and stood beside the carriage with a handkerchief, fussing over an imaginary spot of dust. My heart leaped momentarily into my throat when I thought I saw a familiar hulking profile in the shadows behind the carriage. But no sooner had my mind put the profile together with the name "Collins" than the illusion dispersed.

"Dr. Goddard," I said, "Did anyone accompany you here this evening?"

"No," he said.

He seemed to be evaluating the composition of the crowd now—perhaps making notes of who might cause problems, and which of his men would be in a position to solve those problems. Seemingly satisfied, he turned to me with a wry expression.

"Though I'm hoping someone might be persuaded to accompany me home tonight when it's all over."

I smiled in spite of myself, and was opening my mouth to say something clever, when Goddard cursed under his breath. I followed his gaze back to Narrow Street, where a dour-looking man was stepping out of a cab. He was perhaps fifteen years older than Goddard, with great, graying sideburns like whole legs of lamb, an uncharitable expression, and possibly the most unfashionable suit of clothing known to man.

"Who's that?" I asked.

"Behold, the chancellor and head of the Committee for the Promotion of Moral Virtue. He's a great promoter of the fighting arts. Thinks my club will provide another place for the deserving poor to learn discipline and develop character."

"And yet he refuses to promote the careers of deserving academics," I said. "Bollocks to his charity."

Goddard's shoulders sagged. No matter how many athletic clubs he built, no matter how much ill-gotten lucre he cached away, whatever had transpired between him, St. Andrews, and Sinclair back at Cambridge would always haunt his academic career.

"All the same," he said, "I suppose I should say a few words to the old hypocrite before we begin. Do wait for me afterward. Please."

I watched him trudge off toward the person who, in my opinion, least deserved his consideration before returning my attention to the shadows around Goddard's hansom. I could swear Collins had been standing there just minutes before. It might not have been him, of course. Goddard said no one had accompanied him, so Collins was either sacked or back at York Street, his dismissal imminent. Darkness was falling. There was every chance my eyes had misinterpreted the deepening shadows. And yet I couldn't shake the feeling the manservant was there, watching and waiting for his chance to avenge the humiliation he'd experienced at my hands.

"Evenin', Mr. Adler," said a voice to my left.

I jumped. A ginger-haired man in a short coat and cloth cap grinned at me. When I'd seen the man sparring with Goddard at the athletic club, I'd taken him to be one of Goddard's students from the university. His accent, though, was pure East End. Which meant in all likelihood, Goddard was grooming him for a position in his organization.

"Watkins," he said by way of introduction. "'Enry Watkins."

"You mustn't sneak up like that, Mr. Watkins," I said.

"Sorry, Mr. Adler."

His grin widened, but his eyes never stopped scanning the crowd.

I wondered whether Goddard had asked him to look after me. The idea gave me a little *frisson* of excitement.

"It's a big night for the Fighting Society," I said.

"That it is, sir."

"A big night for Dr. Goddard."

"And for Mr. Zhi Sen, too, I'd imagine. They been workin' real 'ard."

"Indeed," I said.

We both turned our eyes forward as Goddard stepped up to the lectern. He cleared his throat.

"Friends," he began. He ran his fingers over his notes, but kept his eyes forward. The notes were for security. No doubt he'd memorized the speech a week in advance.

"Colleagues, members of the press. You see before you the culmination of a dream many years in the making: London's first school of the Oriental fighting arts. Starting next week, this school, which is equipped with the most modern equipment and facilities, will open itself to the young men of the city, regardless of background, who wish to develop themselves physically, morally, and spiritually through the application of ancient techniques. But before I go any further, allow me to introduce you to Mr. Zhi Sen, our instructor and a personal friend."

There was a light shower of applause as Zhi Sen joined Goddard at the lectern. He'd been to the tailor recently—the quality of his suit rivaled Goddard's. His long, thin beard had been combed until it shone, and his hair had been slicked back with Massacar oil. Ah, the sweet rewards of treachery!

While Goddard told the story of how they met, I examined the old man's every move, expression, and gesture for a clue of how far his betrayal had gone. But Zhi Sen's round face was as impenetrable as ever.

"It was during that fateful voyage," Goddard continued, "that I resolved to master the art of unarmed combat, and to bring it back to London, so that my countrymen might benefit from what I had learned…"

Zhi Sen's daughter was nowhere to be seen. She hadn't any reason to be present, I supposed. Still, with the way she kept turning up when least expected, it wouldn't have surprised me a bit to find her lurking about. I wondered whether Lazarus was having any luck with his promise to find her.

The sun had now fully set behind us, though the eastern sky retained a faint residual glow. The canal was steeped in shadow. Only the sound of water lapping against the concrete dock behind the warehouse gave any indication of its presence. The shadows had descended over the building as well, obscuring its planes and angles, darkening the windows, and turning the bright white paint to gray. The clouds, which held in the heat of the day so oppressively, now seemed to release it. The air remained as poisonous as ever, but darkness was at least bringing some relief from the heat.

Beside me, Watkins yawned surreptitiously into his sleeve. Like Goddard, he was built for action rather than indolence. When the shadows to the left of the warehouse shifted, my muscles tensed in readiness. But Watkins relaxed—as if the possibility of trouble had finally brought a purpose to the evening.

"Anyone supposed to be back there?" I murmured.

He shook his head. As Goddard droned on about international friendship, I craned my head to get a better look. There were at least two people behind the building—though between the shadows and their dark clothing, one could have discounted their presence as a trick of the lanterns. It was clear Watkins wasn't about to make that mistake. From the furtive movements, he had obviously deduced the people were not part of the decorating committee.

As had I.

I opened my mouth to speak, but with a jerk of his chin, Watkins caught the attention of a pair standing off to the side of the lectern. There was a quick exchange of gestures, and one of the men jogged around the side of the building to investigate. The other whispered into Goddard's ear. Goddard frowned, but continued speaking.

"Over the past decade, the liberalization of trade between Great Britain and China has resulted in unprecedented opportunity for both Her Majesty's subjects and those of the Empress. Let this humble school, therefore, stand as a symbol…"

The scout was taking too long to return. Warning prickled at the back of my neck. Watkins sensed my intention almost before I did.

"Now, you let us 'andle it, Mr. Adler," he said in a low voice. "Dr. Goddard said you was to be protected at all costs. 'S prolly nuffin'," he added, though he didn't sound convinced.

"Of course you're right," I said.

But I bolted the moment he glanced away.

I hadn't gone five steps when the right side of the building exploded.

Goddard was thrown forward into the lectern. I ran toward him but was wrestled to the ground by a burly kid.

"Get off me!" I cried as the orderly crowd erupted in chaos. Out of the corner of my eye, I saw a few of Goddard's men spring into action, but they were too few and too far between. People surged away from the building. Others, blind with panic, ran toward it.

"Dr. Goddard said we's to keep you safe, Mr. Adler," the young man panted into my ear. "Jus' come quiet-like an' it'll all be over soon."

Feet pounded the ground near my face, kicking up dirt. I spat out a mouthful of grit. The young man continued to hold me, but bent over to protect us both from the crowd. I twisted loose and threw myself backward into him. There was a satisfying, wet crunch as the back of my head hit his face. I rolled free, only to have a more familiar pair of hands lay hold of my shoulders.

"Come, now," Watkins said, voice straining to stay above the din. "We's 'ere to 'elp."

"Then help me up," I growled.

In response, he put his knee to the middle of my back. All around us, people ran past as charred debris rained from the sky.

"Not until you promise—"

"I promise your life won't be worth a farthing if you don't unhand me."

"Dr. Goddard telled us—"

Watkins didn't have a chance to finish before I snaked an arm behind my back, grabbed a handful between his legs, and gave a twist his grandchildren would feel. I threw him off and scrambled to my feet. I searched the crowd frantically. The lectern was crawling with Goddard's men, but Goddard himself was nowhere to be seen. I had to find him. He needed me. Somewhere behind me, Watkins's colleague was moaning, his face a mess of blood and teeth. It was his own damned fault. If he complained, I'd send him a bouquet of whatever flower signified *serves you sodding well right.*

The bells of a fire wagon sounded in the distance. Footsteps rang out along the docks. Unless I wanted to be pressed into firefighting service, it was time to leave. A flaming piece of paper floated past, landed near my feet, and curled to ash. I turned toward the lectern, but Goddard was gone. So were his men. On the street, a horse pawed the ground impatiently. There was the sharp crack of a driving whip. I looked over in time to see Goddard's hansom pull away, two men leaping onto the running boards on either side.

"Wait!" I cried.

I couldn't see Goddard's head in the back window. He must have been lying across the seat. Was he that badly injured?

Panic squeezed my chest. It couldn't end like this—not with him lying injured with only his employees for comfort. Not with him wondering if I still cared. A lump rose in my throat. My eyes burned and the street blurred.

His physician had been summoned, I told myself. By the time he arrived home, Eileen would already be serving up tea and sandwiches to Goddard's inner circle, and to the best medical personnel money could buy.

But Cain deserved more than that. Our disagreements didn't matter now. The future would take care of itself in time. If the worst happened…dear God…if it came to that, he couldn't…I wouldn't let him…not alone. Not when I loved him. And I did love him, I realized. If I could do nothing else for him, I could let him know it.

Swiping a sleeve across my eyes, I took off after the hansom. My heart pounded, my arms and legs pumping as I followed it down Narrow Street, only peripherally aware of the bloody, blistered mess my feet had become. The driver slowed to make the turn onto Horseferry.

I leaped.

Only to be tackled by a third imbecile.

"What the *fuck*?" I cried as we both went down hard.

I rolled across the cobblestones trying to dislodge him, but he clung fast.

"I'll kill you!" I shouted, swinging blindly. "Cain!"

The carriage was getting away. I flailed my arms, trying to find a soft spot with either fist or elbow. Eventually I came up on my stomach and pushed myself onto my knees. I threw my weight forward, hoping to toss the cretin over my shoulder, and promptly found myself on my back. I tried to rise, but couldn't move.

"Care to reconsider your response, Adler?" Lazarus asked, standing over me while I choked dust and blinked up at the night. He looked exhilarated—he hadn't even wrinkled his jacket. He held out a hand to help me up. I slapped it away.

"I..." I gasped as I struggled to my feet. My chest felt like a clenched fist.

"Don't panic," Lazarus said. "I just knocked the wind out of you."

I stood there doubled over while Goddard's coach disappeared. As my breath returned, I lunged at him.

"Why did you stop me?" I shouted. I shoved his chest hard. He staggered back. I stepped toward him again, then, thinking better of it, thrust my hands in my pockets so I wouldn't strangle him. "I should be with him," I said miserably. "He needs me."

"He needs a doctor, and no doubt has the best in London. Our real concern now is who caused the explosion. Because they're behind that building."

I swallowed. Taking a deep breath, I followed his gaze to the warehouse. Smoke was billowing from a hole in the right side of the roof. Flames were shooting up into the dark sky. Lazarus was right. There'd be no catching the carriage now. But we could get the son of a bitch who'd blown up the building.

"All right," I said.

Signaling for me to follow, Lazarus took off into the crowd. When we reached the left side of the warehouse, he flattened himself against it and pushed me back with an arm across my chest. The air was acrid there, as hot and dry as the wood at my back. Inside the warehouse, the beams crackled and groaned. There was a crash as a pane of glass exploded from the heat.

"What the devil are you doing here, anyway?" I hissed.

"Shh," said Lazarus.

A few yards ahead of us, the ground dropped off sharply where the back wall of the warehouse ended in a concrete loading dock. A small boat bobbed up and down in the water behind the building—not much more than a glorified punt, really—too small to be safe even within the confines of the canal. In the rough, congested waters of the river just a few yards south, it would be a death trap.

"Your Mrs. Wu, I believe," Lazarus said, nodding toward a tall, thin figure illuminated by the flames.

"She did this?" I cried. "But what? Why?"

"Shh," he said again.

Like the two men standing with her beside the boat, Mrs. Wu was wearing black trousers, boots, and a pullover, but her long rope of hair was unmistakable. She had a sack slung over one shoulder. Goddard's scout lay, unmoving, on the ground nearby. Something was huddled in the belly of the boat. A sudden rain of sparks revealed several pairs of frightened eyes. In the whisper of flames across timber, Nate's dying words came back to me: *Mrs. Wu...ware'ouse...the children...*

I elbowed Lazarus. "The children from the brothel," I whispered. "They're in that boat."

"We have to leave, now," one of the men said to Mrs. Wu. "The fire brigade will be here any minute, and the police won't be far behind."

"We can't leave without Turnbull," said Mrs. Wu.

"Where is he, then?"

"The river is jammed," Lazarus said to me. "They'll be smashed to bits in that little thing."

"Mrs. Wu has the porcelain dog. If we let her get away, we may never find it."

Lazarus looked at me, the seriousness of our situation heavy in his deep brown eyes. He drew a Webley service revolver from beneath his coat.

"Then we can't let that happen," he said.

"Where did you get that?"

"When Christopher James Parker perished in a snowstorm outside of Caboul, his weapon found its way into the hands of a certain Timothy Lazarus. How exactly I'm not at liberty to say."

With a quick smirk, he stepped down onto the concrete path running alongside the canal. Farther down, the conversation between Mrs. Wu and the men had turned to argument.

"We can't wait any longer," said one of the men.

"Mr. Turnbull has put himself at great risk to get us this far," Mrs. Wu argued. "We can't leave without him."

"You'll have to," Lazarus said, coming up behind them. "Mr. Turnbull died in my surgery earlier today."

"He's dead?"

I turned at the sound of the voice behind me. Soft. Sad. A burst of flame illuminated the figure on the cement walk beside the canal, not far from where I was standing. He wore a magnificently cut coat that clung to his thin torso, a top hat, and a face full of blond whiskers that formed a point at the end of his chin. It was difficult to make out his features in the dark, but it wouldn't have been a stretch to imagine that years ago, he might have been Goddard's "rat-faced little upstart."

But now Nick Sinclair sounded like a child who had lost his favorite toy.

"My men brought him to the clinic as quickly as they could," Sinclair told me.

"After watching him take a beating like that," I said. "Very decent of you."

We stared at one another for several long moments. Behind me, the muted voices of Lazarus and Mrs. Wu carried on a terse exchange. There was a great clatter of hooves and bells as the fire wagon pulled up Narrow Street, and the shouts of firemen as they bullied the remaining onlookers into work crews. Behind Sinclair, a wave sloshed up over the concrete, pooling around his expensive boots.

"I did everything I could," Sinclair said. "But Acton was there. I'd have been killed."

Some bogeyman, I thought with disgust, reduced to sniveling over his own inaction.

"But they killed Nate instead, and you didn't do a thing to stop it." I hopped down onto the concrete walk so that I could look into his face. "Blackmail is a coward's game, Mr. Sinclair." I spat on the ground near his feet. "It suits you."

His face went white with fury.

"What do you know of it? What do you know of anything? Who are you?"

"The friend of an enemy," I said.

Rage burned inside me, bubbled up my gullet, and tinted the entire world red. I'd never killed a man. I doubted I could have killed in cold blood. But at that moment, my blood was anything but cold. Nate was dead, Goddard was dying, and it was all Sinclair's doing.

"This is for Cain," I said as I stepped toward him. "This is for Nate."

Recognition lit his face as I threw myself on him. The last vestiges of fear drained away as a sense of righteousness settled over me. He had threatened my lover and my home, and stood by while Acton's men beat my best friend to death. Whether the explosion was his doing or Mrs. Wu's was immaterial—he could carry the blame for that as well. As long as Nick Sinclair had breath in his body, I would not rest. All it would take was one good bash to the head. A crack, a splash, and it would all be over. I pulled him off the railing and flung him into the concrete wall of the dock. Behind me, there was a loud boom as a ceiling beam split inside the burning warehouse. The flames shot higher, lighting up the dock like daylight.

"Now!" Sinclair shouted. "Never mind me, go now!"

Footsteps slapped on the wet concrete as two men rushed out of the shadows and pushed past us.

"Tim!" I called.

"Over there," Sinclair shouted. His voice was filled with triumph. "Make sure to get the woman! She's the one you want!"

He pushed off from the wall, slamming me against the metal railing. Pain shot up my spine.

"This had nothing to do with you, boy," Sinclair sneered.

One of my arms was pinned against the railing, the other trapped between us. Sinclair's face was so close to mine I could see the cracks between his uneven teeth.

"If you'd kept out of it, you'd have been out of prison in two years, and no worse for it. I might even have let you come work for me."

"Over my dead body," I said.

"Yes, well, these things can't be helped."

Gunshots rang out near the boat. I glanced over, only to be rewarded with a punch to the kidney. My boots slid on the wet concrete as I struggled to stay on my feet. Sinclair rammed me against the railing again. I felt the barrel of his revolver beneath my chin.

"Tim!" I shouted again.

"You don't understand anything," Sinclair said.

"I understand that Nate—"

I didn't see the fist coming, but felt the crack of my jaw and tasted the warm, coppery flood. I saw stars out of my left eye. For an instant I floated outside myself. More gunshots came from the direction of the boat. There was a shout, a splash, and then—nothing.

"Don't you dare say his name," Sinclair growled. "Nate was dead from the moment he cast his lot in with her." He jerked his chin toward the boat. "She and her anarchists have been a thorn in my father-in-law's side for a long time. Blowing up buildings, stealing valuable property…He'll be very pleased when I bring her, and his property, back to him."

"People aren't property," I spat.

"Some people are." He caressed my cheek with the muzzle of the gun. "But you'd know more about that than I would."

I hazarded another glance toward the boat. Mrs. Wu's men lay dead on the ground beside Goddard's scout. One of Sinclair's men had Mrs. Wu's head in a solid lock, her arm pinned painfully behind her. The other stood at the edge of the water, the little boat's mooring rope in his hand. Lazarus stood back from the water, training his gun first on one man, then the other. He was holding them for now, but sooner or later one of Sinclair's men would find his advantage and take it.

"Giving her to Acton might get you back in his good graces," I told Sinclair, "but what will Zhi Sen do when he learns that you've handed over his daughter to a murderer?"

"Zhi Sen was a means to an end," Sinclair said. "He doesn't matter in the long run."

"No. In the long run you want it all: Goddard and St. Andrews in prison, Acton dead, and the entire criminal underworld yours for the taking."

Sinclair laughed mirthlessly.

"Is it wrong to aim high?"

"And in the meantime, you're wasting your time with the woman, when the one Acton really wants is over there." I nodded toward Lazarus.

The split-second glance was his fatal mistake. I brought my knee into his groin so hard that it met bone. His eyes went wide, and he slumped against me, gurgling insensibly. I pushed him off and relieved him of his gun as he stumbled back.

"Adler!" Lazarus called.

The man holding Mrs. Wu was backing up a staircase, putting her between himself and Lazarus. I pointed Sinclair's revolver at the man by the boat and pulled the trigger. The shot hit his shoulder and pushed him backward into the canal. There were a few horrible seconds of screaming and splashing before he disappeared for good.

"I'm going after them, Adler!" Lazarus shouted as Sinclair's man pulled Mrs. Wu up the stairs. "If I'm not back by dawn, give the ledgers to the police. Tell them they'll find Acton at the East India Officers' Club, St. James's!"

Shots rang out from the direction of the staircase. Lazarus disappeared into the shadows.

"Tim!"

His head popped up, and with a quick wave toward me, he darted up after them.

I let out a long breath. Sinclair was moaning in a heap at the edge of the dock. Before I could think of my next move, I realized I was not alone. A broad, muscular chest pressed against my back. Hot breath ruffled my hair. Before I could cry out, thick arms wrapped around my shoulders, enormous hands closed around my gun-hand, and my attacker spun us both around to face Sinclair. I squeezed my eyes shut as he pulled my finger against the trigger. When I opened my eyes, there was a mass of blood and bone and brain where Sinclair's face had been, and the muzzle of the gun was burning into my face just in front of my left ear.

"One down," Collins said, his breath eerily intimate on the top of my head. "I can't tell you how satisfying this next one is going to be." His right arm circled my neck. His other hand trembled, as if he were savoring the last seconds before my murder.

"Cain…" I gasped as he subtly crushed my windpipe in the crook of his arm.

"Dr. Goddard should have listened to me in the first place. It was one thing to satisfy his unnatural urges with the occasional renter, but trying to build a life around perversion only leads to tragedy. He should have learned his lesson at Cambridge."

I gasped for breath and clawed at his arm. Inside the warehouse, something heavy crashed to the ground. The diamond eyes of my golden snake ring flashed orange in the firelight.

"You've cost me my position, Mr. Adler," Collins said. "Twenty years of service without a reference to show for it. What am I to do now?"

Hysterical laughter bubbled up inside me. If he hadn't been slowly strangling me, I might have told him the names of a few gentlemen who would have paid handsomely to feel his impossibly muscled chest against their backs.

I struggled, but it was no use. He was stronger than a team of oxen, and I was going to die at his hands.

"It's nothing personal," he said gamely. "If it's any comfort, I always thought you were the best of the lot."

There was a roar as the roof of the warehouse collapsed. Flames shot up, raining down sparks and debris. Collins threw a hand up to shield his head. I ducked out of his grip and managed a long, sweet breath before those massive arms pulled me back and crushed my face into his chest. Something Zhi Sen had once said about momentum and acquiescence came back to me. Instead of pulling away, I charged forward into his chest, not stopping until I heard the crack of his tailbone against the railing. The manservant's height made him imposing, but also top-heavy. While I struggled to slip free, his feet scrambled for purchase on the wet concrete. When one of his hands reached for the railing, I gave a violent twist. There was a cry, and I looked up to see the manservant's boots disappearing over the edge of the railing.

I stood discharging the gun into the filthy water until red bubbles rose up through the water and the empty chambers of the revolver clicked past again and again.

"Mr. Adler!"

I swung the empty revolver toward the staircase. A man was running down from the warehouse. Fire still raged, but the smell of wet ash was creeping into the air. The firemen would soon have the blaze contained. The man reached the bottom of the staircase and started toward me. A few yards later he saw the gun and stopped.

"Mr. Adler?" Watkins said.

I lowered the revolver. My fingers were locked so tightly around the handle, I couldn't have holstered it if I'd wanted to. As Watkins bounded toward me, he gave a low whistle.

"Wot 'appened 'ere?"

"Best not to ask," I said with a shaky laugh.

There were five men dead—two in the canal and the other three clearly dispatched with prejudice.

"But you've got it all under control," he said.

I shoved the gun into my waistband. My eyes burned from the smoke. The struggle with Collins had wrenched my back. My feet were raw and bleeding stumps. There'd be a garland of bruises around my neck in the morning, and I would surely vomit the moment I was alone.

"Yeah," I said. "'S under control."

"Then wot about them poor blighters in the boat?"

Chapter Eighteen

The water was thick, scummy, and cold as fuck. I sank like a stone and spluttered to the surface some yards away. Daylight would show the canal to be the color of strong coffee. The smell would fell an ox. But Nate had died to get the brothel children this far. Mrs. Wu had been dragged off by a sadistic criminal. And now the children were drifting toward a rough, heavily trafficked river in a craft that would shatter into toothpicks at the first sign of resistance.

"All right, Mr. Adler?" Watkins called, his tone peevish.

He'd understood what I'd meant to do and had tried to stop me from jumping. I hadn't let him. After hurling the gun and Mrs. Wu's bag, I'd flung the coat at him and leaped. Goddard would have his hide. If Goddard survived. As I swam toward the little craft, Watkins paced back and forth along the walkway like a schoolboy outside the headmaster's office. Something brushed my foot. I shook off the image of Collins, bloated and pale, reaching up to grasp my ankle.

In the light of the burning warehouse, I could make out four small shapes huddled in the boat. God only knew where Mrs. Wu had been taking them when Lazarus and I interrupted. In any event, the man holding the mooring rope had dropped it when I shot him. Now the unlit boat was drifting toward the treacherous, crowded waters of the Thames.

"Jus' wave if you needs 'elp, then," Watkins called.

I wasn't a strong swimmer, but with some effort, I managed to flail my way to where the vessel had run up against a mass of debris in the center of the canal. As I hooked my arm over one side, I saw a black puddle of water gathering around the children's feet.

"Well," I panted. With my other hand, I gave my face a vigorous rub. "Shall we bring this pleasure cruise to an end?"

Towing a small boat across half a canal is more difficult than it sounds, but somehow, I managed without drowning anyone. There were four children—three boys and a very small girl who blinked at me with liquid black eyes that caught the fire. With Watkins's assistance, I hauled myself out of the water and looped the boat's soggy rope around the mooring post. My feet, which had been merely raw earlier, began throbbing. I was suddenly desperate to remove my boots. There'd be no getting them back on again, I realized.

"Wot's all this, then?" Watkins asked, eyeing the cargo warily.

"This," I said with a grimace, "is your good deed for the week. Perhaps even for the year."

My belongings lay in a heap at the foot of the staircase. The two bodies that had been there when I'd jumped were conspicuously absent. Rubbing his hands clean on his trousers, Watkins crouched beside the boat and one by one lifted the children onto the walkway with the gentleness of a father.

Our young passengers were frightened, begrimed, and surrounded by a miasma of opium and urine, but their skin was clear of bruises. More importantly, none looked back at me with that haunted, violated expression Nate had schooled his face not to show. The fact they'd been spared both violations only to ensure a higher selling price didn't lessen my relief. Nothing would erase from my mind the image of that basement cell where Nate had met his end in his ill-fated rescue attempt. Nor would anything make me stop wondering how many children had passed through there before.

"Well?" Watkins asked, his voice hard with protectiveness.

"They're very far from home," I said. "The less you know about why, the better."

I stripped off my shirt and wrung it out over the canal. I was about to give my trousers the same treatment, when I noticed Watkins performing the same quick inspection of the children I had. I settled for twisting the water out of my trouser legs as best as I could while still wearing them.

"Whatever happened before, they're safe now, thanks to you," I said, after Watkins turned back to me. "Take them to Stepney Clinic, and Nurse Brand will see they're cared for. Go immediately. Don't stop along the way, and speak of this to no one. If Dr. Goddard asks, they drowned in the river."

His eyebrows drew together at this, but he grimly nodded. Even if he eventually did tell Goddard the truth, Goddard had more to worry about right now than some incidental property of Acton's. And the delay would give Pearl time to remove the children to a safe location.

"Wot 'bout you?" Watkins asked.

"I'm going to find the man responsible for bringing them here, and put a bullet in his brain."

He nodded.

"You'd better take this, then." He handed me his own pistol. "Yours is spent."

I thanked him and tucked it into my waistband. I hobbled over to the staircase to retrieve my things. I pulled on the tweed coat and slung Mrs. Wu's bag over my shoulder. The little rag doll was still in the coat pocket. I'd return it to its owner at the nearest opportunity, but first it had one last job to do. I made to tuck Sinclair's pistol into the other pocket when I remembered its owner.

"One more thing, Mr. Watkins," I called.

He looked up from the little boy whose tunic he was straightening.

"There's another…er…one in the shadows a few yards to the west. Dr. Goddard would prefer it not remain there."

"Understood, Mr. Adler," Watkins called back. "Good luck to you."

I considered the empty revolver in my hand then pitched it into the canal. As I made my slow, painful way up the staircase, I watched Watkins stride toward Sinclair's body, to deliver it to his final destination. If Goddard made it through the night, and if I made it back to Goddard, I would see that Watkins received a handsome reward.

The staircase ended some yards from the ruined warehouse. The fire brigade had cleared all the idlers from the area and had settled down for a long, laborious night. Amid the crackling wood and firemen's cries, I heard a faint splash from the canal behind me as Watkins sent Sinclair to his watery grave. How many of Goddard's men would meet the same fate? I hoped Watkins would not be among them.

I skirted along the edge of the property until I came to Narrow Street. Somewhere in the darkness a clock struck ten. The burst of energy that had carried me through the last three hours suddenly dissolved, leaving me exhausted in body and mind, and my nerves shot to hell. I forced my throbbing feet to continue until I reached a well-traveled section of Commercial Road, and then I slumped against a lamppost and hailed a cab. The first driver slowed until he got a good look at me, and nearly ran me down in his effort to get away. The second didn't bother to slow. When a third cab rattled by—one wheel larger than the other and the left door hanging by one hinge—I tottered off the curb into its path.

"Ye gods, what a stink!" the driver cried by way of greeting.

"Take me where I need to go," I said, "and this is yours."

The driver gaped at the sovereign in my hand.

"Or you can choose this."

I flashed my pistol, but the driver was too busy scrambling down to open the door to take offense. The seat was ripped, the stuffing compressed to nothing. I sank down onto it gratefully, and the half-doors clicked shut in front of my knees.

"Well, then, sir." The driver grinned, eyes fixed firmly on the dosh. He could skive off for the rest of the week and still come out on top. "Where to?"

York Street was the obvious answer. Cain had been lying there for some time already, waiting for me. My chest clenched at the thought. I wanted nothing so much as to crawl into bed with him and take him in my arms—or to sit at his bedside if he was too injured for that. I imagined holding his warm, dry hand between my own while he slept. After everything he had done for me, I could at least tell him honestly and confidently that his affections were returned in full. The corners of my eyes burned at the thought. How useless I was, if this was the only thing I could do! And what an utter bastard I was for having taken this long to even consider the question!

On the other hand, even if I couldn't put Cain Goddard back together again, perhaps I still had a role to play. Southeast of York Street lay St. James's. An hour ago Lazarus had gone armed with nothing but courage and an ancient pistol to rescue Mrs. Wu and take back his name. Our blackmailer was dead, and Goddard was under the supervision of the finest medical minds in London. And though Lazarus would sooner have died than admitted it, he couldn't handle Acton by himself. It was settled, then.

"The East India Officers' Club," I said, "St. James's Square."

Like many gentlemen's clubs, the white three-story building from which Edward Acton directed his own criminal network maintained a number of rooms for its members' temporary lodging. It was no surprise to find the front door attended even at that late hour. But nothing could have surprised the weasel-faced doorman more than finding me on his doorstep.

Except, perhaps, the stench I brought with me.

"Edward Acton," I said without preamble.

A long moment passed during which the only sound was the drip-drip-drip of brown canal water onto scrubbed steps. So offensive was my presence the man had been struck dumb. Then his lip curled.

"I cannot imagine any contingency that would force Dr. Acton to interact with the likes of you," he said, stepping behind the door.

He was an over-pomaded little prick in his forties, with arms and legs like pencils and a neck that might that might have snapped in a strong wind. At the same instant he moved to close the door, I shoved it back hard. He hit the wall behind with a satisfying thud and slid to the floor.

"You will take me to him now," I said, as he skittered backward, "If he asks, you'll say it's about this."

I brandished the little rag doll. In the haste of his retreat, the doorman bumped into the wall. Remembering his dignity, he slowly rose along it, never taking his eyes from the doll.

"You've seen its like before," I said as I advanced. "How many times?"

He knew all about Acton's vile trade—it was written on his face. I kicked the door shut behind me and drew the pistol.

"You'll take me to him, by God, or you'll wish the constables had got here first."

He fixed me with a black scowl, but glancing from the gun to the doll, he reluctantly signaled for me to follow down the narrow corridor. A fire was blazing in the visitors' hall, though the room was empty. We turned at the end of the corridor. He stopped before the last door on the left, but rapped so ineffectually I was forced to push him aside and put my shoulder to it.

The door burst open. I caught a glimpse of an old man behind his desk before a foot swept my legs from under me and a set of hands threw me to the ground.

"Mr…Adler, is it?" a voice asked.

The hands lifted me to my knees and wrenched away my pistol. The air was hot and smelled of blood. Someone groaned. I caught sight of Lazarus slumped in a chair at the back of the room before the hands forced my face straight ahead.

Edward Acton sat behind a desk at the back of a sparsely but expensively furnished office. In the center of the desk was a paraffin lamp turned low, and behind that an immaculate blotter. A black leather case sat on atop the blotter—too large for spectacles, but too small for papers. Beside it was a small, stoppered bottle. From Lazarus's story, I'd expected a giant. Acton looked more like a pixie, with his delicate limbs and translucent skin, which, seemed to glow in the lamplight. He was dressed in a silk *robe de chambre*, though his cloud of hair and thick silver mustache had been combed, and his ice-blue eyes were bright.

"I've seen you in Dr. Goddard's company, of course, but what on earth are you doing here?"

I glanced from Acton to Lazarus seated behind him. Lazarus's left eye was purple and swelling. Someone had broken his nose again. Blood spattered the scarf they had used to gag him, as well as the front of his once-white shirt. As he met my eyes, he shook his head almost imperceptibly.

"You'll forgive my caution, Mr. Adler," Acton went on. "I'd no idea when I retired to my rooms this evening, that fate was about to drop two of my greatest irritants into my lap—Dr. Parker, there," he nodded toward Lazarus. "And Zhen-zhen Wu. When I heard the front door, I wondered, quite frankly, if it weren't that useless son-in-law of mine, coming to make the evening complete."

"Sinclair's dead," I said.

Acton's eyebrows shot up.

"Dare I hope?"

"I killed him," I said.

"Well, then." Acton's tone was suddenly warm. He made a gesture, and the hands at my elbows, now gentle, lifted me to my feet. "I suppose I owe you a debt of gratitude. How kind of you to inform me in person."

"Actually," I said, "I'm looking for Mrs. Wu. I saw your men apprehend her, and followed them here."

"Oh?"

Acton folded his arms across his chest and leaned back in his chair. I hadn't intended to ingratiate myself to the man, but he seemed so pleased I'd snuffed Sinclair I wondered whether I might be able to broker Lazarus's freedom as well as Mrs. Wu's.

"Zhen-zhen Wu and her friends have made it their mission to disrupt a very lucrative arm of my business," he said. "I was looking forward to dispatching her in the same way that I had her husband. What's your business with her?"

Up until that evening, my only interest in Mrs. Wu had been the porcelain dog. But if I was correct, she and Nate had been working together to get the brothel children to safety. There was no doubt Pearl could eventually find a place for them in a workhouse or an orphanage. But if Mrs. Wu had better plans, she had to have the chance to execute them.

Of course I couldn't tell him that.

"Sinclair stole something that belongs to Dr. Goddard," I said. "A porcelain statue. I recovered the statue from Sinclair, but Mrs. Wu recovered it from me."

"I see." He steepled his fingers beneath his chin. "And what's the significance of this statue?"

"It's not my business to know. However, Dr. Goddard is very anxious for its return."

Lazarus moaned softly in his corner. What had he been thinking, coming to beard Acton in his den with nothing more than a decade-old service revolver and a tintype of his girl? He was lucky I was there, and not at the bottom of the canal. I shifted my weight from foot to foot. The leather was cutting into the sides of my feet. My toes felt like pincushions.

Acton cleared his throat.

"Dr. Goddard has been a valuable associate for a long time, and you, Mr. Adler, have done me a great favor. I shall extract the location of your statue before I send Mrs. Wu to hell to see her husband. Morrison?"

The man behind me made an affirmative grunt and moved toward the door.

"Wait," I said. "Time is of the essence. Dr. Goddard is most insistent about that. If you'll release Mrs. Wu long enough to lead me to the statue, I'll take care of her once I have it."

He cocked his head. The man definitely wasn't stupid. I wondered whether I had just signed my own death warrant.

"That's a kind offer," he said after a moment. "But I have plans for Mrs. Wu, just as I do for Dr. Parker. All the same, for Goddard's sake, I suppose I could postpone my enjoyment for an hour or two." He stood. "You may borrow Mrs. Wu to find your statue, but I'll send a man with you. Once you have what you need, you'll disappear, and Mrs. Wu shall return to me."

"Agreed," I said. It wasn't optimal, but it was better than nothing. "May I have my gun back?"

Acton laughed.

"I'm generous, Mr. Adler, but I'm not naïve."

Acton instructed Morrison to prepare a car, and to put Mrs. Wu in it. I followed him to the door, then stopped and turned.

"What are your plans for Dr. Parker, if I might ask?"

Acton frowned. "I can't see how that's any of your concern."

My heart raced. As quick as Acton had been to extend his good graces, he would be even quicker to retract them. But he was going to kill Lazarus, and I had used up my favor. I hoped what I was about to do wouldn't bode ill for Goddard.

"Dr. Parker is a friend of mine," I said. "As was Nate Turnbull, before you had him killed."

Lazarus's eyes went wide as I took the little Afghan doll from my pocket, tossed it into the air, and caught it in the other hand.

"You may not be aware that Nate was keeping records of your basement visitors at Fitzroy Street. When he died, those records came to me. If you release Dr. Parker, I shall turn them over to you. Otherwise, they'll be on some constable's desk by morning, whether by my hand, or by that of the friend whom I've instructed to deliver them, in the event that I don't return."

Acton's face went white. When he spoke again, his voice was quiet with fury.

"I wonder what your employer would think if he knew he had a blackmailer on his staff."

"Dr. Goddard employs several blackmailers," I said. "We're cheaper than assassins and get better results."

Behind me came the metallic click of a pistol. A cold steel barrel pressed into the base of my skull. I wasn't sure which was more appalling—the gun at the back of my head, or the fact the law that nearly sent me to prison might now save my skin.

"Labouchere's amendment is four years old," I said, trying to keep my voice steady. "But no one has forgotten why they passed it. If you think that your connections can protect you once word about those children reaches the papers, you are delusional."

Mr. Labouchere's opus had addressed indecency between men. However, its success had come from equating, in the mind of the public, adult indecency with the sort of exploitation of children that Nate had documented. Once proof of Acton's crimes had been published, he would never be safe again, and he knew it. Hatred seethed behind his ice-blue eyes.

"Very well," he said through clenched teeth. "Morrison, you shall accompany Mr. Adler and Mrs. Wu to retrieve the statue and the documents. If there's any foolishness, shoot Mr. Adler with his own gun." He turned to me. "Satisfied? Then get out. Not you, Doctor," Acton said as behind him, Lazarus began to rise.

Acton removed a hypodermic needle from the leather case on his desk. The light of the paraffin lamp danced over the metal as he drew clear liquid from the bottle into the chamber. Two men wrestled Lazarus to the desk.

"I, too, employ blackmailers, Mr. Adler. It pays to take precautions when dealing with them."

Lazarus struggled, but Acton's man held him tightly, while another rolled up his sleeve and held his arm still against the desk. Acton pushed the plunger home, withdrew the needle, then turned to me with a cold smile.

"Dr. Parker will remember the impressive effects of elapid venom upon the human constitution. Fortunately, in the years since he witnessed it, an antidote has been developed. Bring me the documents, and I will administer the antidote. You have two hours before he loses consciousness, but if he really is your friend, Mr. Adler, you'll be back well before then."

The men pushed Lazarus back toward his chair. He stumbled, collapsed against the wall, then slid to the ground beside it. As he looked up at me imploringly, a large drop of blood gathered below one nostril.

"I'll hurry," I promised him.

"Yes," said Acton, "And in the meantime, I shall decide to what degree I shall allow this incident to reflect upon your employer."

Chapter Nineteen

Acton's carriage cut through the darkness as silently as a shark. The chassis rose slightly, then dipped as the smooth streets around St. James's gave way to more-traveled pavement. On the bench across from mine, Mrs. Wu clutched her bag in her lap.

"I'm surprised they left us alone in here together," I said.

"Morrison knows better than to shut himself in a small space with me."

The carriage swayed, and the curtains swung open, briefly bathing her bruised face in gaslight. She'd learned Zhi Sen's fighting system at his knee, and I'd no doubt Morrison had come out the worse for their struggle. He'd been disappointed when Acton had instructed him to bring us back alive.

Before they'd packed us into the carriage, Mrs. Wu had told the driver the statue was back at the shop on Dorset Street. I couldn't fathom why she'd return it to the very place from which it had nearly been stolen, but as long as I'd eventually have it in my hand, I supposed it didn't matter. She glanced at me warily. She had no reason to trust me. She'd picked my pocket, and her father was stabbing Goddard in the back. She probably thought I'd rescued her from Acton's wrath so that I could indulge my own.

"All I want is the porcelain dog," I said. "Then I'll find some way for you to slip away."

"Why would you do that?"

"To thwart that prick, Acton, for one."

I was also doing it for Nate's sake. Not to mention Pearl would be stuck with four Afghan orphans if Mrs. Wu wasn't able to eventually retrieve them.

I rubbed my bleary eyes, shuffled my throbbing feet. The stink of the river was thick inside the carriage. If I had it to do again, I'd still have jumped in after the boat, but selflessness wasn't going to spare me a world of pain.

"That, and Nate told me everything before he died. The opium, the children, everything," I said.

"You were there when he died?" she asked.

"I was at the clinic when Sinclair tossed him out of a carriage. Nate was a friend of mine. He wasn't alone."

"I'm glad," she said.

I opened the thick curtains on each side of the carriage and secured them. The shadows and treetops of the embankment gardens flashed past on the left. To the right, the new road rolled by beside the river.

"Nate was a good man," Mrs. Wu said. "He used to carry messages between Sinclair and my father. That's how we met, how he became involved with my husband's organization."

"The organization that's been such a thorn in Acton's side."

She nodded. "The children are casualties in a much larger war. I'm not certain if you're aware, Mr. Adler, of the devastation that opium has caused in my homeland. Since your government will not listen to reason, and our own has been overruled by force, our group, and others like it, have taken matters into our own hands."

"You blew up the warehouse," I said.

"The Duke of Dorset Street didn't choose that location for his school simply because he liked the view."

It made sense. Goddard rarely used anything, or anyone, for only one purpose. I wondered if Zhi Sen knew.

"It would be a convenient place for receiving and distributing shipments," I admitted.

"And for exporting high-alkaloid opium back to China," she said.

"Does your father know about your group?"

She shook her head bitterly.

"Zhi Sen is blind to everything but his own ambition. He'd

probably hand me over to Acton himself if he knew what we'd done. Of course, that's exactly what you'll do once you have what you want."

True, it's what Goddard would have done. Acton was his master, and Mrs. Wu was an annoyance on a number of levels. But I wasn't Goddard. I couldn't pretend his indifference to suffering, and I couldn't see human beings as commodities to be bought and sold. I'd spent the better part of the last two years building a life around Goddard's philosophy, and yet it hadn't taken but this short, strange week to show me how meaningless such a life actually was.

"No. I meant what I said," I told her. "Get me the statue, and you'll go free, if we have to kill those two with our bare hands." I gestured toward the seat at the front of the carriage, where the driver and Morrison sat. "I already know you're good in a fight."

This earned a small smile.

"You're an honorable man, Mr. Adler," she said. "We, too, strive for honorable goals. You should join us. Change the world, rather than living at the sufferance of those who control it."

Goddard's words came back to me: *saving the world is a losing battle, and not nearly as much fun as running it.* But it wasn't about fun anymore. My friend was dead, and I'd come face-to-face with four young people whose innocence had been the price at which my life of luxury had been purchased. At the same time, I was still living at Goddard's sufferance. He might have found my new scruples amusing, but he wouldn't tolerate them for long if they began to interfere with business.

"Perhaps we should save ourselves before taking on the international opium trade," I suggested.

The carriage turned left onto Bishopsgate, the wheels sloshing through abattoir sludge as we passed by dark-windowed warehouses. The slaughterhouse smells of Cheapside eventually gave way to the ambrosial fragrances rising from the carts and barrows serving theatre-bound crowds in Shoreditch. My stomach growled. Above us, the driver cursed loudly as traffic slowed to a crawl.

"The children are safe, by the way," I said. "I sent them to Stepney Street after pulling them out of the river. Not sure what Pearl's going to do with them, but they'll be fed and given a bed for the night."

"Is this why you stink like a barge full of offal?" she asked.

"I prefer to think of it as the strong smell of heroism."

Her lips twisted wryly. "Then I shall give you the porcelain dog with a clear conscience. And, since your presence here tells me Sinclair must be dead, I have no further need of it."

"Because you were using the evidence inside to blackmail him, to keep him from going to Acton while you and Nate got the children to safety," I said.

"We should have killed him a long time ago, but Nate wouldn't hear of it."

"You'll be happy to know that his death was most unpleasant," I said.

Once the streets cleared, it was a short, silent ride to Miller's Court. Foremost on my mind, of course, was exactly how we'd go about freeing ourselves once the statue was in our possession. Mrs. Wu had already demonstrated her fighting prowess. Knowing this, both Morrison and the driver had surely armed themselves—one with my own weapon. Though Acton's orders would make them think twice about shooting me, they'd probably leap at the opportunity to rough us up a bit. As for Mrs. Wu, Morrison had likely been planning her death since he made the mistake of tangling with her back at the warehouse.

Eventually, the carriage turned onto Dorset Street and came to a stop. The door opened, and Morrison's great, scarred face appeared in the window.

"You might be interested to know," Mrs. Wu said as she stepped onto the running board, "that my father pays the owner of this shop a handsome sum to store the opium that he was buying from Sinclair behind Goddard's back."

"Thank you," I said. Goddard would be most interested indeed.

She set her bag near my feet and hopped down. Morrison took her arm, holding her away as if she might bite.

"Forgetting something?" I asked, nodding at the bag.

"Keep it safe," she said. "I have a feeling you'll be needing it more than I will."

Once they disappeared into the alley, I eased myself out onto the running board to survey the situation. The driver was a stout fellow, but the stout that comes from chips and beer rather than hard animal bulk like Morrison. He was in his fifties, and looked as if he'd have given his left eye to be putting his feet up somewhere rather than babysitting the likes of me. It wouldn't take much to overpower him, provided he didn't draw the gun that bulged obscenely in his jacket pocket. And provided that he didn't raise a cry, for if he did, Morrison would put Mrs. Wu down like a rabid dog before running out to finish me.

I slid back onto my bench. My feet felt like hives of angry bees. My head pounded. I tugged at my collar. Jumping into the canal had been a mistake. The Thames was the toilet of London. Excrement, factory runoff, slaughterhouse remains—it all ended up there. I'd been careful not to swallow a drop, but in my haste to get to the boat before it drifted into the river, I'd forgotten how the afternoon's unaccustomed walking had turned my feet into an engraved invitation to any number of infections lurking in that vile soup. A shiver ran through me, even as a sudden flood of sweat ran down my neck. But this wasn't the time to indulge in panic. Once the porcelain dog was back in Goddard's hands, and Lazarus free from Acton's clutches, once Mrs. Wu had been released to fight the scourge of opium on every shore, only then would I have the luxury of worrying about some wretched infection.

I'm not sure how long I sat there, fingers pressed to eyelids, trying to replace morbid thoughts with a workable plan, but when distant chimes tolled one, I sat up. We had left Acton's club a little after midnight, by my estimation. Even allowing time for travel, Mrs. Wu should already have found the statue. The storeroom simply wasn't that large. Above me, the driver let out a long sigh. The carriage rocked as he shifted in his seat. This was taking too long. Acton had said that Lazarus had two hours before he lost consciousness. In the meantime, who knew what he was going through? I considered making a run for Miller's Court, but that would have only given the driver an excuse to shoot me. Instead, I took a deep breath and lifted Mrs. Wu's bag into my lap.

There was something heavy inside the rough black sack. My heart leaped with the thought that it might be a gun, then sank, when loosening the drawstring revealed a bundle of most decidedly the wrong shape, wrapped tightly in rags. I cursed under my breath. What on earth could she have thought that I'd need at this point more than a weapon?

I brushed a damp clump of curls back from my forehead, then addressed the complicated series of knots. Whatever it was, someone had trussed it up like a mummy. Perhaps I'd manage to unwrap it in my afterlife. A few moments later, I lifted away the last of the rags, and the porcelain dog fell into my lap, grinning, its gold-touched eyes aflame with gaslight.

"I'll be damned," I said.

Something rattled inside. A note? A photograph? Documents? My heart raced. Whatever it was, was the only known evidence that could be used to convict Goddard of criminal sodomy. I felt around the statue for some way inside, but the hole in the bottom had been plastered over. I was about to smash it on the floor when shots rang out in Miller's Court.

Shoving the statue back into the bag, I slung it over my back and crept to the door. Above me, I heard the driver cock his gun. Were I to run for the storeroom, I'd have a bullet in my back before I hit the alley. And if I somehow escaped the bullet, I'd either find Mrs. Wu dead and Morrison standing over her with another bullet ready, or Morrison with a hole in his skull and Mrs. Wu vanished like the wind. I'd done what I could for her. I had the dog. Now I had to concentrate on getting Nate's documents and springing Lazarus.

I slid silently to the ground, wobbling on numb feet. The driver was peering down the alley, the gun resting on his thigh. Before I could change my mind, I swung up onto the coachmman's step. He gaped for a second before I smashed his nose with a quick punch. I shoved his pistol into my waistband, then half dragged, half pushed him over the side. I slapped the reins. As we tore off down Dorset Street, he began to shout.

❖

Stepney Clinic wasn't far. Once I got the horses going in a straight line, it couldn't have taken long at all, though urgency made every moment feel like an hour, and every block like a mile. When the horses finally stumbled to a stop at the mouth of the alley, I was nearly blind with panic.

"What took you so long?" I demanded when Pearl opened the door.

"Could be them four patients you sent me," she said as I pushed past. "Who are they, anyway? Where'd they come from?"

The clinic was empty, but in the stillness, I could hear the faint sound of hushed breathing coming from the infirmary. It amazed me that they'd be able to sleep in a strange place after what they'd been through. On the other hand, I didn't dare sit down for fear that I'd do exactly the same.

"Poor mites," she went on. "They look like they ain't ate in a week. Have you seen the doctor, by the way? He had the night shift, startin' at nine o'clock, but as you can see, he ain't here." She narrowed her eyes. "Don't have nothin' to do with you, by any chance?"

It had everything to do with me, but no good would be served by admitting as much. If Pearl murdered me, then Lazarus was worse than dead.

I pushed past her and hurried toward the dispensary. Lazarus hadn't told me where he'd hidden Nate's documents, but I had a good idea. Pearl followed, close on my heels.

"I know you don't have a lot of room here," I said, turning suddenly. My fingers brushed against the little Afghan doll as they rifled through the coat pocket for coins. "Perhaps this will make things easier until Mrs. Wu comes to retrieve them."

Her eyes went wide at the stack of coins I pressed into her hand.

"If she comes," I added. "By the way, do you have the keys to the dispensary?"

"But what…who…what…" She stared at the lump in her hand as if she'd never seen money before. Then she looked up. "The dispensary?"

"Never mind."

I fished my picklocks from the other pocket. There was a tobacco canister on the top shelf of one of the cabinets where Lazarus squirreled away precious oddments that had no other rightful place. I let myself into the dispensary, made quick work of the cabinet lock, and then found myself a stool.

"No, the doctor doesn't know," I said as Pearl opened her mouth to protest this invasion. "But I can't imagine that he'd object. Excellent," I said, as I lifted the lid and saw the familiar reddish brown cover of the client book.

Both ledgers were there, as well as the letters, and, to my surprise, Nate's watch. The papers went into my right coat pocket. I dropped the watch into the left with the picklocks. I was about to close the lid on Tim's little treasure box when my eyes fell on something that I couldn't imagine anyone would consider worth saving. And yet as I plucked it from beneath an extra set of house keys, it was painfully obvious why Lazarus had.

After nearly four years, the cork was shriveled and dry. Yet it was still redolent with the scent of the mid-priced bottle of Bordeaux that Lazarus had bought for my twenty-second birthday. We had shared it, and a small spread of bread, sausage, cheese, and liquor-filled chocolates, on a wobbly table in the sordid little room that Lazarus had called home at that time.

"Ira?" Pearl asked.

Feeling a strange combination of nausea and guilt, I dropped the cork back into the canister. I replaced the canister on the shelf and hopped down.

"Lazarus won't be coming in tonight," I said.

"But—"

"I don't know when he'll be back. Is there a relief doctor?"

"Yes, but—"

"Then send for him. One more thing," I said.

The one thing that had kept Acton from putting a bullet in me was the threat that his crimes would be exposed if he did. It was an idle threat, but now that I had the documents in my hand, there was no reason it had to remain one. Aside from the client book, Acton had no idea what manner of documents Nate had been keeping. And the client ledger and the opium book looked much the same, both inside and out. I tucked one of the letters into the client ledger and thrust it into her hand before she could say a word.

"Make as many copies as you can," I said. "If Lazarus and I don't return by first post, send them to all of the major newspapers and to Scotland Yard."

"But what about the children?" she asked.

"You must have ten quid in your hand, Pearl. If Mrs. Wu doesn't come for them, you can open a bleeding orphanage. Oh, and there's this." I handed her the doll. "I believe it belongs to the little girl. What time is it?"

She frowned at the watch pinned to the front of her apron.

"Half past one."

Good God, Lazarus had half an hour left. And that would depend upon how much of the poison was in his system, and how much blood it had caused him to lose. I remembered Lazarus's description of the Afghan prisoners at Bala Hissar and shuddered. He might already be dead by now, and it would be my fault.

"Ira?" she called as I half ran, half stumbled toward the front door.

The stinging sensation in my feet had been replaced by an ominous cold, but the carriage was still there, unmolested, to my surprise, quite frankly.

"I'll explain it all later," I said as I clambered into the driver's seat.

Pearl had followed me to the mouth of the alley, muttering objections the entire way. Now she stood on the sidewalk, arms folded under her substantial bosom, features stony with the disapproval that covered worry.

"I don't like the look of that limp," she said as I pulled the carriage away from the curb.

"First post," I repeated. "Then send those letters to every newspaper in London."

❖

The Great Clock was striking two when I shambled up the front steps of the East India Officers' Club. The door swept open before I could raise my fist, and the doorman didn't so much as raise an eyebrow as I stumbled past him down the corridor to Acton's office. The door was open. Acton looked up from his desk as I slumped against the jamb.

"Ah, Mr. Adler, right on time. Dr. Parker will be happy to know you're as good a friend as he thought you would be, if he wakes up."

Lazarus was unconscious, as Acton had predicted he would be. Blood had crusted along the bottom of his face and his neck, and every now and then he twitched in his chair, as if poked by a hot needle. Something dark and dangerous stirred inside me. I touched the pistol through the stained tweed of my jacket.

"The antidote," I said.

I shook out one foot, then the other. My face felt like it was on fire. I could smell my own sweat above the stink of the canal.

"Is there something the matter with your feet?" Acton asked.

"Blisters…canal water…it's none of your business, really. We had a bargain."

"Then give me the papers."

I slipped my hands into my pockets, caressing the documents with one, and the pistol with the other. There was no one else in the room except for Lazarus, and he was in no position to object to a bit of instant justice. Between his dead weight and my increasingly useless feet, though, I wondered how far we'd get before the sound of gunfire brought Acton's men running. Lazarus shivered violently. Cursing under my breath, I thrust the documents toward him.

"Well, Mr. Turnbull was certainly busy," Acton said as he examined one of the letters. "*I'm gon tell em all startin wiv the Times.* Charming."

My heart stopped when he glanced at the ledger, but apparently it hadn't occurred to him that there could be more than one. He slipped it into the pocket of his robe without comment.

"There are letters here to every major newspaper," he said, looking up. "I am truly in your debt."

"Just get the antidote."

My teeth were starting to chatter, though the night was far from cold. All I had to do was get Lazarus to the carriage, and I'd be in a hot bath before the hour was out.

"Wouldn't you care for a cup of—" Acton began.

"Now," I said.

Only after I'd drawn the pistol did I understand the gravity of my error. The last time Acton had seen me with a gun, his man had been taking it away from me. Now he looked from it to me, his face darkening with rage.

"Where's my driver? Where's Mrs. Wu?"

"You might ask Morrison that," I said. "He took her out of my sight. Moments later, I heard gunfire. I assumed that I was next. I was forced to take matters into my own hands, but I did keep my end of the bargain. You will give Dr. Parker the antidote, and you will give it now."

"And if I don't?"

Sweat seared my eyes. My shirt felt damp beneath my arms, but I kept the gun trained on Acton as he circled around toward Lazarus's chair.

"I've killed three people tonight," I said. "Four is a nice, round number."

"My men will be on you like flies on a corpse."

I thought I detected a quaver in his voice, but one couldn't be sure. Lazarus twitched again, and a sudden stream of blood ran down from his nose to his chest. I tightened my finger around the trigger.

"Mrs. Wu was part of the bargain," Acton said. "You're not getting the antidote. Leave now, and we're even."

It took an unprecedented act of will not to shoot him where he stood. But if I had, then neither Lazarus nor I would have left that room. If I did as Acton said, however, there was a chance that I could get Lazarus to a hospital, and that someone there might be able to help him. If the hospital stocked antidotes for the venoms of rare Asian vipers, that is, and if it wasn't already too late.

"I'm taking him with me," I said, stepping toward Lazarus.

Acton laughed. "Be my guest, Mr. Adler. There's no sport in tormenting a dying man. You'll save me the trouble of disposing of his remains."

He moved aside as I tottered to the back of the room. Still keeping the gun pointed at Acton, I looped Lazarus's limp arm around my neck and lifted him to his feet. I'd no idea how such a slight man could be so heavy, and even less idea how I'd manage to shift him all the way to the carriage without assistance. The first numb-footed step almost sent us both to the floor. The second step was only slightly less excruciating. Leaning against his desk, his lips curled with amusement, Acton watched us make our pathetic way toward the door.

"I do believe, Mr. Adler," Acton said as we reached the hallway, "that I'll leave your discipline to Dr. Goddard. That is, if the infection of your feet doesn't solve the problem for him."

❖

I stumbled twice as we descended the front stairs. The second time, Lazarus slipped out of my arms, which was actually a blessing; it was a lot easier to just roll him the rest of the way down and to the edge of the pavement. He was starting to come to as I heaved him onto the running board of the carriage, or perhaps it was convulsions. Either way, between my pulling and his flailing, I managed to get him onto the carriage floor. I leaned against the open door and mopped my face with my sleeve.

"Don't worry," I said. "We'll go straight to London Hospital. Someone will remember you. Someone has to be able to help."

Every inch of my body was aflame. I was dangerously light-headed. When he spoke, I was half-convinced it was hallucination.

"Home," came his dry hiss of a whisper. "Just take me home."

"But—"

"Home, Adler," he said. And then he said no more.

I drove the horses hell-for-leather to St. Andrews's Baker Street residence. When the butler came to the door, hair askew, a robe covering his pajamas, he looked as if he'd have been happy to give me a good thrashing. But at the mention of the doctor's name, he came to the carriage without delay or complaint. I opened the door, petrified of what I might find.

What I did find was Lazarus perched on the edge of the bench, eyes tired but bright, his shirt-sleeve stained by his attempt to clean the blood from his face and neck. He winked at me.

"Fenwick," he said, with a weak smile, as the butler offered him a hand. "Completely unnecessary for you to come all the way down the stairs." He stumbled on the running board, then gratefully took Fenwick's proffered arm. "But welcome, nonetheless."

"What in blazes?" I demanded as they began the long creep up the front stairs.

Lazarus turned, a spark of mischief in his eye. "I've been injecting myself with small amounts of venom from the carpet viper since I returned from Afghanistan. The immunity isn't perfect by any means," he said, dabbing at his nose, "but I'm happy to see that, despite ruining a shirt once a month, the experiment ultimately paid off. Sorry to have frightened you, Adler. Do come in for a moment. You look as if you're about to drop."

I followed them up the stairs on numb feet. Now safe, the surge of energy that had brought me this far began to drain away. I shut the front door behind me and slumped against it. Goddard and St. Andrews had similar taste in vestibule furnishings. Chinese vases, colorful fish, grandfather clock. I wondered what Goddard was doing right then. I hoped he was well.

"Ah yes, your ring," Lazarus said as I absently fingered the golden snake. He was looking almost chipper by that point as he hung his jacket on the rack. "The jeweler was unable to give us any additional information about Mr. Turnbull's watch, as I predicted. However he could say with confidence that your ring had been cast last December. It caused quite a stir, as you can imagine: a copy of Her Majesty's, but with, as you pointed out, more expensive materials. You have quite an admirer, it seems."

His voice sounded far away, but the note of envy was unmistakable. No matter. My business with Lazarus was over. I had to get the statue back to Goddard.

I reached behind me for the doorknob, but somehow my arms had become tangled in the strap of Mrs. Wu's bag. I struggled to free myself, but found myself sliding toward the floor instead. There was no time for this nonsense. I had to get home. But my body simply wouldn't obey. My knees buckled and I went down.

"Adler?"

Fenwick wasn't quick enough to stop my fall, but he did slow it considerably. He laid me gently down beside the coat rack.

"Adler?"

"Extraordinary, Tim," I mused. The floor tiles were so cool against my cheek. "I can't feel my feet."

Chapter Twenty

I didn't object to the laudanum upon which Lazarus insisted prior to removing my boots. By the time it took effect, my feet had swollen to the point that poor Fenwick was sent to fetch the garden shears. The next few hours passed by in a blur of cold, carbolic-laced baths, dubious herbal concoctions, and leeches. I rather hoped that the latter was a figment of an opiate-addled imagination, but knowing the good doctor's vigilance regarding bad blood and every other manner of impurity, I suspect that it was one of the most real things that happened that night. At last, having been half drowned in frigid, tarry-smelling water, bandaged to within an inch of my life, swaddled in one of St. Andrews's outsized robes, and liberally dosed with a foul-tasting potion, I was put to bed, where I remained, gratefully.

When the smell of bacon and coffee pulled me out of my dreams two days later, my first thought was of Goddard. According to Lazarus, he had commissioned the ring seven months ago—which meant that he'd had it made for me and me alone. And while I'd been lying abed in the home of Goddard's enemy, Goddard was on his side of our bed, injured, and wondering where the devil I was. These thoughts caused me to nearly bolt through the door, and I would have, had Lazarus not been walking through it at that very moment with a tray piled with enough food to fortify the British army.

"I thought this might bring you around," he said.

He set the tray on the bedside table, removed a newspaper, a silver coffeepot, and two china cups, then placed the tray over my lap. In addition to half a pig, sliced and fried, there were three poached eggs, two kinds of fish, and a mound of buttered toast. As he poured my coffee, Lazarus hummed a little tune. He'd cleaned up quite nicely. Between his starched white shirt, pressed waistcoat and trousers, and freshly shaven chin, one would never guess that he'd not three days ago been tugging at St. Peter's hem.

Once he'd creamed and sugared my coffee, he crossed the room to address the curtains. I winced as searing midmorning light poured into the chamber. When he opened the window itself, I groaned.

"Current wisdom holds that fresh air and light are the worst thing for a patient, but I've found their effects to be quite salutary. Behave yourself, and you might even get out for a walk this evening."

"I have to go home," I said.

His cheerfulness vanished, and was replaced with a disappointment so unexpected and so deep that it was painful to behold. Poor Lazarus. He didn't belong there, surrounded by St. Andrews's fussy clutter of lace and antiques. And yet I couldn't picture him installed in some house in Brixton with a wife and a new baby every year. Perhaps this was what our previous association had represented to him—the opportunity to create something new and unprecedented: a place where he truly belonged. Perhaps having me under his care had stirred up these thoughts once more.

"Of course," he said. He cleared his throat and rearranged his features into a professional mask.

"Thank you for everything, though. You can tell St. Andrews that Sinclair is dead. I'm sure he'll be relieved to hear it."

"Good news, good news. And the porcelain dog?"

"It's safe," I said.

Specifically, it was safe in Mrs. Wu's sack, which Fenwick had stowed with my coat, wherever that might be. But I wasn't about to tell him that. I'd nearly lost my life so many times over that blasted thing that I'd be damned if I let St. Andrews get it now.

"I see," he said.

"I'll dispose of it as soon as I'm able. Tell St. Andrews that he has nothing to fear from us."

"I'm sure," he said coldly.

"Tim—"

"Eat your bacon."

St. Andrews's cook had outdone herself. Not even released from Goddard's strict rules regarding healthfulness and frugality could Eileen have prepared such a feast. And not even Lazarus's sulking could impede my enjoyment of it. I was a little more than halfway through, when Lazarus said,

"The newspaper may interest you almost as much as the food, that is, if you haven't devoured it in your haste."

I dabbed at my mouth with the napkin and glanced toward the bedside table.

"I wouldn't have thought that St. Andrews would dirty his fingers with *The Daily Telegraph*," I said.

Lazarus shrugged.

"He usually reads *The Times*. But in this case, he thought that you would prefer to receive the news from a source more familiar to someone of your background."

When I read the headline, I nearly choked on my haddock.

Midnight Mob in St. James's

> *Late last night, a group of enraged citizens armed with truncheons and broken bottles broke down the doors of the East India Officers' Club, and dragged Dr. Edward Acton from the building. Documents first published in these pages had accused Dr. Acton of providing children for purposes too vile to detail here, to highly placed members of government and the aristocracy. The police were summoned, but arrived too late to prevent the mob from carrying Dr. Acton off. Scraps of clothing, flesh, and hair have been found, but it is doubtful that enough of Dr. Acton's remains will be recovered to provide positive identification.*

My heart stopped. I'd instructed Pearl to distribute Nate's documents to the press and police, in the event that Lazarus and I failed to show, and she had done just that. I should have at least sent word to her when we arrived at St. Andrews's home. On the other hand, given Acton's connections, what were the chances that justice would have been done, had justice been forced to grind through normal channels? The thought of Acton sliding through the system on greased palms made me grit my teeth. The world was a better place without him.

"Good," I said.

Lazarus smiled.

"I must admit to a most unchristian glee," he said, helping himself to coffee. "And relief. I can't tell you how relieved I am."

I could imagine. He had been hiding from Acton for nearly a decade. Now he could reclaim his name, start his own practice, and make a real life for himself.

"I'm sure your Bess will be happy that there are no further obstacles to your marriage," I said.

At the mention of her name, Lazarus's chest swelled, and his face flushed with pleasure. Perhaps there really was more to this marriage nonsense than the desire for respectability. He patted the waistcoat pocket where he kept her portrait.

"I spoke to her this morning. She's been ever so understanding."

"How understanding?" I asked.

I had no intention of making trouble for Lazarus. If he wanted to marry a carthorse, I wouldn't stand in his way. But he'd hidden his identity from Acton since the war; the degree to which it weighed on him was etched into his face. Was he prepared to hide from his wife for the rest of his life? It was possible, though I couldn't fathom it, that he harbored carnal desires for this woman. Even if he didn't, he seemed willing to put that part of himself aside for now. But would it ultimately be enough for either of them?

Lazarus met my eyes.

"Bess and I have no secrets, but we've agreed that the past belongs in the past."

"Then I wish you both the best." I mopped up a puddle of yolk with some toast and shoved it all into my mouth. "Are you going to call yourself Parker now?"

"Do swallow before you speak, Adler." He sighed. "Only my mother still knows me as Parker. Of course I'll set my civil records straight. But I've been Lazarus for so long now that I'm not sure I know how to respond to anything else. Perhaps I'll change it legally."

I made a noncommittal, food-muffled noise and shook the newspaper out in front of me. I was about to fold it over when four lines in the bottom left-hand corner caught my eye.

"By God," I said.

No doubt Lazarus had passed over the little article because it hadn't meant anything to him. It meant the world to me.

> *The body of a man shot dead two nights ago in Miller's Court remains unidentified. No witnesses to the shooting have come forward. Due to the position of the wound, the police do not consider the death a suicide. The pistol has not been recovered.*

"She did it." I laughed.

Lazarus frowned.

"The body is Acton's man, Morrison," I said, slapping the paper. "Mrs. Wu got away after all. By God!"

"Well, then," Lazarus said with obvious satisfaction.

"Has she returned for the children?" I asked.

"No," he said. "Actually, Pearl seems to be taking your suggestion about starting an orphanage to heart—more of a shelter, really, for young people trying to make their way out of the flesh trade. She's already twisted the arms of a number of donors. I've volunteered my services as needed, and Bess trained as a teacher in America. Did you know that?"

"No," I said.

"The only thing left is to find a building and give it a name. Any suggestions?"

I took a thoughtful bite of bacon and washed it down with the rest of my coffee.

"Turnbull House," I said.

Lazarus's face broke into a grin.

"Yes. I think that would suit very well indeed."

He grinned at me for a moment more, and then, as if remembering himself, straightened his waistcoat and muttered something about crumbs in the bed. Nothing more remained of my excellent breakfast, and so, like the excellent host that he was, he stacked the plates neatly and set the tray back on top of the bedside table. St. Andrews's guest room was expensively furnished, though the thickly painted wood and the gold-touched curlicues were not to my taste. If anything, they reminded me how very much I was missing my own modest room.

"I meant what I said about going home," I told Lazarus.

He narrowed his eyes. He seemed to have resigned himself to my leaving, but there was something else bothering him.

"Yes," he said, chewing a nail thoughtfully, "about that… The thing is, Adler, St. Andrews sent Goddard a message the moment you were out of danger. He's sent two per day since then, but there's been no reply."

It took a moment for his words to register. My first thought was that Goddard had thrown the messages onto the fire unread. But Goddard wasn't stupid. He disliked St. Andrews, but, given the past week, he'd have recognized the importance of any communication from the man. My second thought was much worse: that following the explosion, Goddard was in no shape to respond.

"Oh, God," I whispered.

I wasn't sorry I'd chosen to go after Lazarus two nights ago instead of following Goddard's carriage home. Tim would have died horribly at Acton's hands. Mrs. Wu, too. And we wouldn't have recovered the porcelain dog. But I should have returned to York Street after delivering Lazarus into Fenwick's capable hands. Instead, I'd fainted like a lady and spent the last two days playing patient while Cain…God. My own selfishness was nauseating.

Where would I be without Goddard? Without his strength, his direction…without his companionship? Not to mention that I had no legal right to remain at York Street. If he was dead, where would I go?

And if he was alive, he needed me now more than ever.

"I've got to go to him," I said. "Stop me at your peril."

Lazarus took a step back at the violence in my voice. Then he nodded. "Then let's have a look at those feet."

I swung my legs to the side of the bed and threw off the blankets. As I did, an earthy odor of carbolic and sweat rose from the bedcovers. I'd been wearing the same robe for two days and a night, but the bandages had been recently changed. Lazarus found the end of the fabric strip and carefully unrolled the bandage from my left foot first, then from my right.

"Not bad," he said, nodding. "Not bad at all. Yes." He looked up. "You won't be comfortable, but the danger is over. I'll have Fenwick bring you some of St. Andrews's old clothes."

The larger blisters were still raw in the centers. The marks left by the leeches were unmistakable. But the smaller wounds and lacerations had healed under Lazarus's diligent care. Shoes would hurt, but I didn't have far to walk.

"Thank you," I said as he wadded the soiled cloths into a ball.

"All in a day's work."

"No, Tim," I said, pausing until he met my eyes. "Thank you."

❖

The short walk from St. Andrews's abode to my own felt interminable, but it gave me time, once my initial panic had dispersed, to think.

More than anything, I wanted to find Goddard unharmed. Bruised, perhaps, possessed of some lingering injury, which might inspire him to turn his attention to different facets of his business—or perhaps to remind him that the harm resulting from his actions might be visited upon his own house. If this were the case, then I could take my place at his side without reservation. But if he refused to acknowledge the suffering that he'd caused, then I'd no idea how I could be convinced to stay. It was an unsettling conclusion, for I couldn't very well repair back to Baker Street. And yet I'd never been more certain of anything in my life.

From the outside, the house looked exactly as it always did: clean red bricks, scrubbed steps, lace curtains, and unblemished windows. But the moment I stepped across the threshold, I knew that something was wrong. There were no flowers on the vestibule table. The air was thin and stale. Though Eileen hadn't allowed a speck of dust to settle, the house was clearly unoccupied. My stomach began to sink. Had Goddard been recovering upstairs, the vestibule would be filled with flowers and well wishes. Had he been on his deathbed, it would have been bursting with members of his organization jockeying for a position in the new hierarchy. Five unopened letters lay on the vestibule table where the silver vase had once stood.

"Mr. Ira, sir?"

I whirled at Eileen's voice behind me. Standing in the doorway to the servants' stairs, she wore a plain black dress with a black band tied around her upper arm.

"No," I whispered.

And yet the truth was all too plain. The house was deserted, the maid in a mourning dress. I felt the blood drain from my face. Shaking, I lowered myself onto the bench beside the hat rack as panic overtook me. Goddard was dead. How could the world go on without him? How could *I* go on?

"When, Eileen?" I demanded. "How? How on earth could this have happened?"

She frowned as if my questions were completely out of line. Eileen was only sixteen, and yet, between her severe expression and the contrast of her pale skin against the black, she presented a formidable figure. She smoothed down her apron indignantly.

"I 'as it on good aufority wot Mr. Collins ain't comin' back," she said, her voice defiant. "The master says wot I earned it."

"He says…"

Says, not *said*.

My heart leaped. My panic cleared. And for the first time I saw things as they actually were. The girl-of-all-work wasn't wearing a mourning dress at all. And Eileen was no longer a mere maid. She was clad in the crisp uniform of a housekeeper. After Collins's departure, she had stepped into his place.

And if Goddard were dead, he couldn't have promoted her. The armband was for Collins.

A small smile tugged at her thin lips. Her dignified coif, unmarred by a lowly mobcap, suited her. She was actually quite a bit taller when she held herself erect.

"Then…then…Cain is…"

"In Buda-pesth," she said. "Wot'd you think, silly? 'E weren't back 'alf an hour when 'e gets a message. 'Pack me bags,' 'e tell me. I say 'e don' look so good, maybe 'e should go lie down. 'Pack me bags,' 'e say again. I say ain't you gon' wait for Mr. Ira, and 'e says, 'Things is movin' too fast to wait. Tell Mr. Ira to meet me in Buda-pesth.'"

"Of course," I said with a nervous little laugh. "Of course. I knew that."

Weak-kneed I stood, my heart pounding with relief now rather than terror.

Goddard was alive and waiting for me in the flat he kept in Montmartre. He called the place 'Buda-pesth' because of the building's distinctive architectural style—and because telling someone as honest as Eileen where he was really going would have been like sending it in letters to whoever he believed was pursuing him.

"'E left this for you, sir," she said, producing a letter from the pocket of her new uniform. The wax seal was still intact. Fingers trembling, I ripped it open.

> *My dear boy,*
>
> *Urgent business compels me away. I know you disapprove of EA, but if this succeeds, I shall personally drown your conscience in Perrier-Jouët. In the meantime, I am in most desperate need of your services. Come at once.*
>
> *C*

My heart sank again, and I sat back down on the bench.

A year earlier I'd have flown out the door without a second thought. But that day the note made my blood run cold. Knowing how I felt about Acton and why, Goddard had left on an errand for him. And though the news of Acton's death had, no doubt, reached Paris by now, it was all too clear how Goddard would respond when I insisted he leave the opium trade. I crumpled the note in my hand.

"Shall I pack your bags, then, Mr. Ira?" Eileen asked.

"No," I said, numb. What now? What now? Resignation settled over me as I realized what I had to do. I suddenly felt so tired. "Just set up my desk in the blue room."

I seated myself at the desk in my bedroom. I hadn't slept in the bed since that cold night so long ago. How I had delighted in the soft mattress, in the crisp, lavender-scented cotton that had surrounded me as I'd drifted off to sleep, safe for the first time in my life! How I had clung to that taste of security, vowing that I would sell my very soul if somehow I could remain there. I suppose I had done just that.

Pen in hand, heart in throat, I must have lingered over that empty page for an hour. How could I explain my desertion in terms that Goddard would understand? And how could I convince myself that I wasn't making the biggest mistake of my life?

In the end it came down to this: my life had been torn apart at an early age because of the business that made Goddard rich. One might argue, rightly, that the same business had later enriched me beyond my wildest dreams. But nothing came without a cost. I'd been able to avoid thinking about that for a long time. But when confronted with the people directly affected by Goddard's criminal activities, I'd seen the true cost of my unearned luxury.

Fate was perverse. Nate had tried to do the right thing, and had died horribly, while I, who had tried my damnedest to avoid difficult choices, had been spared. There had to be a reason. And though Goddard would have laughed at the idea, I knew better than to ignore it.

My farewell was short and to the point. I didn't tell him where to find me, because I didn't know where I would find myself. But wherever I did end up, my conscience would be clear. I folded the letter around my ring, slipped it into an envelope, and sealed it with wax. Then I pulled my portmanteau from underneath the bed. The corners were still sharp, and the leather creaked like new, though Goddard had purchased it over a year ago for our first trip to Montmartre. He wouldn't mind if I took it. He'd want me to have it.

I selected two good sets of clothing from the wardrobe and laid Mrs. Wu's bag on top of them. I could have left the statue. I probably should have. But Lazarus and St. Andrews had been so kind to me that I couldn't bear the thought that, enraged at my departure, Goddard might use the evidence inside to destroy them once and for all. As I closed the portmanteau, my eyes fell on the trunk, where I'd kept the few possessions I'd brought with me from Whitechapel. The hat didn't suit me anymore, even less so my old clothes. Smiling, I scooped up the cloth with Lazarus's surgical needle. I'd return it to him one day. And then there was that page from the *Telegraph*. Was it my mother in the photo of the opium den victims? And had Acton's experiments led to their deaths? I would probably never know.

I carefully folded the page and tucked it into the breast pocket of my borrowed jacket. I shut the door behind me, then found my way down the stairs. The five letters were still on the vestibule table. I scooped them up and put them in my pocket. Then I left my own note in their place. Laying my keys on the table beside it, I let myself out.

Epilogue

Christmas Eve 1890

It had saddened me to sever our connection with something as insubstantial as a note. The lack of finality ate away at me for some time. Ultimately, though, I was grateful that Goddard hadn't been at York Street that day. It wouldn't have taken but a single smoldering look, a moment in his arms, for my nascent scruples to have gone up in smoke like a fine Egyptian tobacco. There were several times over the course of the following year that I'd have happily thrown away my new independence for a mouthful of whisky and a night between silk sheets. The only thing that kept me from doing so was the fact that the house on York Street remained locked up tight. It was miserable to make one's way on a secretary's pittance. But it was better for the soul, as Pearl would say. And it was miles better than accepting the proffered room in the house that Lazarus had purchased after his wedding.

He wasn't so bad for all that, Lazarus. He and Bess were wed in September, and he fell effortlessly into the rhythms of married life. Every few weeks or so, when I allowed myself to be dragged to Sunday supper, their home had glowed with domestic contentment. I suppose my presence served to remind him of more adventurous times—from a safe distance, of course. My exploits provided no end of entertainment for their surprisingly eclectic parade of friends, one of whom would become my first employer. He was a man after my own heart, but fortunately not one to let my rejection stand in the way of an excellent working relationship.

Summer turned to autumn. Winter came and went and came again. And eventually the streets began to whisper of Goddard's return to London. Though in truth, I never expected to see him again, I slept with one eye open for quite a while. But in the end, my worries came to nothing. In addition to his affection, Goddard had set aside his rancor. He had, it seemed, simply relinquished all feeling toward me. His hand was evident everywhere I looked, but as far as my life was concerned, his disappearance was so complete as to make me wonder if any of it had ever really happened.

It was with surprise, then, trepidation, and, yes, a brief, bittersweet flutter in my chest, that I found him Christmas Eve at my door.

"I mean you no harm," he said, before I could speak.

He was pressed and coiffed to his usual perfection and held a large parcel in his arms. Perhaps foolishly, I stepped aside to let him enter. As he surveyed my room, I suddenly saw it as he must have: the peeling paint, the faded rug with patches of floor showing through; the long black crack in the basin of the commode half hidden behind a tattered screen; the narrow bed with its sagging mattress.

"It's only temporary," I said. "My employer says that when his next book is published, he'll have more work for me—"

"Ah yes," he said. "Mr. Wilde. I'm surprised he hasn't offered you a different sort of work."

He had, in fact. But I'd seen too many of my contemporaries take that one last job, only to fall back into the life that I'd clawed my way out of. For all I knew, Oscar Wilde might not have been an entirely unpleasant lover, but I had no intention of allowing myself to be kept by him or anyone else, ever again.

"Forgive me," Goddard said. "That was uncalled for. It just saddens me to see you reduced to…"

"To fending for myself?" I finished. "I don't mind."

It was a lie. Not a night went by that I didn't curse the filthy coal in the grate, the rowing neighbors and their nasal, low-bred accents; and the lack of privacy and indoor plumbing. The latter I missed more than even Goddard himself.

"One might even argue," I said, "that lesser circumstances make a greater man."

He glanced around the room once more. William Shakespeare had once lived on Aldersgate Street. John Wesley had experienced his conversion among these once-stately houses. But the houses had long since been divided into tenements. The glory days of Little Britain were far in the past, and it showed.

"Indeed," he said.

He placed the parcel in my hands. It was heavy. "I bought this in Paris to surprise you. It's been cluttering up my morning room for more than a year now. What I really wanted was to throw it off the roof, but that would have been an unconscionable waste. Go ahead, open it."

I didn't need to open it to know what it was, or that it had cost more than I'd likely earn in five years. The weight of the thing, its shape, and the cold metal plate on the bottom gave it away. Nonetheless, my fingers trembled as I pushed a pile of papers to the corner of my desk, set the typewriting machine beside it, and peeled back the paper that concealed it.

"Cain, it's magnificent."

And it was: a Remington keyboard typewriter, which, when one could find it, cost upward of fifty pounds. A far cry from my two-quid Ingersoll, which still required me to set the letters one by one by hand.

"I don't know what to say," I said.

"Say that you'll put it to good use."

"I promise," I said. "Thank you."

"Nonsense. If you're determined to make a career of this, you'll need the right equipment. At any rate, it's gratifying to see that the time I put into training you wasn't completely misspent."

There wasn't much to say after that, and for a long while we stood on opposite sides of the fireplace, watching the coal in awkward silence. I was grateful for the gift. Beholden, really. Goddard had been quite open-handed when I lived at York Street, but now that he had no claim over me, I wondered what strings this gift actually entailed.

"So this sort of work makes you…happy?" he finally ventured.

I shrugged. It was difficult not to squirm under his scrutiny, but I made an admirable job of it.

"You look happy," he decided after a moment. "You look well, despite the beard."

It would have been dishonest for me to return the compliment. I flatter myself to think that the new peppering of gray in his hair was my fault, somehow, or that I, and not the winter, was to blame for the excessive pallor of his skin.

"You didn't come here to tell me that," I said. "Nor to give me a gift that any trusted messenger might have delivered."

"No." He cleared his throat and began to pace. When he reached the ancient screen that hid the commode six short steps away, he turned. "I understand why you did what you did, Ira. It took extraordinary courage to defy me. I admire that."

The corner of his mouth twitched, no doubt at the astonishmment that must have shone on my face.

"Courage, strength, and integrity."

He made a slow round of the room, hands clasped behind his back, looking for all the world as if he were sizing the place up for investment potential. Eventually, he returned to his place at the opposite end of the imitation mantel.

"I came with a proposition," he said.

"Cain, I—"

He cupped my cheek with one gloved hand. My blood rose at the familiarity of the gesture, and I closed my eyes, allowing myself, one last time, to revel in his touch. Notes of jasmine and bergamot danced above the smell of burning coal, then disappeared.

"Not that kind of proposition, Ira."

His expression was kind but adamant. Releasing me, he reached into his coat and withdrew an envelope.

"What's this?" I asked.

"Courage, strength, and integrity are in short supply in this world, especially in combination. I'm prepared to pay handsomely for them."

"I don't understand."

"It's all in here." He nodded toward the envelope. "Read it at your leisure. I think you'll find the duties to your liking. The terms, it goes without saying, are generous."

What an infernal temptation came over me then! Integrity be damned! I wanted it all back again, wanted him back. But that wasn't what he was offering. An eternity passed while Goddard waited for me to take the envelope. Then, sighing, he walked it over to the desk.

"I'll consider the offer open until you tell me otherwise," he said, laying the envelope atop the new typing machine. "The Remington is a gift, regardless of your decision."

"Thank you, Cain."

His gaze flicked over the papers that littered my desk, looking for what, I couldn't imagine. I said nothing; I'd nothing to hide.

"I don't suppose you still have the statue," he said.

"It's at the bottom of the Thames."

His shoulders relaxed. A decade's worries fell from his features.

"I knew I could depend on you," he said.

He looked as if he wanted to say something more, but, of course, there was nothing left to say. So, without the exchange of pleasantries that most people find so necessary, he showed himself out.

Once Goddard's footsteps had faded into the noises of the street below, I fished a small key from behind the clock on the mantel. The porcelain dog was in the deep left-hand drawer of my desk. At one point, a mere quarter-inch of cheap wood had stood between it and Goddard, and I couldn't shake the superstitious feeling that it had somehow left with him. But it was there, where I'd placed it the day I'd moved in, and as I opened the drawer, it stared back at me with eyes of malice and fire.

The porcelain was cool in my hand. The seal was intact, and the paper that could have cost three men their freedom still rattled faintly inside. If not for this monstrosity and its contents, I'd have been at that very moment curled up in my chair in Goddard's morning room, a tumbler of expensive whisky in one hand and a book of erotic art in the other. And yet until that day, I hadn't been able to muster the anger to smash it to bits, nor the curiosity to pry loose the seal. Why I was still hanging on to it, I couldn't say. Perhaps it was nostalgia. Perhaps I'd felt the need for some sort of insurance. But Goddard seemed to have made his peace with me. If I turned down his offer, I'd not hear from him again.

"A Fu dog!" a woman's voice suddenly cried out behind me.

I started upward. The object that had been the cause of all of my troubles slipped from my fingers and crashed to the floor. From the doorway, the redoubtable Mrs. Lazarus winced. Her husband peered apologetically over her shoulder. It was a testament to the woman's persuasive powers that I'd agreed to spend the holiest of all nights working with them in a soup kitchen in Bethnal Green, and a testament to my own abstraction that I'd forgotten. How fortunate that they were late.

"Sorry about that," she said, as she bustled to my side. "But it couldn't have been expensive. My parents dragged me all across the Orient saving souls. I've seen more than my share of the things, and that one's a fake. Here, let me help you clean that up. Do you have a broom?"

Muttering to myself, I snatched a few sheets of Wilde's latest article from the desk and crouched down beside the wreckage.

"Didn't mean to surprise you," Mrs. Lazarus said. "I thought you were expecting us."

"I wasn't expecting you to let yourselves in," I said.

"The door *was* open. Well, no matter."

Her deft fingers piled the larger pieces onto the paper, while I used a few more sheets to sweep up the smaller bits. There was something disarming about her enthusiasm, about the way she kept stuffing her unruly ringlets back beneath her bonnet, while melting snow dripped from her oft-mended coat onto my pathetic excuse for a carpet. The whole time, her wide mouth kept threatening to break into an unseemly grin, and I found it impossible to remain angry.

"Mr. Adler, please tell me you didn't pay more than a few pennies for that horrible thing."

"It was a gift," I reassured her. "From someone with whom I'm no longer on speaking terms." I fixed Lazarus with a pointed look.

Recognition dawned on his face, and he blanched.

"I should hope not," she tutted. She raised the head of the beast on two fingers like a puppet. "Really, Mr. Adler, I'd never have suspected you of harboring such appalling taste. Something this ugly must have a cracking good story behind it. Come on, then, out with it."

"Well…I…er…"

"That's enough, now, Bess," Lazarus said.

"Oh, Tim, don't be—oh, look!" Mrs. Lazarus suddenly cried. "There was a photograph inside! Now this *is* intriguing!"

No sooner had she plucked up the photo than Lazarus was across the room, snatching it from her fingers and shoving it at me.

"That was Mr. St. Andrews," she accused, as I slid the picture up my shirt-sleeve.

"I'm sure I don't know what you're talking about," said Lazarus.

"It was! And that was Cambridge. I'm certain of it!"

While they bickered good-naturedly, I crossed to the fireplace and tossed the cursed thing into the fire. It was a shame to destroy such a lovely picture. They looked so happy together, so young, in love, and without a care in the world—or a stitch of clothing on their bodies, though that part had been artfully concealed by trees and shadow. How ironic that such an expression of beauty and joy would be considered so indecent that it would have spelled prison not only for its subjects, but for the photographer as well.

"Who was that other man?" Mrs. Lazarus demanded as the photo blistered and charred.

"It doesn't matter now," Tim said. He had turned from her, and was taking a most unusual interest in the letter on top of the Remington. I cleared my throat, and he looked up, sheepish.

"Then why won't you tell me?" Mrs. Lazarus asked.

"Because it's none of our business," he said. Then he looked at me. "Though I can't say that I'm surprised."

And neither was I, if I thought about it. If I really thought about it, I'd known all along.

Snow began to fall outside my window. A rowdy group of youths stumbled past on the sidewalk below, drunk on gin and Christmas cheer. There would be no roast beef for me that year, no blazing fire made from fragrant wood, no warm arms to collapse into when the wine was drunk. All the same, things could have ended much, much worse.

"Come on, then, Adler," Lazarus said, guiding his wife to the door by her elbow. "The soup isn't going to serve itself."

"I do hope Mr. Booth is there tonight," she said, the photo now forgotten. "I have a few ideas to put to him."

"I'll just bet you do," said Tim.

I ushered the Lazaruses into the hall and then went to put out the fire. As I stirred the coals, what remained of the photograph—of my past—blackened and disappeared. Some people believe that patterns in the coals can reveal clues about what's to come. However, all I saw was ashes.

Lazarus and his wife were at it again, their animated discussion blending in with the wailing babies and ominous clatters and bangs as they made their way down the hallway. It was a long way from York Street, to be sure, but it was a long way from Whitechapel as well. Leaning the poker against the wall, I reached for my coat and hat. Then I pulled the door shut behind me, squared my shoulders, and went out to meet the future.

About the Author

Jess Faraday has earned her daily bread in a number of questionable ways, including translation, lexicography, copy editing, teaching high school Russian, and hawking shoes to the overprivileged offspring of Los Angeles–area B-listers. She enjoys martial arts, the outdoors, strong coffee, and a robust Pinot Noir. *The Affair of the Porcelain Dog* is her first novel.

Books Available From Bold Strokes Books

Wild by Meghan O'Brien. Shapeshifter Selene Rhodes dreads the full moon and the loss of control it brings, but when she rescues forensic pathologist Eve Thomas from a vicious attack by a masked man, she discovers she isn't the scariest monster in San Francisco. (978-1-60282-227-6)

Reluctant Hope by Erin Dutton. Cancer survivor Addison Hunt knows she can't offer any guarantees, in love or in life, and after experiencing a loss of her own, Brooke Donahue isn't willing to risk her heart. (978-1-60282-228-3)

Conquest by Ronica Black. When Mary Brunelle stumbles into the arms of Jude Jaeger, a gorgeous dominatrix at a private nightclub, she is smitten, but she soon finds out Jude is her professor, and Professor Jaeger doesn't date her students…or her conquests. (978-1-60282-229-0)

The Affair of the Porcelain Dog by Jess Faraday. What darkness stalks the London streets at night? Ira Adler, present plaything of crime lord Cain Goddard, will soon find out. (978-1-60282-230-6)

365 Days by K.E. Payne. Life sucks when you're seventeen years old and confused about your sexuality, and the girl of your dreams doesn't even know you exist. Then in walks sexy new emo girl, Hannah Harrison. Clemmie Atkins has exactly 365 days to discover herself, and she's going to have a blast doing it! (978-1-60282-540-6)

Darkness Embraced by Winter Pennington. Surrounded by harsh vampire politics and secret ambitions, Epiphany learns that an old enemy is plotting treason against the woman she once loved, and to save all she holds dear, she must embrace and form an alliance with the dark. (978-1-60282-221-4)

78 Keys by Kristin Marra. When the cosmic powers choose Devorah Rosten to be their next gladiator, she must use her unique skills to try to save her lover, herself, and even humankind. (978-1-60282-222-1)

Playing Passion's Game by Lesley Davis. Trent Williams's only passion in life is gaming—until Juliet Sullivan makes her realize that love can be a whole different game to play. (978-1-60282-223-8)

Retirement Plan by Martha Miller. A modern morality tale of justice, retribution, and women who refuse to be politely invisible. (978-1-60282-224-5)

Who Dat Whodunnit by Greg Herren. Popular New Orleans detective Scotty Bradley investigates the murder of a dethroned beauty queen to clear the name of his pro football–playing cousin. (978-1-60282-225-2)

The Company He Keeps by Dale Chase. A riotously erotic collection of stories set in the sexually repressed and therefore sexually rampant Victorian era. (978-1-60282-226-9)

Cursebusters! by Julie Smith. Budding-psychic Reeno is the most accomplished teenage burglar in California, but one tiny screw-up and poof!—she's sentenced to Bad Girl School. And that isn't even her worst problem. Her sister Haley's dying of an illness no one can diagnose, and now she can't even help. (978-1-60282-559-8)

True Confessions by PJ Trebelhorn. Lynn Patrick finally has a chance with the only woman she's ever loved, her lifelong friend Jessica Greenfield, but Jessie is still tormented by an abusive past. (978-1-60282-216-0)

Ghosts of Winter by Rebecca S. Buck. Can Ros Wynne, who has lost everything she thought defined her, find her true life—and her true love—surrounded by the lingering history of the once-grand Winter Manor? (978-1-60282-219-1)

Blood Hunt by L.L. Raand. In the second Midnight Hunters Novel, Detective Jody Gates, heir to a powerful Vampire clan, forges an uneasy alliance with Sylvan, the Wolf Were Alpha, to battle a shadow army of humans and rogue Weres, while fighting her growing hunger for human reporter Becca Land. (978-1-60282-209-2)